Scribe Publications
DEAD CAT BOUNCE

Peter Cotton has been the media advisor to three
federal cabinet ministers, worked as a foreign
correspondent for the ABC, been a senior reporter
on the ABC's *AM* and *PM* programs, and had
stories published in most major print outlets in
Australia. *Dead Cat Bounce* is his first novel.

To Claire, with love

DEAD CAT BOUNCE

PETER COTTON

SCRIBE

Melbourne • London

Scribe Publications Pty Ltd
18–20 Edward St, Brunswick, Victoria 3056, Australia
Email: info@scribepub.com.au

First published by Scribe 2013

Typeset in 10.5/15pt Janson by the publishers
Printed and bound in Australia by Griffin Press

 The paper this book is printed on is certified against the
Forest Stewardship Council® Standards. Griffin Press holds
FSC chain of custody certification SGS-COC-005088. FSC
promotes environmentally responsible, socially beneficial
and economically viable management of the world's forests.

National Library of Australia
Cataloguing-in-Publication data

Cotton, Peter.

Dead Cat Bounce / Peter Cotton.

9781922070449 (paperback)

1. Elections–Fiction. 2. Australian fiction.

A823.4

scribepublications.com.au

'Evil is unspectacular and always human,
And shares our bed and eats at our own table ...'

Herman Melville, by W. H. Auden, March 1939

Channel Four Live Cam

Wednesday 31 July, 11.15 am

Hello again, Jean Acheson with the Live Cam, recapping the news that the search for Environment Minister Susan Wright appears to be over with the discovery of a body here by Canberra's Lake Burley Griffin early this morning.

Mrs Wright disappeared on Sunday night after a party in her office. In the two days since, millions of Australians have been affected by one of the biggest manhunts ever conducted in this country. And now this.

A major police operation is underway around the lake below me, and while we've had no official word yet as to the identity of the body down there, everything points to it being Mrs Wright. For a start, journalists monitoring police communications earlier this morning say officers in the first patrol car to attend the scene repeatedly used the minister's name when referring to the deceased. Also, the senior policeman who led the search to find Mrs Wright has now taken charge of things here. And most tellingly, Prime Minister Lansdowne cancelled all campaign engagements in Brisbane this morning, and his jet touched down in Canberra just minutes ago.

Susan Wright was Michael Lansdowne's most effective minister. She was also his best performer in the parliament, and her efforts over the past three weeks are the only reason his government's still rated a chance in this election. If she is dead, as seems likely, then Mr Lansdowne's hopes of a come-from-behind win must surely have died with her. This is Jean Acheson. Back with more in a moment.

1

THE ENVIRONMENT MINISTER lay on her side in the mud. Her head rested in the crook of her left elbow, her slits of eyes almost closed, and her mouth half open. It might have been fatigue after the hours I'd spent in the tent with her body that morning, or maybe the halogen lights were playing tricks on my eyes, but, as I stared at Susan Wright's mouth, ticking off an urgent to-do list in my head, her lips suddenly began to quiver a bit. I stretched my eyes, trying to adjust them to the light. Then her mouth started tremoring at the edges, and, in that instant, Wright looked to have come alive somehow. I swung away, slapped my cheeks hard with both hands, and when I looked back, was relieved to see she was nothing but dead again.

It was time to let the body contractors have her — they were lined up outside on the access path, waiting to go to work. I was about to call them in, but for some reason I suppressed the impulse, and instead lowered myself down for one last look at her.

In life, Susan Wright had been a political celebrity — one of Australia's best-known faces. And while she seemed to pop up on the box every other night, only the most cynical punters were sick of the sight of her, if the polls measuring personal approval were to be believed. Her appeal went beyond the sparkle in her eyes and her high cheekbones. She seemed like a warm and caring person, and she was obviously smart and on top of her game — all of which inspired confidence. 'A safe pair of hands', the commentators liked to say about her. And now she was dead.

As I gazed at her face, I knew that if we didn't resolve this case in double-quick time, the outside pressure on us would become immense.

I tried to dislodge this thought by focusing on the big patch of lividity that spanned the right-hand side of Wright's face, from just below her eye socket down to the line of her chin. That lividity had had everyone in the team talking throughout the morning. It had a cherry-red edge to it — a classic sign of carbon monoxide poisoning, and something that most of us associated with stationary cars and suicide. The thing was, apart from the lividity, everything else about this case pointed to murder.

For a start, Wright had been missing for the best part of three days. That fact undercut any suicide theory, especially since those close to her reckoned she'd been mostly happy and that she'd had everything to live for. Happy and fulfilled pollies didn't voluntarily go missing in the middle of an election campaign, and they were even less likely to choose such a time to top themselves.

Thankfully, this crime scene had already thrown up some leads. These included evidence that at least two people had been involved in dumping Wright on this sodden little mudflat overnight. They'd immediately become our prime suspects, as there was no way they could have left her like this and still be entirely innocent. The first thing I'd want to know when we caught up with them was why they'd chosen to dump her here. The very nature of the place meant that they were going to leave footprints.

If we were lucky, it could mean that they'd been incredibly incompetent, and that their prints would soon give us a break in the case. Or maybe they were easily spooked, and something had panicked them into disposing of the body in a hurry. Both scenarios were possible, though I didn't see either as likely. If the two who'd dumped Susan Wright were the same ones who'd held her these past few days, they'd already managed to elude one of the biggest manhunts ever mounted in this country. That fact alone meant they were probably very good at what they did, and very careful. I figured that all we'd get from their prints was their weight — and as it was winter, who knew what their clothes weighed, or what else they'd been carrying at the time — and we'd get the size of the shoes they'd been wearing.

What we already knew from their shoe prints was that only one of them had been involved in hauling Wright to the water. The gouges that their heels had made in the mud had survived the body being dragged over them. And the drag marks were unbroken, so the workhorse had done the job with apparent ease. It meant that he was strong and fit, and if the prints were true, he was also very big.

The second suspect had left much shallower impressions in the mud, so he must have been lighter. He'd followed as his mate had dragged the body to the water, then he'd walked along the shore to where we'd found a recently dead tortoiseshell cat draped over a fallen tree. Maybe suspect number two had placed the dead animal there, or maybe it had been left by someone else and he'd merely walked over to have a look at it. We'd know everything there was to know about that cat once our Forensics people were finished with it.

My mobile vibrated. It was a text from McHenry — Assistant Commissioner Len McHenry, the Australian Federal Police's chief of operations. Having headed the search for Susan Wright, he now had charge of investigating her death, and he'd co-opted me and most of the Territory Investigations Group to the task. During the morning, McHenry had pulled me aside to say that he wanted me at a media conference he'd scheduled for noon.

I'd worked with McHenry a few times before he went up to the top floor, and I knew that he rated me. We also got on fairly well, basically because, unlike most people, I wasn't intimidated by his size or by his manner. My stepfather had been a big bloke, too. And he'd been just as testy as McHenry. In fact, you could say that, growing up, I'd developed an immunity to fearsome authority figures who were a bit oversized.

McHenry's text informed me that he was sitting on a bench immediately up the hill from the crime scene and that he wanted me up there. It was still twenty to twelve, so I figured he was after a final word before he fronted the journos. I stepped from the tent into tepid sunlight, and again eyed the news choppers that were clattering in a tight line out over the lake.

The cameramen up there would have all been waiting for any movement from the tent, and by now live images of me would be showing on all the networks. I secured the tent flap to ensure that the body stayed out of shot, and then texted McHenry to tell him that I'd be straight up.

A team from Forensics was still working the area between the small carpark on the rise where the body had been unloaded and the spot by the water where it had been dumped. They were mostly picking up bits of blue plastic fibre that they suspected had come from a tarpaulin used to haul the body. I walked one hundred metres around the lake path to avoid them, and then climbed the steepest part of the rise to where more Forensics people were packing away casts they'd made of every mark in and around the carpark.

From there, I made my way up the hill on a crushed-granite path that snaked through a succession of terraced islands full of low shrubs. The path had been eroded by recent rain, and it was muddy in places. The mud forced me to concentrate on my footing, which meant that for the first time in hours I wasn't totally consumed by the case.

As I emerged from the third planting, I spotted McHenry

sitting on a narrow bench to the side of the shrubbery. He was scribbling in a notebook. A couple of guys from media liaison hovered nearby, eyeing him intently. Four senior cops huddled some distance away, deep in conversation. And thirty metres further up the hill, eighty or more media people — journos, cameramen, and various production teams and assistants — milled around at the edge of the road, waiting for things to happen.

When he saw me coming, McHenry slid his bulk along the bench, patted the modest bit of space he'd vacated, and then went back to his notes. His massive thighs were spread so wide that they hardly left any room for me to sit down, so I pushed against him to secure a perch, and then ran my eyes over the journos.

'We'll get to them soon enough,' said McHenry, casting his gaze up the hill. 'But first, tell me, do you still reckon it's murder dressed up as suicide, or has your thinking changed in the last little while?'

If the question had come from almost anyone else, I would have told them that we still had the post-mortem to come. And toxicology. And that we had to wait to see what we got from Wright's clothes. That would have been the reasonable response, but this was McHenry asking, and he wanted to know what my gut told me. So I took it slowly, knowing that any ill-considered words could come back to haunt me.

'Well, the edge on her lividity does *suggest* suicide,' I said. 'But given that she disappeared, and the fact that she was dumped, I'm with everyone else on this one — I'd discount suicide for now. And it doesn't look like an accident to me, either. I mean, if a high-profile person like Susan Wright killed herself, either on purpose or by accident, what would an innocent person do if they found her? Panic, and bring her down here and dump her?

They'd be much more likely to call it in. Either that, or they'd walk away, say nothing, and leave her for the next person to find.'

'Right,' said McHenry, nodding. 'So you think it's murder?'

'Well, there's a lot pointing to it. At the very least, it's highly suspicious. And the people who left her here? They're a brazen pair, you'd have to say — the way they went about it. So, murder? It's nothing like firm yet, but it *is* likely. And, of course, we'll know a lot more in a few hours.'

'Yeah, but that mob's not going to wait till then, are they?' he said, again eyeing the journos.

He grimaced, dropped his gaze to his feet, and took a deep breath. Then he went back to his notes. I looked at my watch. It was a few minutes before twelve, so the pressure was on. The two media advisors were feeling it, too. They'd moved away from us when I sat down, but now they were shuffling back towards the bench. I glanced over at the heavies. They still had their heads together in a tight little circle.

I was taking the whole scene in when Jean Acheson, the Live Cam girl, bobbed into view at the back of the media pack. She was wearing a black brimless hat with a long black feather sticking up out of it. The hat looked a bit frivolous, even out of place, given the nature of the story she was covering, and the feather added to that impression by swaying languidly from side to side as Acheson made her way down through the press of bodies. Eventually, she found a position on the police tape next to a line of cameras, and, once she'd settled in there, began chatting to a young woman who had a bulky recorder hanging from her shoulder.

Most of the women journos on TV were attractive. It was part of the job description. But of all of them, only Acheson did it for me in any way. Maybe it was her green eyes. They were slightly misaligned, which gave her a vulnerable air. You might say those eyes brought out the inner cop in me.

Like most of her colleagues, Acheson glanced down at McHenry and me every few minutes, anxious for a sign that the media conference was about to begin. The thing was, each time she moved her head to check us out, her feather swayed back and forth a bit, and caught my eye.

It happened like that a few times: me, looking up at her and her swaying feather while she looked away to avoid eye contact. Then I looked up, and she was staring at me. She nodded, and her face softened into a smile. Confused, I stared back at her blankly. She held my gaze for a second, and then her face slumped into neutral and she went back to talking to her friend.

The feather flicked again. I looked up, our eyes met, and this time I nodded and gave her a smile of my own. The one she returned had me looking around for anyone who might misinterpret the exchange, although I had no idea myself what it meant. One thing was certain, though. This was no time for flirting, so I took out my mobile, and, just as I did, the thing vibrated with a call.

It was Smeaton, my partner, letting me know that the post-mortem was set for Kingston at three, and that a team meeting had been scheduled for immediately after. I thanked him for the info, and smiled as I hung up, visualising him scratching another to-do item from *his* list.

'Okay,' said McHenry, slapping his notebook shut. 'Let's get on with it.'

Without another word, he pushed himself off the bench and strode up the hill towards the journos. The pair from media liaison immediately fell in behind him, and I brought up the rear. It took the group from the top floor some seconds to notice that we were on the move; but, once they did, they quickly made up ground and were soon striding past me. Meanwhile, the swollen mass of journos and cameramen were putting such strain on the police tape that it looked set to snap.

We were about ten metres from the cameras when McHenry suddenly stopped, bringing the rest of us to a jarring halt behind him. He turned his back on the journos — which instantly had them groaning as one — pulled his mobile from his coat pocket and examined the screen, and then quickly marched down the slope and handed the thing to me.

'Dunno who it is,' he said. 'Get a number, will you?'

Then he swung around, and he and his little entourage resumed their march towards the cameras, leaving me standing there, holding the vibrating phone. The call was from a private number, so I pressed the answer button and put the thing to my ear.

It was Commissioner Jim Brady's assistant. The commissioner wanted to talk to McHenry, she said. It had me wondering why the general headquarters number hadn't come up on the screen. I told her that McHenry was about to kick off a major media conference, and that she should turn on a television so she'd know when to call back. She asked me to hold, which had *me* groaning. I glanced up the hill at McHenry and saw that he was well into his spiel, so I walked back down the slope with the phone clamped to my ear. I was almost at the bench again when a rasping voice came on the line.

'You there, Glass?' said Brady, sounding doubtful that I would be.

'Yes, commissioner,' I said, in a voice that, even to my ears, sounded vaguely irritated.

'Glass, I'm here with Prime Minister Lansdowne, at The Lodge. I understand Mr McHenry's not available at this point in time, so we'll be talking to you. You'll be on the speakerphone for this.'

Blood Oath subscription news

Wednesday 31 July, noon

Will the body bring a bounce?
by Simon Rolfe

When Susan Wright went missing a few days ago, it had everyone fearing the worst.

So now that the worst has come to pass, what should Michael Lansdowne do? Well, given that his government is six points behind in most polls, dare I suggest that a gorgeous state funeral for the 'much loved one' would be a good start.

Assemble a choir of a few hundred pre-pubescents, all decked out in their flouncey bits. Get Archbishop Pickford back from England to officiate. Pack St Andrews with more flowers than Floriade. And don't forget a good producer, one who'll get the cameras in close when the tears start to fall. Then, when the words have all been spoken and the prayers prayed, have her hauled off in a horse-drawn hearse. Eight animals minimum. Big white ones with feathered head-dresses.

If the prime minister does all this, and the show goes off without a hitch, you never know — a dead Susan Wright might just deliver the electoral bounce his government so badly needs.

2

I PAUSED AT the bench I'd shared with McHenry, but the prospect of speaking to the prime minister had brought on such a surge of nerves that I couldn't sit down. So I walked back through the island of shrubs and down the hill again, with McHenry's phone pressed to my ear. As I made my way around the patches of mud that pocked the path, I worked to calm myself by imagining how Lansdowne might be feeling. That wasn't too hard, really. He'd be devastated, of course. He'd lost a close colleague who'd also been one of his best and most popular ministers. And while some commentators had still been giving him a fighting chance in this election, Wright's death would surely put an end to such talk, and that'd be it for his brief and messy prime ministership.

Michael Lansdowne had always seemed destined for The Lodge, although his elevation, when it came, had been anything but orderly. After winning the previous election, his predecessor as PM had used his victory speech to reveal that he was dying of prostate cancer. The jubilant party members who'd gathered to celebrate his win had taken a moment to digest his dreadful news. Then they'd surged towards him, there'd been a terrible crush at the front of the stage, and dozens of people had been injured — some seriously.

When the shell-shocked members of the parliamentary party gathered in Canberra a few days later, they elected Lansdowne as their new leader, and he thus became the new prime minister. The narrowness of his win meant that the early months of the Lansdowne government were marred by in-fighting and a general lack of discipline. Cabinet ministers brawled openly over policy. There were some high-protein leaks. And several junior ministers were forced to resign over a travel scandal. It all added to the picture of a tired and divided party in need of a rest after fourteen years in power. And soon the opinions polls began to reflect the party's malaise.

Worse still for Lansdowne, the opposition was a unified force for the first time in years, thanks to its popular new leader, Lou Feeney. And Feeney had not only produced a swag of appealing policies — he also had the Irish gift of the gab, and a wit to go with it.

And so, behind in the polls, with a quality opponent breathing down his neck, leading a geriatric government, and facing his first election as PM, Lansdowne now had to deal with the death and possible murder of a star minister. I fully expected him to be feeling the pressure.

There was a scraping sound on the other end of the line. And a loud click. Then the prime minister spoke.

'Good afternoon, Detective Glass,' he said.

Like everyone who immersed themselves in the media, I knew the voice well, though I'd only ever heard it in full attack-mode in the House or when he was jousting with the journos. It was weird to have this gentler version of it saying a simple hello to me.

'Good afternoon, Prime Minister,' I said, trying to control the nervous tremour in my own voice.

'Detective, I know you're busy, so I won't keep you long,' said Lansdowne. 'I've convened a special meeting of cabinet this afternoon to discuss this tragedy, and I thought our deliberations might benefit from your assessment of what happened to Susan.'

Contrary to what I'd expected, the prime minister didn't sound like a man under pressure at all. In fact, his calming tone and apparent humility eased some of the pressure I was feeling. I flipped through my notebook and gave him and Commissioner Brady a run-down from the crime scene. My last entry simply read: 'A humane murderer?' I'd intended keeping that thought to myself, but Lansdowne's next question milked it from me.

'So who are we looking for here, detective?' he asked. 'What sort of person would do this?'

'I'm sorry, Prime Minister,' I said, 'but that's not something we've been able to put much work into yet. We're still establishing what happened to Mrs Wright. I mean, we haven't even had the post-mortem. And there's the physical evidence to be analysed, so it'll be a while before we have a clear picture ...'

'Detective Glass, the commissioner here tells me you're one of his best, so I know you've got some ideas. All I want is your sense of who might have done this to Susan.'

He wanted my gut feeling, like I'd given McHenry. Well, okay. He could have it. After all, he was the prime minister. I left the cover of the ghost gum where I'd taken refuge, and walked to the edge of the carpark, keeping my distance from the Forensics guys who were still working nearby.

'Well, sir, given what we know, we're obviously treating Mrs Wright's death as suspicious,' I said. 'But we can't say yet if it was murder. It might turn out to be manslaughter, involving a greater or lesser degree of culpability. But if it went beyond that, if it was murder, then it doesn't look like a hate crime. That is, I don't think Mrs Wright suffered, and she ...'

'What do you mean, it wasn't hateful?' said the prime minister, a note of anger entering his voice. 'They murdered her, didn't they?'

I waited for Brady to intervene, but he remained silent, so I continued with my point, sounding as consoling as I could.

'With respect, sir, it's as I said. We don't know yet if she was murdered. But if she was, then whoever did it didn't display much emotion in the way they went about it. There's no obvious trauma to the body, and no indication that she resisted. Death either came as a complete surprise to her, or she was unconscious at the time. And, sir, if this does become a murder investigation, an analysis of how the murderers went about their business will be one of the things that leads us to them. As I said, this doesn't look like a crime of passion. It was more like an execution. And a relatively humane one, at that.'

I walked along the edge of the carpark. Brady finally spoke.

'We'll know a lot more by the end of the day, Prime Minister. Then it's only a matter of time before we get to the bottom of this, one way or another. And, of course, we'll be throwing everything at it.'

'I appreciate what you say, Jim,' said Lansdowne. 'And I'm certain you've got things under control, but how long before you find the people responsible for this? Days? Weeks, heaven forbid?'

'I wish I could tell you, sir,' said Brady. 'But I can't. It's not something we can ever know. To claim we did would raise unreal expectations, and that would be unfair to you. And to ourselves.'

The line went silent for a minute or more, and, as I waited, I pictured the two of them at The Lodge, sitting in overstuffed leather chairs, gazing pensively at the floor. We'd eventually get to interview the prime minister as part of the investigation, but his hectic campaign-schedule meant it wouldn't happen for some days. The thing was, he might have something valuable to offer us right here, right now. That thought prompted an impulse that I found impossible to repress.

'Prime Minister, while you're on the phone,' I said, in as neutral a tone as I could muster. 'No doubt Susan Wright upset a few people with some of the decisions she made. Do any of those people stand out for you in any way?'

Brady exhaled loudly into the speaker, clearly bristling at this question without notice. But it was Lansdowne who responded, and he sounded sad and reflective.

'Detective, I have no idea why anyone would want to kill Susan,' he said. 'What I do know is, she's dead, and the loss is immeasurable. We're talking about a woman who would have led this country, had she lived.'

It was a rote response and of no use to us at all, so I tried again.

'What about anything environmental that's been before the cabinet in recent times — the policies you were planning to announce in the next week or so? Is there anything there that might have really upset someone who got wind of it?'

'Nothing springs to mind, detective. Now, if that's all ...'

This golden opportunity was turning into a fizzer. Brady growled on the other end of the line. So I took one last shot.

'Just finally, sir, how did Mrs Wright get on with her cabinet colleagues? Especially the ones who might have felt threatened by what they saw as her leadership ambitions?'

This was a step too far — an interrogator's question aimed straight at his throat, and I knew I was in the shit the moment the words had left my mouth. Excuses immediately cascaded through my brain. I could say that the prime minister's call had been unexpected and that I'd been full of adrenalin after an intense and exhausting morning. It was an acceptable excuse, if a bit predictable.

I could also blame the phone itself. Not being face-to-face with Lansdowne had made me forget who I was talking to; the disembodied nature of the contact had flipped me into detective mode. That was better. I'd blame the phone. There was a moment's silence, and then Brady hissed my name down the line.

'Glass!' he said. 'You watch how you …'

'That's okay, commissioner,' said Lansdowne, controlled, but clearly angered. 'Detective Glass, I find that question both odd and offensive. I was warned that you were tactless. Now I find myself agreeing with that assessment. I just hope for Susan's sake that your investigative talents far outweigh your obvious social deficiencies.'

'I think we can let Detective Glass go now, Prime Minister,' said Brady. 'But, first, let me apologise for his, ahh, his eagerness. I can assure you that he's very talented, and that he'll give his all to this investigation.'

'Yes,' said Lansdowne, sounding sceptical. 'I've no doubt that's right.'

They hung up without another word, and I pocketed the phone and tried to calm myself — not the easiest thing to do when you've just challenged two of the most powerful people around and been rebuked by both of them for your trouble. I took a minute to settle my breathing, and then walked back up the hill, quickening my pace as I went, hoping to catch the tail end of the media conference. But as I emerged from the shrubbery near the bench, I saw McHenry walking down the slope to where his mates from the top floor were waiting for him. The five of them put their heads together, with the boss's big noggin sticking out above the rest.

Most of the journos were scurrying off — some to their vehicles, others to a quiet spot where they could file an update over the phone. I looked for Jean Acheson, but couldn't see her anywhere. Probably doing a Live Cam piece, I thought. Then her feather flicked above the movement of bodies, and there she was, at the rear of the thinning scrum, giving instructions to a young woman who seemed to be writing down every word. She turned, our eyes met, and she nodded and smiled at me again.

Given that I'd just harassed the prime minister, a media goddess held no fears for me now. And anyway, who'd she think she was kidding? We'd just kicked off a huge investigation, and here she was, suddenly showing an interest in me? It prompted the obvious question: Did she really think I was that cute? I would have loved to have believed it, but that was fool's thinking. So I forced a smile onto my face and returned her nod, my mind brimming with images of pigs in orbit.

Channel Four Live Cam

Wednesday 31 July, 12.45pm

Good afternoon, Jean Acheson with the Live Cam, and just minutes ago the police confirmed that the body found here by Canberra's Lake Burley Griffin early this morning is indeed that of missing Environment Minister Susan Wright.

The police are treating Mrs Wright's death as suspicious, and if the scale of the search that failed to find her is anything to go by, their investigation into her death will be massive.

Flowers are piling up along the roadside here as word spreads of the minister's tragic demise, and opposition leader Lou Feeney says he'll follow the prime minister's lead and suspend his campaign for at least twenty-four hours as a joint mark of respect.

Prime Minister Lansdowne and most of his cabinet will meet in Canberra later today to discuss the security implications of their colleague's death. This is Jean Acheson. Back with more in a moment.

3

DR MARJORIE ROWAN dabbed some gauze at a weeping incision that traversed the top of Susan Wright's head. She then worked a small, spade-like instrument into the incision and lifted the skin away from Wright's skull. She paused, examined her progress, and worked at the incision for a bit longer. Satisfied, she downed her tool. Then she took the skin of Wright's forehead in both hands and slowly peeled back the dead woman's face to reveal red tissue and skull, and two clouded eyeballs peering from their sockets.

Rowan picked up a small electric saw from a side table, and, with everyone in the room craning for a view, she hit the switch and gently manoeuvred the machine around the edge of the skull. She put the saw down and dabbed more gauze at the furrows she'd created. Then she used another shiny instrument to separate the section of skull from the head.

'Skullcap removed,' she said into a microphone overhanging the table. 'Brain exposed.'

She picked up a scalpel and cut through the tissue connecting the brain stem to the spinal cord. Then she took the brain in both hands, lifted it out of the skull, and put it into a tray, which she placed onto a set of scales.

'One point four three kilos,' she said.

An assistant took the organ away, and Rowan peeled off her surgical gloves and threw them into a bin.

'That's it for now, Mr McHenry,' she said. 'I'll be over your way as soon as I've got something for you.'

Taking that as our marching orders, McHenry thanked Dr Rowan, then led us from the post-mortem room down the main corridor of the Forensics Centre and out through a pair of sliding doors into the carpark. A huge pack of media was pressed against the security fence that surrounded the building, and they immediately began shouting questions at us — which we ignored.

McHenry had arrived at the centre with a couple of uniformed guys, but he dispensed with them and headed straight for the car that Smeaton and I had driven over in. I unlocked the vehicle, and McHenry squeezed himself into the front passenger seat. I figured he'd joined us so that he could give me a bollocking for the way I'd dealt with the prime minister. Perhaps I was even in for an official warning.

I drove slowly through the mass of media people milling around the front gates, and when we'd cleared them, and I had the vehicle up to speed, I braced myself for a whacking. But it didn't come. In fact, once we'd hit the road, McHenry pushed his seat back as far as it would go, then silently stared out the window. Having been displaced by the boss, Smeaton sat cramped up behind me, his legs folded to his chest, his spidery arms wrapped around his knees. He didn't say anything during the drive back, either. Watching someone have their innards outed will quieten most people. And maybe that was why the boss wasn't getting stuck into me. Or maybe Brady hadn't spoken to him yet. Whatever the cause, I knew it was only a reprieve and that I'd soon cop it for my trouble.

When he'd led the search for Susan Wright, McHenry had worked from a Major Incident Room at City Station. Thirty of us now sat behind desks in that same room, waiting for our analyst, Ruth Marginson, to set us up on PROMIS — the Police Realtime

Online Management Information System. It was a sophisticated program that would collate and cross-reference everything we did, everyone we spoke to, and every bit of evidence we'd collect during this investigation.

McHenry leaned over Marginson as she tapped away. Occasionally, he asked her for a change or made a suggestion. When they were satisfied with what they saw on the screen, she leaned back in her seat, and he returned to his desk at the front and raised his hand. The room was immediately silent.

'Dr Rowan'll be here soon,' he said, looking around the group. 'So, while we're waiting, I suggest you all go into PROMIS and see what Ruth's set up for you there.'

McHenry sat down at his desk and began tapping away, and I fired up the computer in front of me and opened PROMIS. The task force that'd searched for Wright had been through her Canberra residence. There was a write-up documenting that effort, and one for the door-to-door work that had covered Wright's possible routes home on the night she disappeared.

There were scanned copies of Wright's phone records, and those of all her staff, as well as copies of letters she'd received from angry greenies, disgruntled farmers, and fruit loops who were obsessed with her or her portfolio. One of the fatter files documented a search of all her office computers. And there were transcripts of interviews with the lobbyists she dealt with, as well as reports on those of them who'd recently suffered a serious knockback.

'Ladies and gentlemen,' said McHenry, rising from his chair. 'I need a minute now.'

He moved to the front of his desk and waited till he had everyone's attention. Then he looked us over again. *Now for the pep talk*, I thought.

'We've got a lot to get through in the next twenty-four hours,' he said. 'So stay focused, be methodical, and follow correct procedure. Do that, and we'll crack this case. And remember — everything that happens in this room, stays in this room, until I clear it. Everyone'll want to know what you're doing in here, but you don't say anything to anyone. Do I make myself clear?'

'Yes, sir,' we said in unison, as though we were all police cadets again.

'Right! Assignments are on the board. As for rosters, there won't be any. We're on this, twenty-four-seven, until we crack it. Having said that, I want everyone to take a few hours off each day to refresh. Fatigue leads to sloppiness, and that's one thing I will *not* tolerate. We'll be setting up stretcher beds in the rec room. Kip when you need to. And people with families, get home when you can, but keep it brief. And check with Ruth or me before you go. There's a dozen people from major crime on the way over. That'll ease the pressure a bit.'

There was a sharp knock at the door, and Dr Rowan walked in, wearing a formless dark suit that she'd dressed up with a single string of pearls. With her was the head of Forensics, Peter Kemp. He wore the same mud-spattered overalls he'd had on at the crime scene. McHenry directed the two of them to the row of chairs beside his desk, and once they were seated, Rowan took a purple folder from her briefcase. She turned to McHenry, who swept a hand in her direction, giving her the go-ahead.

'Thanks, inspector,' she said, adjusting her half-moon glasses. 'Well, ladies and gentlemen, there's been a rare outbreak of unanimity back at the lab. Everyone there, including me, thinks Mrs Wright was murdered.'

She paused while the buzz in the room swelled and died.

'We knew it was carbon monoxide that killed her,' said Rowan. 'But an hour before her death, somewhere around midnight last night, Susan Wright consumed a substantial quantity of sloppy pasta mixed with vegetables. There were traces of maize starch, yeast extract, and cheese in the food, so we're thinking it was tinned soup. And mixed with the soup was a large dose of ketamine, a potent veterinary anesthetic favoured by date-rapists. In other words, Mrs Wright was unconscious when the carbon monoxide got to her, and therefore she had no hand in killing herself.'

Rowan turned to McHenry, and he nodded at her grimly, thus launching a murder investigation without a word. It was what we'd all been expecting, but this confirmation changed the mood in the room in an instant. Like all terrible news, it made the past seem a much simpler place.

'So, let's get to what else we know,' said Rowan. 'The X-rays were normal, and apart from the ketamine, and the carboxyhemaglobin that killed her, there was nothing notable in her blood. And from what we can tell, she hadn't eaten for a while before she ate the soup. In other words, whoever killed her starved her to make sure she'd eat whatever she was offered. That's all from me for now. Peter?'

Kemp thanked her, and, before he spoke, opened his briefcase and took out a plastic evidence bag.

'We're still working our way through most of the physical evidence,' he said. 'But I thought we should bring this mixture of fibres from the victim's clothes to your attention straightaway. There seem to be two things in it. The first is some sort of animal fur — maybe from a dog or a cat. The vet'll have more for us later.

'The second is a bluey-grey manufactured fibre. We think it's probably carpet fluff. The thing is, there was almost twice as much of this fluff on the minister's clothes as there was fur, a fact which gives this mixture a unique signature. In other words, if you find the carpet that this fluff came from, and if that carpet has a healthy amount of animal fur on it, then you're probably in the place where Susan Wright died.'

Channel Four Live Cam

Wednesday 31 July, 6.00pm

Good evening, Jean Acheson with the Live Cam, repeating for those of you who've just joined us that the death of Environment Minister Susan Wright is now the subject of a full-blown murder investigation.

A market summary follows shortly, but first we go to Parliament House, Canberra, where the prayer vigil for Mrs Wright continues. Here's a bit of what Prime Minister Michael Lansdowne told a packed Great Hall just a few minutes ago:

'When we get to the bottom of what happened to Susan, we'll find some measure of peace. Until then, I ask everyone to remain steadfast and courageous in the face of our tragic loss.'

Prime Minister Michael Lansdowne there. Police are yet to say exactly how Mrs Wright died. No doubt they'll let us know in due course. What I can tell you is that the investigation into her murder will be known as Operation Attunga. The name comes from Point Attunga, a feature on the lake near where Mrs Wright's body was found. I'm Jean Acheson. Back with more soon.

4

SUSAN WRIGHT HAD last been seen alive on the previous Sunday night after she left a party in her office. The party had been organised to celebrate a World Environment Prize she'd been awarded the week before. McHenry's team of searchers had assembled six CCTV packages from the party, including vision that tracked the movements of each of the sixty-three guests who'd attended. It meant we knew who'd been where in the office throughout the night, and what they'd done while they'd been there. McHenry's team had also interviewed all the partygoers in the days following the minister's disappearance. After reading the transcripts, the one I most wanted to speak to was Alan Proctor, a senior advisor in the prime minister's office.

According to some witnesses, Proctor had been pissed when he turned up to the party, and, once there, he'd quickly gotten into an argument with Mrs Wright. The two of them had then retreated to the minister's private office. A short time later, Proctor had stuck his head out the door and had ordered an assistant to go and get him a file from his office downstairs.

CCTV didn't cover ministers' private offices, so we had no idea what happened in Wright's office once the boxy-looking file was delivered. But eighteen minutes after it went in there, Wright had emerged with it wedged up under her arm. The time on the footage was 11.18pm. As well as the file, Wright had a small purse dangling from her shoulder, and a briefcase in her hand. She said quick goodbyes to some of her guests as she headed for the door. Footage from a corridor camera showed her entering a lift. There was a grainy shot of her in the lift, and one of her emerging at the ground floor. The lighting was better where she drove out of the building. In that footage, she was alone in her car and looking relatively relaxed. She gave the security guard a nod as he raised the barrier for her. And then she was gone. Sensing the finality of it, I stared at the screen for a few seconds. Then it went to black.

Wright's car had been found in Yarralumla mid-morning the next day. There was nothing in it, except for a street directory and some easy-listening CDs. We assumed the killers now had Wright's purse and briefcase, as well as Proctor's file. Some who'd seen the file when the assistant walked it through the party were convinced it was from Proctor's legendary dirt collection; however, Proctor had told McHenry's search team that it merely contained mundane material from the campaign trail. Regardless of its contents, that file had immediately become an object of interest to our investigation.

Also of interest were seven partygoers we'd dubbed 'The Early Leavers'. CCTV showed them leaving the party and clearing the Hill by the Melbourne Avenue exit, just before or just after Susan Wright had driven off the same way. The Early Leavers weren't suspects as such, but, as McHenry put it, they were a good place to start, and he'd assigned me and Smeaton to re-interview them.

The Early Leavers were Proctor; Wright's senior person, Ron Sorby; her receptionist, Helen Stannage; her environment advisor, Marie Staples; another advisor called James Manton; Proctor's deputy, Penny Lomax; and the journalist Simon Rolfe. The only Early Leavers not available for immediate interview were Rolfe and Proctor.

Rolfe was travelling in far-west Queensland and wasn't due back in Canberra until Friday morning. I'd considered flying some people up to talk to him, or even interviewing him myself over the phone, but McHenry had said he'd keep till Friday.

Proctor was out of town, too, on the campaign trail in Perth. McHenry wanted him brought back to Canberra immediately, but he said to hold off on interviewing him until after we'd spoken to all the other Early Leavers, other than Rolfe. That way, he said, we'd have a firm idea of what went on at Wright's party when we talked to him.

'Okay, Glass,' said McHenry, as he walked past my desk carrying a cup of coffee. 'It's time to see where we're at.'

His even tone told me that if Brady had been on to him about my tangle with the PM, I wasn't in too much trouble — yet. I watched him as he made his way up to the front of the room, his eyes not moving from the cup that he lowered onto his desk. He gazed down at the group that had now swelled to more than forty.

'Ladies and gentlemen,' he said. 'Attention here, if you will. First up, given that Susan Wright was the environment minister, there's been a thought circulating that the perpetrators may have been greenies of some sort. Well, ASIO's assessment is in, and they don't give much credence to that theory. The fact is, they haven't got anyone on their books who fits the bill. But Foreign's looking for any nasties who might've left the country in recent days, so you never know your luck.'

McHenry then asked for progress reports. Soon after the body had turned up, he'd dispatched a team of detectives to the Canberra Yacht Club, which was situated on the lake shore about two hundred metres around from the crime scene. The detectives had interviewed the staff and a handful of early-morning yachties, but, according to the team leader, no one at the club had noticed anyone hanging around or anything out of place in the early hours. And none of them had noticed any strange vehicles parked in the area, either.

Another team was re-examining Wright's mail, but so far they'd found nothing new. Essentially, while a lot of people were very passionate about the environment, no one had made any serious threats against the minister in recent times.

We were also reviewing her phone records, but there were no surprises there yet, either. Nor was there anything helpful in the CCTV footage of roads around the crime scene. Like most security cameras, the ones in question had been set up to monitor buildings, not the roads around them.

'Anything else before we get back to it?' said McHenry, his mouth slightly open in anticipation.

I had something to say.

'Just one thing,' I said, attracting every eye in the room. 'And I guess I already know your answer to this, but if Susan Wright *was* doing a runner with Proctor's file, shouldn't we be accessing the rest of his files, if only to get a sense of why she wanted that one? And, of course, her having that file might've been what prompted the killers to nab her — which makes Proctor's files even more relevant to us.'

'I hear what you're saying,' said McHenry, 'but if we go for those files right now, the government would see it as disruptive to their campaign, so you could expect them to resist. And if we persisted, the barney we'd be buying into would doubtless become a campaign issue. The question is, are those files worth that sort of distraction for us? I think not. So, no, Glass. We won't be going after Proctor's files. Not yet, anyway.'

With that, McHenry closed the meeting, and people headed off to the kitchen for the coffee that would keep them going through the night. I got another one myself, then went back to promis and a package of shots from the party. The drink-fuelled figures who'd danced that night away would probably have been much more inhibited had they known that a bunch of cops would later assess their every move and shake.

I was still studying the party vision when my landline rang. It was Colin Stevenson, an old schoolmate who'd worked on the Hill for as long as I'd been a cop. I ran into Stevo every now and then, in a bar or in a supermarket, and we always shared a laugh recalling the years we'd spent as teenagers hanging out together on the south coast.

Stevo was a political advisor to the minister for immigration these days, but his influence extended far beyond that. How far, I wasn't sure. He said that Susan Wright's murder had floored everyone up on the Hill, and when he'd seen me on the news, it had prompted him to call. If there was anything he could do, he said, I just had to ask — as long as it was all off the record.

Cops and journos have a similar approach to information. Both use secret sources to get it, but good cops, like good journos, always hesitate when offered the good oil 'off the record'. No one wants to be the pawn in someone else's game. So I applied the 'what's in it for him' rule to Stevo's offer, and conceded that I had no idea of his motivation. And as I had little sense of the people we were about to interview, nor any solid background on any of them, I thanked Stevo, and asked him about Wright's senior private secretary, Ron Sorby.

'There's lots to say about Sorby,' said Stevo. 'Just let me grab out some stuff.'

'You've got a file on him?' I said, almost laughing into the phone.

'Not really a file,' said Stevo. 'More like notes. Look, we should get together sometime. For a drink or something. But you need this now, don't you? Ahh, here he is. Sorby. Well, the first thing to say about Ron Sorby is, don't judge him by his looks — the bad hair and the dated get-up. The thing is, he's got great judgement, and he gets things done. Mostly because he knows everyone up here worth knowing. Susan Wright needed more than good looks and a bit of charisma to get her where she did. She needed someone like Sorby. Funny, then, but the word around the traps was that she was getting rid of him after the election. But I guess you'd say he's safe for now. So there you go.'

No, Stevo. There *you* go — pointing the finger at Ron Sorby. I was going to tackle him on it, but then I figured I'd get a better sense of what motivated him if I kept the conversation amicable. So I asked him about the other Early Leavers. He seemed to have 'notes' on all of them. Some of it was complimentary, but mostly it was neutral stuff and had more to do with their abilities than their personalities. Except for the prime minister's man, Alan Proctor. No one seemed to like him very much.

'Here's something I'd ask you if I had you in an interview room,' I said. 'Do you know anyone up there who seriously had it in for Mrs Wright? Anyone who would've done something extreme to get her out of the way?'

'Not really,' said Stevo. 'I mean, a few of her cabinet colleagues will be breathing easier with her gone. You know — one less hurdle between them and the top job. Then again, no matter what happens on Saturday week, they'll all still have Lansdowne to contend with. He waited a long time for the leadership, and he's been letting everyone know he plans to hold on to it — win, lose, or draw.

'But the interesting thing here is, Wright told our people that if the government lost, no matter what the margin, she'd be shifting her support to Malcolm Redding. So everyone's devastated that she's dead, but for some it has a very definite silver lining to it.'

Blood Oath subscription news

Wednesday 31 July, 10.00pm

Proctor should tumble if he doesn't come clean
by Simon Rolfe

First, a declaration: I hate Alan Proctor, and he likes me even less. Gentle readers might remember that it was Proctor who got me sacked as media advisor to transport minister Terry Sarmen some years ago. He said at the time that Sarmen would end up in the shit with me managing his media.

Well, I found my true calling as the scribe who keeps the bastards bull-free. And Terry didn't last, anyway. Which brings me back to my old mate Alan Proctor, and the fireworks between him and Susan Wright on the night 'The Popular One' disappeared.

As regular readers will know, I was at Wright's party, and having witnessed the said fireworks, it's clear to me that Alan isn't telling all he knows.

So let us in on your secrets, Alan. What was it you said to Susan Wright that had her crashing out of her party the night she went missing? What was in the file you showed her? And where's that file now? And how would you feel if it suddenly popped up somewhere? Like on Blood Oath. And finally Alan, tell me, who's in the shit now?

5

'Susan Wright looked good,' said Stevo. 'She worked hard. And she could've easily leapt over the lot of them, and they knew it. She only ever stuffed up once, but that didn't really hurt her.'

'What was that about again?' I said. 'When she stuffed up?'

'The Mondrian affair,' he said. 'You'd remember it.'

I remembered the affair, but only vaguely. It was early in the government's first term, so it must have been about fourteen years ago. Susan Wright, as the then minister for housing, had introduced a voucher scheme to give homeless people a nightly bed in budget accommodation. The move had enjoyed bipartisan support, and it was certainly good policy, given that the turn-away rate for shelters at the time ran at something like 90 per cent. I remembered Wright launching the scheme on TV, in the foyer of a backpacker hostel. She'd been hugging two skinny kids as they held up books of vouchers for the cameras.

I was a bit hazy on what happened next, so Stevo refreshed my memory. He said the publicity for the bed scheme had transformed Wright into an instant media darling, but that didn't last long. Not after a newspaper revealed that a few months before the scheme was launched, Mondrian Investment Bank had secretly acquired Dolman Holdings, the owner of Australia's biggest chain of backpacker hostels.

The story highlighted Mondrian's vocal support for government policy, and its generous contributions to the government's re-election coffers. And it went on to accuse Susan Wright of 'borderline' corruption, given that her bed vouchers would boost Mondrian's income by tens of millions of dollars a year, thanks to the hostels that the bank had acquired through its Dolman purchase.

Stevo said Mondrian's share price had soared in the days following the story, prompting the opposition to withdraw its support for the voucher scheme. Then it boycotted all parliamentary debate on the matter.

'Things went quiet for a while after that,' he said. 'Then *The Chronicle* got hold of some purchase documents which showed that the Dolman deal had been brokered for Mondrian by Mick Stanton. Of course, everyone knew that Stanton was Michael Lansdowne's nephew, but what *The Chronicle* told the world was that Stanton had been working in Susan Wright's office when the voucher scheme was being developed. Well, you can imagine what the rest of the media made of that. Adding to our woes was the fact that Lansdowne was justice minister at the time, so he had responsibility for any probe into the Dolman purchase.'

'But he ordered an inquiry into it, didn't he?'

'Of course he did. He had no choice. And, in the end, the Securities Commission found nothing untoward in the whole affair. No smoking gun, anyway, so it all died a natural death when parliament rose for Christmas that year. Susan Wright ended up a bit tainted by it all, and that delayed her move into cabinet. But Lansdowne came out of it smelling like a rose. And, of course, Mondrian's made heaps from those vouchers ever since.'

Someone tapped me on the shoulder. It was Smeaton. He leaned over and whispered that he was going down to the front desk to fetch our first Early Leaver, Ron Sorby. I thanked Stevo for the call, took his number, and agreed that we should catch up. But after he'd hung up, I wondered about his motives in fingering Sorby. And why he'd raised the Mondrian affair, given the damage it could do the government if we had another look at it — especially at the tail end of an election campaign. It was all beyond me at this point. Walking to the interview room, I resolved to delve into the Mondrian business, but on the quiet. And if I found that Stevo had been playing me, I'd hammer him hard.

When Ron Sorby entered the interview room, he looked every bit the diffident chap that Stevo had described. He watched the door close behind him, then he slumped reluctantly into the chair on the opposite side of the table and promptly dropped his eyes to his lap.

'Thanks for coming down at this hour, Mr Sorby,' I said.

Sorby flicked me a look, then went back to examining his lap. All of the political staffers that I knew decked themselves out in the latest office gear. Sorby's get-up, by contrast, was drab in the extreme: a grey cardigan over a white shirt, with a blue stripey tie and light-grey trousers. Even his hair, which was shortish on top and long at the back, was done in a style favoured by old-time public servants — the sort who'd go out for a big Friday night and paint the town grey.

Smeaton hit 'record' and named the three of us in the room. Then he gave me the thumbs up, and I eased Sorby into the interview by asking how long he'd worked up at the House.

'I started in late '99,' he said, making eye contact for the first time. 'As deputy secretary to the Joint Standing Committee on the Environment. And I've been up there ever since. At one thing or another.'

'How'd you come to be working for Susan Wright?'

'I stepped in after the last election, when she shifted from Home Affairs to Environment. She was going to recruit for the position, but things worked out between us, and after a few months she asked me to stay. That's almost three years ago now, and we were still going strong. Until this.'

Either Sorby was unaware of Susan Wright's plans for him, or he was in denial. Or maybe Stevo was wrong, or being mischievous. But with the election imminent, Sorby's job security was tenuous at best, anyway. He was gone if the government lost. And if it won, would Wright's replacement keep him on? I had no idea, but given where we were at in the electoral cycle, job security seemed like a pretty pale motive for murder. But I put the question anyway.

'It's interesting hearing you so upbeat about your relationship with Mrs Wright,' I said. 'Especially when people say she was going to sack you after the election.'

'I know what people say,' said Sorby, some steel entering his voice. 'But, detective, this town's full of bullshit. And, mark my words, we'll all be *wading* in it by election day.'

'So you and Mrs Wright were solid?' said Smeaton, looking doubtful. 'No tension? No drama on the job front?'

'It can be heavy going up there,' said Sorby. 'You get snakey with someone over something, and it's hard to let go. And yes, sometimes she got impatient. But she never wanted me gone.'

'Mr Sorby, you left the office party just after the minister,' said Smeaton. 'And you were only a couple of minutes behind her when she left the building. Can you tell us where you went after you left that night?'

'Straight home. My wife and I've been having some problems, so I went straight home.'

'Your wife can vouch for you, then?'

'Well, actually, she wasn't there in the end. She'd gone to her sister's.'

'And where were you between eight o'clock last night and eight this morning?'

'I was in the office till about six last night. Then I dropped in at the Kingo for a couple, and I was home by eight. And I was still in bed this morning when the call came through. About the body.'

'Was anyone home with you last night?' I said.

'No. The wife's still away.'

'Mmm. Okay. Well, do you know of anyone who may have wanted to harm Susan Wright? Any threats made against her? Any particular enemies?'

'Look, detective, everyone in this game's your enemy,' said Sorby. 'No matter what side they're supposed to be on. And if you give some bastards up there the space to swing an axe, they'll chop your head off if it suits them.'

'With respect, Mr Sorby,' I said, leaning across the table towards him. 'That sort of stuff probably goes down really well with kids doing politics 101, but it's not what I want to hear from you right now. So I'll ask you again. Do you know anyone who had a reason to murder Susan Wright?'

'No. I don't know anyone capable of killing her. It was so, so … I don't know. So over the top.'

'It was that,' I said. 'Now, I know you've been through this before, but let's talk about Sunday night. Mrs Wright left the party abruptly, and we're told she was visibly upset at the time. Do you know what caused her early exit?'

'No, I don't. She and I had been in the corridor with Alan Proctor from the PMO, going through the environment launch with him. And we'd just got onto discussing the PM's involvement when my wife rang on my mobile, so I took the call in my office. With the door closed.'

I loaded PROMIS, and adjusted the screen so that we could all see the layout of Wright's office suite.

'So the three of you were about here,' I said, pointing to the section of corridor between Sorby's office and the minister's.

'Yes,' said Sorby. 'And when I finished the call I came out, and someone said the minister and Proctor had gone into her office. And the door was closed. She generally kept it open unless she had something confidential going on, so I hung around and waited for them to come out. And when she did, about a quarter of an hour later, she was obviously upset, and she said a quick goodbye to everyone and left. And the show effectively broke up after that.'

'What did she have with her when she walked out?'

I pictured the CCTV images of the minister heading off carrying her briefcase and purse, with the boxy file under her arm. Sorby's eyes dropped back to his lap. Then he looked up.

'Her briefcase,' he said. 'And her purse. And she had a file with her. But you'd know about that.'

'The file,' I said. 'Do you know what was in it?'

'No. I wish I did.'

'But it was a red prime-ministerial file?'

'That's right. And I'm pretty sure it was Proctor's. But that's all I know.'

'Were you surprised to see her leave with it? The file?'

'Well, yes, I suppose I was. But I didn't say anything about it. She was upset. That's what concerned me most. It was rare to see her like that.'

'And you reckon a lot of people left soon after she did?'

'Yeah. Most of them were only there because of her. Once she went, there was no point in most of them hanging around. The same with me, too. I called the office after I got home, some time after midnight, but only the diehards were left by then.'

'The diehards?' said Smeaton.

'Five or six of the boys,' said Sorby. 'Blokes who work long hours, who love a beer and who're never desperate for the night to end. Blokes like me, I guess.'

In any other context, this semi-confession might have provoked sympathy, or at least a moment's silence. But I pushed on.

'Back to the party, then,' I said. 'Did you speak to Alan Proctor after he came out of her office?'

'Yes, I did,' he said. 'He looked very unhappy, and I asked him a couple of times if he was alright, but he ignored me and just staggered off like the rude bastard he is.'

'And do you know why he was unhappy?'

'No, I don't. Maybe the file being taken? I don't know.'

We finished the interview by asking Sorby to outline the roles of the various people in his office, just to fill in the picture of how the place worked. I warned him not to talk to anyone about the interview, and let him know that we might need to talk to him again. He rose from his seat and thanked us, and Smeaton ushered him out.

Sorby's daggy clothes and diffident manner clearly masked some special qualities. Maybe, just maybe, one of them was the capacity to murder a boss who'd been planning to give him the flick. Then again, he didn't strike me as a bloke who would have the nerve for it, especially when a murder charge would put him under a national spotlight in the middle of an election campaign.

Blood Oath subscription news

Thursday 1 August, 6.00am

A bounce comes early
by Simon Rolfe

Prime Minister Michael Lansdowne will be celebrating this morning's Aztec poll, which has his government surging to be just three percentage points behind the opposition, on a two-party-preferred basis.

One obvious explanation for this remarkable turnaround is the sympathy the government has garnered following Susan Wright's tragic demise. If her death is the cause, the prime minister should know that sympathy is an emotion that quickly dissipates, and in no time flat, he may find himself back where he started this campaign. Eight points behind and heading south.

Another possible explanation for the government's good numbers is a nasty little rumour that's doing the rounds. The rumour targets Opposition Leader Lou Feeney, and the question for those who've heard it is this: is it a tale concocted for electoral gain, or does it indicate something truly dark about our alternative leader? I'd hope to have an answer for you all in coming days.

But back to the government's better-than-expected poll numbers. And my advice to Mr Lansdowne is to capitalise on them by flipping the switch to fear. Immediately. It's worked fabulously well for his party in the past, and now that he has a well-known and much-loved corpse to use as his prop, the prime minister can thunder on with true conviction about the disintegration of law and order in our nation. And as you consider this impending assault on your senses, dear readers, please remember. The prime minister doesn't have to fool all of you all of the time. Just the majority of you in the lead-up to polling day.

6

I was scrambling up a muddy slope in fading light. A grey mist swirled in the valley below and expanded towards me. I had to make it to a line of trees near the top, and I was making good ground.

Then I lost my footing and fell on my face, and started sliding backwards on all fours. The more desperate my efforts to halt my slide, the faster I descended the slope. And all the time the mist was closing in.

I got to my feet and was again scrambling up the slope. Then I tripped over a tussock of grass and went over again. I was looking up at the trees on the ridgeline when the mist enveloped me, the ground gave way, a hole opened up underneath me, and I fell in. Then, hurtling through total darkness, I braced for the impact, choking with dread, and suddenly I …

I sat up with a start and pulled in a big breath. My bedding was soaked, my eyes felt sore and heavy, but I was relieved to be awake. Woolly light framed the closed curtains of the rec room. According to the wall clock, it was six-fifteen. I'd had four hours' sleep, and it was time to get moving again. I got up and left the room as quietly as I could so as not to disturb the other sleepers. I had a shower and got dressed, and then made a strong cup of coffee and took it to my desk.

The room was full of people. Some were on the phone. Others were tapping away at their machines. And another lot were deep in discussion in the back corner. I wasn't up to talking, so I drank my coffee and trawled the morning papers. Then I moved onto the websites. All of them carried tributes from Wright's admirers and colleagues, and most photo spreads included shots of me looking very solemn at the crime scene.

I glanced up at McHenry. He was behind his desk at the front of the room, the tip of his tongue moving between his lips as he prodded his keyboard with his index fingers. I'd put a note on PROMIS outlining what Stevo had told me about Mondrian. I'd also noted rumours about Sorby's doubtful tenure with Wright. I waited for McHenry to finish what he was doing, then went up and told him that I wanted to pursue both leads.

'Do it,' he said, slumping back in his chair. 'But use discretion on the Mondrian business, please. And don't let this Stevenson play you. I'll see if there's someone in the opposition we can talk to as well, just to keep things balanced. But leave that for now — I've got something else for you to go on with.'

He signalled for Smeaton to join us, then unlocked his desk drawer and produced an evidence bag with Susan Wright's name on it. The bag held some of the carpet fluff that had come from her clothes. He handed it to me.

'Forensics sent it to their fibre expert over at the uni,' he said, eyeing the fluff. 'The expert reckons it's from high-grade carpet. Axminister, to be precise. Eighty per cent wool. Twenty per cent nylon. The sort of floor covering you find in national institutions like the High Court, the National Gallery, and Parliament House.'

Smeaton usually looked vaguely anxious around McHenry, but, on hearing this news, he gave the boss a rare smile. I thought it sounded pretty good, too.

'And it gets better,' said McHenry, licking his lips. 'A few years ago, this fibre guy got his students to analyse the carpets in ten public buildings around Canberra, including Parliament

House. On the basis of what they found back then, he says he's pretty sure our bluey-grey fluff here comes from carpet made *exclusively* for the House.'

This was stunning news, though it was hard to believe that we'd come up with something so solid so early.

'Let me get this straight,' I said. 'The heaviest concentration of fluff on Wright's clothes corresponded with those areas of her body where the lividity formed. So, presumably, she was lying on a floor thick with this stuff when she died, and it got compressed onto her. Now if this fluff *is* from carpet made exclusively for Parliament House, it either means she was killed up there, at the House, or …'

'Or what?' said McHenry. 'What else can it mean?'

I had no idea, but I gave him the only other possible explanation.

'Or the fibre expert's got it wrong,' I said.

'Maybe, but I don't think so,' said McHenry. 'Anyway, I've got the name of a bloke who helped lay the original carpet at the House. That's the good news. The bad news is, this Barry Waldeck leaves this afternoon for a month in Hong Kong, so you two have about ten minutes before you're supposed to meet him in Fyshwick.'

Barry Waldeck was waiting on the footpath when we pulled up outside Carpet Central. He was a little bloke with badly dyed black hair and a firm handshake. With introductions done, we followed him through his showroom, past a dozen or more giant rolls of carpet and into a small office set into the back corner of the place.

Once we were seated around his desk, I told Waldeck that we were trying to identify an assault victim who'd been found with lots of carpet fibre on their clothes. Waldeck looked at me doubtfully and asked where the assault had occurred. Everything to do with the crime was confidential, I said. He nodded, but I figured he'd seen me in the media and had put two and two together.

When I handed him the evidence bag, Waldeck took it like it was some fragile thing. He placed it on his desk, opened it, and carefully removed the small sausage of fluff. Then he smelt the fluff, rubbed it between his thumb and forefinger, and stretched it a bit. Finally, he put it under his desk lamp and closed in on it with a giant magnifying glass.

'Blue-grey Axminister,' he said at last, easing the fluff back into the plastic bag. 'That's what this lint is. From the same stock we laid up at the House. Tassie carpet. The best. Made especially for the job.'

'So these fibres are definitely from the carpet you laid at Parliament House,' I said. 'Is that what you're saying?'

'No. What I'm sayin' is, I'm pretty sure it's from the same *stock*. But whether it came off any carpet *laid* up there, I don't know. Let me get old Len in 'ere. He'll explain it better.'

Waldeck got on the phone, and soon there was a rap at the door, and a craggy old bloke in faded blue overalls limped into the room. After introductions, 'old' Len slumped into the only spare chair and Waldeck pointed to the bag of fluff and asked him where he thought it was from. Len removed the fluff from the bag and rubbed it between knuckles bulging with arthritis. He stretched it and smelt it, just as Waldeck had done, only more slowly. Then a faraway smile lit his face, as though the fluff had prompted a pleasant memory.

'It's Parliament House stock,' said Len, nodding as he continued to study the fibre. 'This stuff went down in most of the public areas. And the ministerial wing. And the library. And a few other places. I don't remember the dye lot number. I knew it back then, but the memory's a bit like the knees these days. It's from Brindells, though. And they'd have it. The number. Ya see, no two dye lots are the same, so you send them this bit of lint, and they'll give you the details, for sure.'

'And would Brindells have used the same dye on other jobs?' I said. 'I mean, would you find the same-coloured carpet in other places around Canberra?'

'No way they'd do that,' said Len, looking at me doubtfully. 'That was an exclusive run, that one.'

I looked at Smeaton and he smiled back at me, both of us chuffed at this apparent confirmation that Susan Wright had died up at the House. I looked at Len. The semi-scowl on his face told me he was about to set us straight.

'As for where this lint came from,' he said, 'I really can't say for sure. Possibly Parliament House. But those pollies, you know, they're like you cops. Very particular types. They like their offices spick and span, so they get them vacuumed every night. I could spend half a day rolling around on the floors up there and still wouldn't get half as much lint on me as this little bit. Yah know what I'm sayin?'

'No, Len,' I said, my guts in freefall. 'Exactly what are you saying?'

'I think it's for sure that this lint is from Parliament House stock,' he said. 'But I don't think it's from up there.'

Oh no. Snakes and ladders.

'So where do you think it's from, Len?' I said.

'Here's what I reckon,' he said, leaning in close. 'It's from offcuts.'

'Offcuts? What offcuts?'

'There were all sorts of offcuts from the Parliament House job. Bits of granite. Lengths of timber. Plasterboard and the like.

The construction authority sold it all off to a few places around town, and then those places broke it down into smaller parcels and flogged it off to the punters. For souvenirs and the like. Some of it was absolute rubbish, but it sold — boy did it sell. One bloke I know got all the excess granite from the outside walls. He had it stacked up in a paddock out on the Captains Flat Road. Some big pieces, too. That sold so quick it was unbelievable.'

'And don't tell me. There were carpet offcuts, too.'

'Too right there was. And we bought the lot. Barry here did, at least. Ended up with the equivalent of about ten rolls, didn't you, Baz?'

Waldeck nodded and smiled, but said nothing, enjoying the memory.

'We had some little pieces and bigger bits,' said Len. 'And we put a notice in the local rag and sold the lot. Didn't we, Baz? You remember. The place was crawlin' with people. Most of it was gone by midday.'

'That's right,' said Waldeck, now looking a bit sheepish. 'But I'm sorry, detective. Like Len says, it was all a bit mad in here that day, so it was strictly cash sales, and we kept no record of any of them.'

Channel Four Live Cam

Thursday 1 August, 8.30am

Good Morning, Jean Acheson with the Live Cam, and Prime Minister Michael Lansdowne has told Breakfast Beat that security for senior government ministers and members of the opposition front bench will be beefed up following the murder of Environment Minister Susan Wright.

And while the prime minister refused to go into detail, I understand that most of what he has in mind is contained in a Senate report on parliamentary security which he and his cabinet rejected earlier this year.

That report proposed an allocation of four extra police bodyguards for the prime minister, two for each member of cabinet, and two for the opposition leader and his deputy, plus the introduction of dog patrols in the parliamentary precinct.

When asked if Mrs Wright's death had forced him to reverse his position on the Senate report, Mr Lansdowne said her murder had been a shocking lesson for everyone. We've got Morning Brunch coming up on the Live Cam. This is Jean Acheson.

7

THE PROBLEM WITH me sniffing around an old scandal like the Mondrian Affair was that some journo might get wind of it. The last thing we needed was for the media to rehash the whole business by linking it to our investigation. The government wouldn't take that lying down, especially with the election so close. At the very least, they'd wheel out a senior minister to savage us. They might even get Lansdowne to do the job. And if they did that, he'd probably target me personally after our little chat on the phone.

Back from Fyshwick, I had a quick read of the Security Commission inquiry into Mondrian, and then rang an old mate who I thought might have more information on it. Tim O'Brien and I had done three years at Woden station together. He'd gone on to the commission and was now running its compliance effort. Tim's work phone went to messages, so I tried his home number and that's where I found him, sick as a dog with the latest flu. I told him I was interested in Mondrian, but emphasised that it was all strictly hush-hush. He said he understood, and told me that he had a staff member who'd been an investigator on the Mondrian inquiry. He assured me that this Colin Wells could keep his trap shut, and gave me Wells' mobile number.

I immediately phoned Wells, mentioned Tim, and asked if we could talk face-to-face as soon as possible. Wells said he was happy to help, and we agreed to meet at Café del Sol in Garema Place. He said he'd be wearing a long, black coat and that he had a scraggy beard. The beard was why some of his mates called him Fidel, he said.

'Fidel' Wells was easy to spot when he entered the café. His beard was thin on his cheeks and thick under his chin. To my eye, the thing made him look more like an old-time Quaker than a Latin revolutionary. I signalled him over, and we ordered coffees and talked AFL till our drinks arrived. Then we got down to business.

'I've skimmed your report on Mondrian,' I said, 'so I've got a fair idea of what you found. My question is, did you ever feel there was more to it? You know — things you could've got to if you'd been able to use thumbscrews?'

'Not really,' said Wells, smiling and shaking his head. 'I mean, it's possible that Mick Stanton got wind of the voucher scheme while he was working for Wright, but he said he didn't, and we had no way of contradicting him. And as for Lansdowne, Stanton was adamant that he never talked shop with his uncle — not while he was working for Wright, nor later when he went to Mondrian. And Lansdowne backed him all the way on that.'

'And Susan Wright? How'd you see her role in the whole affair?'

'Innocent enough, I guess, if a bit naive. She supported Stanton's claim that he had nothing to do with putting the voucher scheme together. And she said she didn't know anything about his role at Mondrian, either. We had no evidence to the contrary. And, you know, these ex-political types parlay their contacts and knowledge into big bucks all the time. On the face of it, Stanton's only sin was tipping his bank into a scandal.'

'So everyone came out of the Mondrian affair virtually unscathed,' I said, looking up from my notebook.

'Not exactly everyone,' said Wells. 'Susan Wright's senior person at the time took some big hits.'

'That was Dennis Hanley?'

'Correct. The voucher scheme was Hanley's baby, and in the end it buried him. He was a big-picture person, but very poor on detail. Like, he left it to a junior person to examine the corporate beneficiaries of the scheme, and that effectively put the job on hold. The thing was, this mob'd only been in office for about a year at that stage, so the whole ministerial wing was more or less in chaos — everyone leaving it to someone else to do the necessaries. Well, in this case, the buck stopped with Hanley.'

'So what happened to him?'

'He lost his job. And it turned into a double whammy for him, because the story goes that he and Wright had been having it off, and she put an end to their affair once the scandal broke. She'd trusted him to look after her interests, and he demonstrated a shaky grasp of process. So he paid the price.'

'And where's Hanley now?'

'Oh, I thought you'd know,' said Wells, swirling the last of his coffee around in his cup. 'He died a few months after we reported — so, about eleven years ago now.'

'How'd it happen?'

'He had a head-on with a stock transporter out on the Sutton Road. He was pissed at the time, but I understand not so pissed that he didn't know which side of the road he should've been on.'

'And Stanton's dead, too, isn't he?'

'Ahh, so you *do* read the obituaries. Yeah, dead as well. He joined Mondrian as a lean and nosey go-getter, but after five years there, he was so fat and flatulent that his ticker just went pop.'

Blood Oath subscription news

Thursday 1 August, 10.00am

PNG offers Oz aid, no bowstrings attached
by Simon Rolfe

Our nearest neighbour, Papua New Guinea, is a country we love to tut-tut about and lecture, especially when its law officers go AWOL in the face of a disorderly public. Now PNG has returned the favour, and you've got to love a dependant with a sense of humour.

You see, the Commissioner of the Royal Papua New Guinea Constabulary, Mr Iambakey Maladina, has offered to assist Australia in the hunt for Susan Wright's killer.

In fact, Commissioner Maladina says he has twenty officers who are ready and willing to travel to Canberra right now, and he reckons his men's depth of experience would help bring the Wright investigation to a fast and fruitful conclusion.

Long known as an organisation that appreciates a joke, the AFP has thanked Commissioner Maladina, but gratefully declined his offer.

8

FOR PEOPLE BUYING property, it's location, location, location. For cops working an investigation, it's walk, walk, walk, and talk, talk, talk. Cops in the ACT had walked thousands of kilometres since Wright disappeared, sacrificing their soles in several fruitless door-to-doors. Nor had the thousands of callers to our hot line delivered anything substantial. As a talker, I was mostly spared the walking, and that suited me fine. My first interview for the day was another Early Leaver — Susan Wright's environment advisor, Marie Staples.

According to my political mate Stevo, Staples had studied science at Sydney University, where she'd belonged to various left-wing groups, including one that published the *Progressive Green Quarterly*. She'd even edited the magazine for a year and sold it on street corners around Sydney's CBD.

But in her final year of study, Staples surprised her comrades by cutting all ties with 'the movement' and engrossing herself in her books. More were surprised when she graduated with straight As and got a job in the government's National Environment Foundation.

Staples' mum had been at school with Susan Wright. The two had remained close, so when Marie Staples later got a job in Wright's office, some people accused the minister of nepotism. However, according to Stevo, Staples had a lot more going for her than good connections. In fact, she'd shone in Wright's office, thanks to her deep knowledge of all things green and her great negotiating skills.

When Smeaton ushered Staples into the room, it was easy to see how she could win people over. In her late twenties, she was well formed and pretty, with a bob of blond hair that fringed her penetrating blue eyes.

I began by asking her where she'd spent her time at Wright's party. She said that, like most of the staff, she'd hung around the reception area, filtering journos, and monitoring the various comings and goings.

When McHenry's search team had interviewed Staples, she'd given one of the more graphic accounts of the argument between Susan Wright and Alan Proctor, so that's where I went next.

Staples said that at about ten-thirty she'd noticed Susan Wright in a huddle with Proctor and Sorby in the corridor outside the minister's office. The next time she looked, Sorby was gone, and the minister and Proctor had moved to the end of the corridor.

'Did you hear what they were talking about?'

'No. The music was way too loud, and, you know, the minister and Proctor were real heavyweights, so when they put their heads together, everyone gave them a bit of space.'

'And what happened then? Once their heads were together?'

'Well, you could tell things were getting testy between them. The body language. And the way they were looking at each other. Especially the way the minister was looking at him — so pissed off. And at one point she really let him have it.'

'You mean she shouted at him,' said Smeaton.

'She didn't shout really. There was just a lot of, like, emotion in what she said, and it cut through the other noise.'

'And what did she say?'

'It was, "That's not going to happen", or, "That won't happen." Something like that. She said it loud enough so that people looked at her. That's when the two of them went into her office.

Simon Rolfe was with us by then, and, being a typical journo, he said someone should put their ear to the door. We all ignored him, of course, but I would've given anything to have been a fly on the wall in there.'

'And Alan Proctor came out a bit later,' I said, 'and told his assistant, Janet Wilson, to go down to his office and get him a file.'

'That's right. From his security cabinet.'

'He keeps his files in a special cabinet?'

'Yes. The sensitive ones.'

'The dirt files,' said Smeaton.

'That's what some people call them,' said Staples.

'And how did Janet Wilson get access to this cabinet if it was secure?' I said. 'Did Proctor give her a key or something?'

'No, Mr Proctor can open his cabinet remotely with his BlackBerry. And he can use the BlackBerry to release individual files in the cabinet, too. We've got the same system in our office, but our files aren't as, ahh, interesting as Mr Proctor's.'

'And Proctor's files — they're big and red, and look a bit like a box. What else can you tell us about them?'

'Well, we call them files, but, as you say, they're more like oblong boxes. They come in various sizes, and they're locked into individual slots inside a secure cabinet. The whole system's pretty much standard in the ministerial wing these days.'

'Okay. So Proctor got this box file brought up to him, took it into the minister's office, and closed the door. What then?'

'They were in there for about fifteen minutes, then the minister came out and she had Proctor's file with her, as you know. And that was it. She said a quick goodbye and left.'

I visualised the scene again: the minister with her hands full, pushing through partygoers, uttering perfunctory farewells as she headed for the door.

'And you're sure it was Proctor's file she was carrying?'

'Yep. A red, secured file from the PMO. We don't see many of them up here.'

'You left the party straight after the minister,' said Smeaton. 'And we've got you driving out of the Senate-side carpark at 11.27pm — a few minutes before the minister exited the building in her car. You got out of there pretty quickly, didn't you?'

'Yes. I use the stairs rather the lift,' she said. 'And why did I leave straight after the minister? Well, I was tired, and I'm not much of a drinker. So I went home and was asleep by midnight. Sadly, there's no one you can check that with.'

Sad indeed. I put my eyes into neutral and lingered on hers. She stared back, waiting for the next question.

'And where were you between eight o'clock on Tuesday night, and eight on Wednesday morning?'

'I was at home. Alone again.'

'Okay, just one more thing before you go. What can you tell us about Ron Sorby's relationship with Susan Wright? Did they get on, as far as you could tell?'

'Mmm, I'm not sure. They seemed fine to me. Why, what's been said?'

'Nothing. He was her senior person, that's all, so their relationship is naturally of interest to us.'

Staples nodded, seeming to accept my explanation. And that was it for her — another Early Leaver without an alibi. With an environment minister dead, a former radical environmentalist had to rate a high level of interest from us. I escorted her from the building, intent on delving deeper into her past.

Smeaton brought in some coffees, and then collected our next Early Leaver, Proctor's deputy, Penny Lomax. Lomax made good eye-contact during introductions, and there was nothing passive about her handshake, either. I figured her as a person who was used to dealing with new and threatening situations. Or maybe she was just well prepared for this one. The only evidence of nerves was the way she constantly readjusted her glasses as we talked. But she was polite and to the point, and she was very pretty.

Stevo hadn't known much about her — just that she'd worked for a senior government backbencher before she'd joined Lansdowne's staff. Lansdowne had been communications minister at the time, and Lomax's computer skills had helped her leapfrog other contenders into the job. According to Stevo, Lomax and Proctor were close — so close, in fact, that she'd even been touted as a possible candidate in the election after this one.

Like Staples, Lomax had spent most of her time at the party in reception. But unlike Staples, she downplayed the stoush between Proctor and the minister. I figured it was loyalty talking, so I moved on and asked about the file.

'Do you have any idea what was in it?' I said.

'No, I don't,' she said.

'I understand it came from a special cabinet in Alan Proctor's office. Do you have access to that cabinet?'

'No. I work with some of those files, but Alan's the only one who can access them at will.'

'With his BlackBerry.'

'That's right.'

'Do the files stay locked once they've been taken out of the cabinet?'

'No. They're not secure once they're out of their slots.'

I let that penetrate for a few seconds, then nodded at Smeaton.

'So, Miss Lomax,' he said, his long, thin fingers drumming on the table. 'You left the party immediately after the minister. Can you tell us why you chose to go at that point?'

'I didn't leave immediately after her,' said Lomax. 'I left immediately after Alan. He's my boss, and when he goes, I can go.'

'And you beat the minister out of the building,' said Smeaton. 'In fact, you got out so fast I'd say you broke a few records.'

'I like to get home,' she said. 'I've got a great job, but I love my sleep, too.'

'So you went straight home?' I said.

'That's right.'

'Can anyone vouch for you?'

'No, I live alone. I don't even own a cat.'

The word 'cat' stopped me in my tracks. Lomax's eyes stayed locked on mine as she waited for the next question. She was ready, but not tense. Like a tennis player anticipating the return of the ball, she was intent on staying in the game. There was nothing in the cat reference.

'You've worked for Alan Proctor for what, now?' I said. 'Three years, is it? I know politics is a very combative business, but have you ever seen him exercise perhaps a little too much vigour when it came to tackling a political problem?'

'If that's your way of asking whether Alan's capable of murder,' said Lomax, 'let me say that if I were trying to picture the sort of person who might have done this to Mrs Wright, Alan would not feature.'

'Why not?'

'Because I don't think he's capable of violence. He's just not made that way. I mean, he hates football because it's rough. And he can't watch those real-life medical shows on TV. He's just too squeamish. So Alan Proctor and murder? I don't think so. It's not in him.'

It sounded like loyalty talking again, and even if Proctor *was* averse to violence, anyone was capable of anything, given enough motivation and the right opportunity. I took a deep breath, considered asking her more about Proctor, but then decided against it. I'd find out for myself soon enough.

'Finally, Miss Lomax,' I said, 'can you tell us where you were between eight o'clock Tuesday night and eight on Wednesday morning?'

'I spent Tuesday organising a marginal-seat visit for Alan,' she said. 'I finished that at about six. Then I went home, made some tea, and I was in bed with a book by nine. Then on Wednesday morning, I was back in at work by seven.'

And that was that. I thanked her, and Smeaton escorted her out.

James Manton was the next Early Leaver. He was a bright young guy with Jesus-length hair and a well-groomed beard. He'd advised Susan Wright on world-heritage issues. He said he'd spent the party drinking beer with the boys in the open-plan office out the back. He wasn't aware of any 'aggro' between the minister and Proctor on the night, and he said Sorby and Wright had always got on just fine, as far as he could tell. As for why he'd left the party so soon after the minister, he said he'd promised his mum he'd be home by midnight, and he was. And he was also home with her when the body was dumped.

After Manton, I went back to the room and found a cup of takeaway coffee sitting on my desk. I looked around to see who I should thank for it, but no one eyed me to claim the credit. Probably McHenry, I thought, though he was out. Sitting next to the coffee were two documents I'd ordered up. One was a restraining order that had been taken out against Wright's former senior staffer, Dennis Hanley. It had been issued around the time he died in a head-on. The other was the police report on his death. I resolved to drink the coffee before I opened the documents, and was raising the cup to my lips when reception called. Janet Wilson was waiting to be collected.

Wilson wasn't an Early Leaver, but as one of the three people who'd handled Proctor's file on the night of the party, she was a must-see. When I got down to the foyer, she was busily hunting through her bag. She was a small, compact woman in her late twenties, with long, crinkled hair smeared with too much product. She jumped when I said her name, but quickly recovered. We shook hands and she followed me to the lift.

Once we had her seated and settled in the interview room, I got her to tell us about her night at the party. She, too, had spent most of her time in reception, and, yes, she'd seen what she called the 'kerfuffle' between Mrs Wright and Mr Proctor, though she hadn't heard a word of it. And she confessed that when Mrs Wright left the party early, she'd thought the minister was being very rude, and she'd said so to a few people.

Despite her nervy manner, Wilson answered our questions fluently, and the longer the interview went, the more relaxed she became. Of course, I was building up to the question of Proctor's file, and as soon as I raised it, she stiffened again and clasped one hand firmly in the other.

'When Proctor sent you down for the file,' I said, 'how did you know which one to get?'

'That's easy,' she said, too forcefully by half. 'Each file has a dedicated slot, and there's a light that flashes above the slot that's been freed.'

'And once a file's out of its slot, it's no longer secure, is it? Anyone retrieving a file can open it — if they have the opportunity, and if they feel inclined. Did you feel so inclined that night, Mrs Wilson?'

'No. I never. It'd be ... it'd be the wrong thing to do. Those files are full of very confidential material. And they're for Mr Proctor's eyes only.'

'Mrs Wilson, this is a very serious matter, so I'm going to ask you again. Did you look at that file as you brought it up to the party?'

'No, I did not,' she said.

Her eyes were locked on mine, but her mouth was slightly open and her bottom jaw was quivering. The quivering might have indicated that she was hiding something, maybe even lying. It might also have been her usual reaction to pressure. Regardless, we had bigger fish to fry, so I thanked her, and Smeaton saw her out. As I sat there mulling over the interview, I made a mental note to request the CCTV footage for the file's journey from Proctor's office up to the party.

The next interviewee on our list was another Early Leaver — the office receptionist, Helen Stannage. Stannage was a big woman with a fleshy face and dull, brown hair. She groaned as she lowered herself into a seat opposite us; but once she was settled, her eyes met mine with such intensity that she took on the look of a woman half her weight and age.

As with the others, we covered her general actitivities at the party first. She'd spent the whole night at her desk in reception, checking invites as guests arrived. She seemed proud that she'd sent a number of blow-ins on their way. Given her no-nonsense manner and her size, I doubted that any of them had put up much of a fight.

Stannage said she hadn't seen the argument between Proctor and her minister, and had been surprised when Mrs Wright left the party so early. When I asked why she herself had left just minutes later, Stannage said that with her boss gone, her job was done. She wasn't much of a party person, and she had teenagers at home.

'And you went straight home to your kids?' said Smeaton.

'Yes, I did,' said Stannage, wiping beads of sweat from her upper lip. 'My husband left us a few weeks ago, so my youngest has been a bit, you know ... stressed.'

'And Tuesday night through to Wednesday morning?' he said. 'Where were you then?'

'At home. With my daughter. You can ask her if you like, but I'd rather you leave her out of this, if you can.'

'We'll let you know. Now, on another matter, we're looking at people who've worked for Mrs Wright over the years, and I understand you were with her when Dennis Hanley was her senior person.'

Stannage's jowly face slumped at this turn in the conversation.

'Yes,' she said. 'I knew Dennis. But he's been dead for years. What's he got to do with this?'

'We're just interested,' I said. 'What can you tell us about him?'

'Dennis? What's there to tell? He messed up over the Mondrian thing, lost his job, and not long after that, he died. It was all very tragic. And extremely hard on his wife and kids.'

'Do you know if he blamed Susan Wright for what happened to him?' said Smeaton.

'No. He blamed Mr Lansdowne, for some reason,' she said, the sweat running freely down her face now. 'Maybe it was because Mr Lansdowne's nephew worked for Mondrian. And, of course, Mr Lansdowne was the minister who set up the inquiry into the affair, so that might've been it. The thing is, those five were so tight before that voucher business — Mr Lansdowne and his nephew, and Mr Proctor, Dennis, and Mrs Wright. So it was really sad to see Dennis cut adrift like that.'

'And how'd Hanley take it when he lost his job?' said Smeaton.

'As you'd imagine, not well,' said Stannage. 'In fact, he went quite strange. He'd show up at the Hyatt for Friday-night drinks and give everybody a bit of stick, like he thought he was still boss, y'know? But nothing too bad, unless you were sitting with Mr Lansdowne's people.

'Then a month or so after he lost his job, he went into the ministerial carpark and sprayed shaving cream down the side of Mr Lansdowne's car. They took out a restraining order on him for that. Then he had his breakdown. And the next thing I knew, he was dead in his car.'

'Do you know what happened to his wife and kids?' I said.

'Margaret died a couple of years after he, he ... you know, died,' said Sta   'Some idiots at the time said it was the shame that killed her, but I know for a fact she had cancer.'

'And the kids?'

'The older one, Sylvie, she's dead now, too. I can't remember what happened to her exactly, but it was a couple of years after Margaret died. And Tom, the boy, I haven't seen him since Margaret's funeral. In fact, that's the last time I saw either of the kids. Sylvie was really angry, I remember. But no one blamed her — losing her parents like that.'

'And Tom?' I said, prompting her.

'Tom? He was ... well, Tom was not easy to connect with at the best of times, if you know what I mean. But I'm sure he was hurting in his own way. I've got a photo of him and Sylvie at home somewhere. I could dig it out, if you think it might help, and make some calls — see if anyone knows where Tom is now. It was all too sad.'

'It'd be good if you could do that,' I said. 'Get us a photo and make some calls. And sooner rather than later would be best.'

Before Smeaton escorted Stannage out, I asked her about Susan Wright's relationship with Sorby; but, as with her colleagues, she wasn't aware of any problems between them.

When she'd gone, I read through the old restraining order that had been issued against Hanley. If the gossip was true, he and Wright had been having it off. Cue political scandal. Then came the inquiry that turned his life to shit. Soon after it, he'd died. Then the wife died, followed by one of the kids. And Wright, who'd prospered in the wake of the scandal that destroyed the Hanley family, had now turned up dead as well.

So where was Tom Hanley? Stannage's contacts were probably our best bet for finding him quickly. If they failed, there were school records, bank accounts, Medicare, and lots of other ways to track him down.

I trudged back to my desk and logged on to PROMIS. I was flipping between screens when McHenry came up behind me, clamped a hand on my shoulder, and dropped a document onto my keyboard. It was an interim report from the vet who'd examined both the fur on Wright's clothes and the dead cat from the crime scene. The report said that while the fur on the clothes had come from a number of cats, it was possible that some of it was from our crime-scene cat. That animal, a tortoiseshell, had been female, about eighteen months old, and it'd had at least one litter before it was neutered. Our forensic vet had also established the cause of the cat's death. She'd died in the same way as Susan Wright — of carbon monoxide poisoning.

Channel Four Live Cam

Thursday 1 August, 2.00pm

Good afternoon, Jean Acheson with you, and an Aztec poll conducted exclusively for the Live Cam overnight shows the Lansdowne government edging one point closer to the opposition.

Aztec now puts two-party-preferred support for the government at 49 per cent, just two points behind the opposition on 51. And so, just nine days out from the election, the contenders are virtually neck and neck.

Along with the continuing turnaround in the government's fortunes, Aztec also shows an improvement in Prime Minister Lansdowne's personal standing among voters.

He's now just four points behind Opposition Leader Lou Feeney, who's said to have been somewhat listless on the campaign trail this week. I'm Jean Acheson. Back with more in a moment.

9

THE LUNCHTIME CROWD had mostly cleared out of the Manuka café by the time I arrived for a bite with Stevo, my political mate. He turned up five minutes after I did, and stood in the doorway, surveying the place with worried eyes. Then he spotted me, smiled, and marched down to my table. Stevo had put on weight since I'd last seen him. His third chin wobbled like jelly as we shook hands.

We both ordered the salmon pasta and a coffee, and once the waitress had gone I got straight down to business. I told him I wanted to hear everything he knew about Proctor. He checked the neighbouring tables to ensure that we were out of earshot, then leaned in close and gave me the drum.

He said Proctor's parents had both been senior office-holders in the party, and their Point Piper home had long been the unofficial meeting place for party heavyweights visiting Sydney. As Stevo put it, Alan Proctor had learned how to play the backroom while sitting in his lounge room.

'And he was a good student,' said Stevo. 'He impressed important people. Sure, he had a handicap or two. I mean, his sexuality's still an issue with some. And there's his weight. And his looks. But he was the director of the state branch at twenty-eight. And national director at thirty-four. Not bad going for a fat, ugly poof, eh?'

'So how long's he been with the prime minister?'

'He joined the PMO straight after Lansdowne moved into The Lodge, so about three years now. But those two've been tight since they were kids. Both Kings boys, you know. So another win for the old school tie.'

'And what's he do for Lansdowne, exactly?'

'He manages the numbers and keeps everyone in line. Usually by gentle persuasion, but sometimes by threatening them a bit. And he's got dirt on everyone — knows where the bodies are buried. That sort of thing. So it's ironic to see that that little shit Rolfe is trying to bury *him* now.'

Stevo left the comment hanging there, his eyes full of subtle pressure, clearly hoping I'd say something, anything, about Proctor's status in our investigation. But I just stared back at him. Suddenly the waitress loomed over us with plates of food, dissolving the moment.

'I see the government's rising in the polls,' I said, twirling some pasta around my fork. 'They're calling it "The Wright Factor". Is it really that big?'

'Ohh, no doubt about it,' said Stevo, shoving a forkful into his mouth. 'And if you guys collar someone before the tenth, that'll give us *another* boost. We'll be calling that one "The Relief Factor".'

'You make a good poll result sound like a motive for murder.'

That brought a mirthless chuckle from Stevo.

'Stranger things have happened,' he said. 'But murder as a way to influence public opinion? I think it's over-rated. I just hope our numbers from a few weeks ago were the genuine rock-bottom. I mean, I'd hate to see a dead cat bounce in our polling this close to Election Day.'

'A dead cat bounce? What sort of bounce is that?'

'Picture a cat, dropped from a fifty-storey building. It hits the pavement and bounces off it. It's a small upward movement, but you know the cat's always going to hit the pavement again. And when it does, that second impact always seems much worse than the first. More final somehow. That's your dead cat bounce. They use the term on the stockmarket for a share that looks like it's bottomed out, and is on the way back up. But then it goes into reverse again and falls even further than before. In politics, it's when you think the polls are as bad as they can get, and your numbers are on the mend, but then they fall again, worse than ever. In other words, it's when things go from terrible to truly catastrophic.'

Pleading a heavy schedule on behalf of their boss, Alan Proctor's people had asked Brady for the interview to be held at Proctor's home. The commissioner had agreed.

Proctor's place was easy to spot when we turned into his street in Forrest. A dozen media vehicles were parked either side of his driveway, and a crowd of journos and cameramen were loitering on his nature strip. When they spotted us, there was a scramble for cameras and microphones, and we became their total focus as we swung into Proctor's driveway.

The cameras were in close as my finger pushed the button on the intercom, even recording me announcing myself to the woman who answered. And as we waited for Proctor's massive iron gates to swing open, the reporters shouted their questions.

'Is Alan Proctor a suspect in the Wright murder case?' asked one, tapping Smeaton's window.

'When do you expect an arrest?' asked another.

'Have the police looked at Alan Proctor's files yet?' asked a more canny operator.

We ignored them all, and when the gates were fully opened, I drove down the crushed-granite drive, past a big dry fountain and line after line of empty flowerbeds.

Proctor was waiting for us at his front door. I'd seen lots of photos of him, but this was the first time I'd laid eyes on the complete package. He was short and balding, and his tracksuit was a perfect fit for his perfectly pear-shaped body. He shook hands limply and led us down a corridor hung with portraits of people from a much sterner age. The corridor opened out onto a large lounge room at the back of the house where six chesterfields were set around a huge open fire.

A bloke sitting close to the flames looked us over as we entered the room, then went back to the wad of papers on his lap. His pinstriped suit, steel-grey hair, and severe look told us everything we needed to know about him. Proctor motioned for us to sit, and then introduced the seated bloke as Phillip Bailey QC. Bailey made no move to shake our hands, and as we were already seated, we simply nodded at him. There was no offer of refreshments from our host, either, and certainly no social chatter to break the ice — just the stock question from Proctor.

'So, gentlemen,' he said, 'how can I help you?'

'First up, Mr Proctor,' said Smeaton, hitting 'record' on his machine, 'I must inform you that you're a person of interest in our investigation into the murder of Susan Wright. Therefore, I must warn you that you're not obliged to answer our questions. But if you do, anything you say may be used in a court of law against you.'

'Alan Proctor? A person of interest?' said Bailey, barely controlling a snigger. 'Are you serious, detective?'

'This is a very serious matter, Mr Bailey,' I said, my tone appropriately grave. 'Mr Proctor was seen arguing with Mrs Wright at her party on Sunday night. It's also been suggested that she took property belonging to him when she left that party.'

Bailey considered my words for a moment, then gave his client the advice I'd been expecting from him.

'It's entirely up to you, Alan,' he said, shaking his head. 'But I strongly advise you not to go ahead with this.'

I'd prepared an argument to counter his advice. And it was compelling.

'Then I must warn you, Mr Proctor,' I said, 'that if you decline to answer our questions, you'll automatically become the prime suspect in our investigation.'

Proctor turned to Bailey. Bailey merely repeated his advice.

'It's up to you, Alan,' he said.

'Okay, okay,' said Proctor, seemingly resigned. 'Ask your questions, detective, and we'll see how we go.'

It was a predictable response, and no doubt part of the script they'd rehearsed. Proctor was apparently ignoring Bailey's advice, but he still had the lawyer there to run interference for him. It meant they were going to co-operate, to a degree — at least enough to avoid an accusation of stonewalling. Given these circumstances, our challenge was to push Proctor more than we would in a normal interview, but not so far that we gave Bailey an excuse to shut us down.

'So, Mr Proctor,' I said, 'what can you tell me about your argument with Mrs Wright on the night she disappeared?'

'To call our little disagreement an argument, or a fight, as some would have it, is a massive overstatement,' said Proctor, flicking his hand at me dismissively. 'Essentially, any planned event during an election campaign is subject to change, and I wanted changes to her environment launch. She wasn't happy with what I proposed, and the upset that others witnessed was due to that fact.'

'If it was such a minor matter, why was there so much heat in it?'

'There wasn't. Heat, as you put it, detective, is in the eye of the beholder. I'm sure you wouldn't have found it too hot. As for what others think they saw, people have fertile imaginations, and they often see things that aren't there.'

'When you were talking to Mrs Wright in the corridor that night, some people heard her say, "That's not going to happen", or something to that effect. What did you say to provoke that response?'

'I truly can't remember, detective. Maybe I told her that her party was running out of booze.'

He chuckled and I smiled politely, though I was tempted to give him a verbal backhander for what I saw as an attempt to throw me off my game.

'After your "disagreement", you and Mrs Wright went into her office,' I said. 'And then you came out and asked one of your assistants to fetch you a file. What was in that file?'

Proctor turned to Bailey, and the lawyer removed his glasses, nailed me with his steely eyes, and hit me with the line that he'd been brought over to deliver.

'The file you're referring to contained documents,' he said, as if handing down a judgement from on high. 'Those documents are classified "Cabinet-in-Confidence". Given that that's the case, my client is duty bound not to reveal their contents.'

'But, Mr Proctor,' I said, ignoring the lawyer, 'during the search for Mrs Wright, you told our people that the file merely contained "organisational detail" for the campaign.'

'That's right. The file contained campaign documents prepared for cabinet's consideration and approval,' said Proctor. 'Therefore they had Cabinet-in-Confidence status.'

'But did the documents contain proposed government policy? Or did they contain party policy for release during the campaign? Or were they merely full of "organisational detail", as you claimed a few days ago?'

'Detective Glass,' said Bailey, 'your question goes to the

nature of the documents, and I advise Mr Proctor not to answer it.'

This was more than I could take. It was time to give this pair a touch-up.

'Okay,' I said. 'We'll put that question aside, and I'll arrange for a justice of the Federal Court to consider it. Maybe then we'll get something more from you about these documents.'

Proctor frowned at Bailey. This wasn't the script they'd workshopped. Arguing such a case in open court would be a public-relations disaster, especially at the tail end of an election campaign heading for the wire.

'That sounds suspiciously like a threat to me, detective,' said Bailey, sterner than ever. 'Is that your intention here? To threaten my client?'

His question and tone implied a much bigger threat, of course.

'I'm not here to threaten anyone,' I said.

'What more do you need to know, then?' said Proctor, his patience clearly exhausted. 'The file contained campaign documents that I'd prepared for cabinet's consideration. The documents related to certain matters pertaining to the environment. Is that enough for you now?'

'Were these documents central to the discussion you had with Mrs Wright in her office that night?'

'We did talk about them, yes. In the corridor, and in her office. But I can't say more than that.'

'We've established that Susan Wright had your file with her when she left the party. Did she have your permission to take it?'

'No, she did not.'

'Why'd you let her then?' said Smeaton.

'I didn't,' said Proctor, giving vent to his anger now. 'I used her ensuite, and when I came out, she'd gone.'

So that was how Wright did it. Proctor had answered a call of nature, and she took the opportunity to do a runner.

'So we're talking about a secure file here,' I said. 'One of the many you keep in your office. How'd you feel about losing that one?'

'Truthfully?' said Proctor. 'Well, it's as I've said, the file, in and of itself, isn't important. But losing it has caused me to re-think the way I secure my office. After all, the material I hold in there could determine who governs Australia in a little over a week.'

'I'm sure that's right,' I said. 'So, finally, and most importantly, what do you think influenced Susan Wright to run off with your file?'

Proctor pondered the question without looking at his lawyer. When he finally responded, there was a hint of sadness in his voice.

'I have no idea what caused her to act in the way she did,' he said. 'None whatsoever.'

'You left the party soon after she did,' said Smeaton. 'Where'd you go?'

'As you'd already know from CCTV,' said Proctor, 'I went straight to my car in the executive carpark and drove home.'

'Not to Mrs Wright's apartment?' said Smeaton. 'You didn't go over and try to retrieve your property?'

'I considered confronting her, but then I thought that, in the cold light of day, she'd see her error and return what she'd taken. And if she didn't, I planned to involve the prime minister.'

'I'm told you were in Perth on Tuesday and Wednesday. I trust you'd have no trouble getting someone to vouch for that fact?'

'There's thousands of people who can do that. Now, is that it? I've got a plane to catch.'

There were no farewells from Bailey as we left the lounge room, and Proctor walked us to the front door without another word. On the way back to the station, I resolved to have a lot more up my sleeve the next time we saw Proctor. And it would be in an interview room, preferably minus his high-priced attack dog.

I was mulling this over when McHenry called. He said Simon Rolfe was stranded somewhere north of Mount Isa and wouldn't be back in Canberra till late the next day. His interview had been re-scheduled to Saturday evening. And Wright's receptionist, Helen Stannage, had called. She'd supplied something we needed — the contact details for a bloke who might know where to find the only surviving Hanley.

Channel Four Live Cam

Thursday 1 August, 4.30pm

Good afternoon, Jean Acheson here with this Live Cam exclusive. And today I can reveal that Treasurer Alan Stokes spent time at a clinic in the United States, where he received treatment for an addiction to prescription drugs.

Live Cam has obtained a set of receipts from the Bethesda Addiction Clinic in Los Angeles which show that Mr Stokes was an in-patient at the clinic for five days from May seventh last year.

At the time, the treasurer was said to be vacationing in the US with his wife.

Mr Stokes' office has refused to comment on the matter. His spokesman asked that I put my questions in writing. So, Treasurer, here we go: What's the nature of your addiction? What's the current status of your addiction? Why did you use taxpayers' money to fund your travel to your treatment? And why weren't we told about your condition? We await your answers with interest. This is Jean Acheson.

10

IT WAS COMING on peak hour as I drove down Northbourne Avenue, heading for a property out by Lake George where we hoped to find Tom Hanley, the son of Susan Wright's former senior private secretary. Smeaton sat next to me in the front, working his way through a burger and a bag of chips. Senior Constable Eric Bender from Queanbeyan police sat in the back, whittling down a shish kebab. Being in New South Wales, the lake was beyond the AFP's jurisdiction, so we needed Bender with us if we wanted to talk to Hanley.

Information on his whereabouts had come from Ron Pitman, an old schoolmate of Hanley's who Helen Stannage had put me on to. According to Pitman, the Hanley family had long owned some simple cabins out by the lake. He said the cabins were connected to the town water supply and electricity, but they'd never had a phone on out there. So, with no other way of contacting Hanley, we'd been forced to take a drive. And while we were probably on a wild-goose chase, Pitman had been confident his old mate still owned the cabins.

'If Weereewaa Lodge had ever come onto the market,' Pitman had said, 'I'd certainly have bought it. Those lake properties are very tightly held. You'll understand why when you get out there. It's an amazing bit of country.'

Smeaton switched the car radio from a news station to classical music, then he pushed his seat back and closed his eyes. Twenty kilometres north of Canberra, I turned off the highway onto Macks Reef Road, an undulating stretch of blacktop that had once been the main route to the local gold diggings.

Macks Reef Road ended at a T junction, where I turned right, and about five kilometres out of Bungendore I took a left onto Lake Road. The blacktop soon gave way to a graded track that skirted the vast lake bed. The tree-lined track was narrow, with regular blind corners, so I eased my foot off the accelerator, turned on my lights, and Bender gave me some of the history of Lake George.

Weereewaa was the Aboriginal name for the lake, he said. The word meant 'bad water', and the blacks, and the Europeans who took their land, had plenty of reasons for thinking there was something bad about the lake. Before it was upgraded in the mid-1980s, the section of federal highway that skirted the lake's western shore had been a notorious killer. Bender reckoned some of the drivers who'd died there had been mesmerised by the size of the lake.

'Or maybe they just got distracted trying to see if there was any water in it,' he said. 'Whatever it was, lots of them ran off the road or piled into oncoming traffic. We dealt with the carnage on a regular basis.'

I'd driven along that section of highway countless times, and had never found the lake a distraction. This bumpy stretch of gravel road was different, though. It passed within twenty metres of the dried-out lake bed, and it was only a couple of metres above it in elevation. And though the full expanse of the lake was only visible through gaps in the trees, it was riveting when it flashed past — the sheer immensity of it. And, strangely, given how cold the day had become, the low line of mountains that bounded the far side of the lake shimmered in the late-afternoon light.

Like most Canberrans, I knew that the lake was very dangerous when it was full of water. Five Duntroon cadets had drowned here back in the 1950s. And two groups of hunters had died in more recent times when their tinnies, weighed down with shot deer, had sunk as they motored back to the western shore. There were even hang-gliders who had fallen in and gone under.

However, according to Bender, the worst tragedy happened in the early 1940s when a man and his wife, their two kids, and the parish priest ventured out onto the lake on a Sunday morning after mass. Soon after they set out, the wind picked up, the waves rose, and all of them ended up clinging to the upturned boat. The dad swam for help, but he disappeared under the waves. The mum followed him in, and she went under, too. Bender said that the priest had then weighed up his options — whether to swim, or stay with the kids. He decided to swim, and he was barely alive when the shore party stumbled across him. They immediately put a big boat out onto the water, but by the time they found the dinghy, it was deserted. When news got back to town that the priest had deserted the kids, he was run out of the parish.

Smeaton nudged me as the sign for Weereewaa Lodge flashed past. I slowed, did a three-point turn, and headed back to the sign. Then I swung the vehicle down a sandy track hemmed in on both sides by a low forest of skinny eucalypts. The track finished abruptly about seventy metres in — and there, parked under some taller trees, was an old BMW sedan. I got out and gave myself a minute to stretch while Smeaton and Bender had a look at the car. The registration was current, and the tyre tracks it had made coming in looked relatively fresh. It gave us hope that Tom Hanley might be around.

At the far end of the carpark, we found an old walking track that had been cut through another dense stand of eucalypts. The track seemed to head towards the high country overlooking the lake. We walked the perimeter of the car park looking for other options, and when none presented themselves, we headed down the track to see where it took us. After a few minutes walking through a tunnel of overhanging trees, we emerged into a clearing, and, sure enough, there was the Hanley place, just as Pitman had described it — seven cabins set either side of a wooden stairway that ascended to the top of the ridge about fifty metres above us.

Smeaton let out a few cooees, then we climbed the stairs to the first cabin. I knocked on the door and, when no one answered, I turned the door handle and gave it a push. It was a simple, single-room affair, with mouldering clothes strewn across the floor, and some magazines piled up in a corner. Most of the magazines were more than a decade old. I followed Smeaton and Bender back to the stairs, and we climbed to the next cabin — which was in the same condition as the first one. As was the next one up. It had me thinking our drive out might prove fruitless after all.

I was following Smeaton out of the fourth cabin when he stopped so suddenly I almost ran into the back of him. He tapped his ear urgently a couple of times and pointed to the cabin directly above us. Then I heard it, too — someone clearing their throat. We made our way back to the stairs and climbed to the fifth cabin, warily eyeing its open doorway and the dark corners under its eaves.

Then a pale, skinny bloke in an oversized grey tracksuit stepped from the cabin and spat into the bush below. He spat again, and then stood and gazed out over the treetops to the massive expanse of lake bed. At first I thought he hadn't noticed us, but then he turned and casually nodded in our direction.

'I'm Senior Constable Eric Bender from New South Wales police,' said Bender, taking a few steps forward. 'And this is Detective Sergeant Darren Glass. And Detective Joe Smeaton. They're from the Australian Federal Police in Canberra. Are you Tom Hanley?'

Helen Stannage had emailed us a fourteen-year-old photo of

Tom Hanley. Back then, he'd been a young man with nice teeth and an engaging smile. The disheveled guy in front of us bore some resemblance to the Hanley in the photo, except that this guy's hair was matted and grey, his face was cracked with lines, and the purple sacks under his eyes completed the picture of a life stuck on spin cycle.

'Are you Tom Hanley?' said Bender, this time more insistent.

'Yes, I'm him,' said Hanley, sounding intoxicated or medicated, or both.

'Mr Hanley, these two detectives are investigating the murder of Mrs Susan Wright. Would you mind sitting down inside with them and answering some questions?'

'Questions? What questions?' said Hanley, as if testing the notion. 'And why d'yah wanna talk to me?'

'If we could just go inside, sir,' said Bender, indicating the open door.

'I haven't done anything,' said Hanley, suddenly so enlivened it had me thinking that maybe he was *under*-medicated.

'If we could just go inside, Mr Hanley, we could get this over with,' said Bender. 'And it's very cold out here.'

'That's true,' said Hanley. 'It is cold. Okay. Come in. But not for long, mind. I've got things to do.'

And with that he swung around and stepped back inside the cabin, and the door slammed shut behind him. Never one to take chances in the face of erratic behaviour, Smeaton unholstered his Glock, and I followed suit. We readied ourselves on either side of the doorway, then Smeaton turned the door handle and gave it a push.

I silently indicated that I'd go in first, but Smeaton shook his head. I responded by nodding furiously. He took a deep breath, jabbed his bony index finger into his chest a couple of times and silently mouthed a count to three. Then he stepped inside and quickly swung his Glock in an arc to target the far end of the room. What he saw there caused him to lower his weapon, and he motioned me to join him.

When I stepped into the room, I was immediately hit by the musty smell of an unwashed human animal. Hanley was sitting in one of three old lounge chairs arranged around a picture window at the far end of the room. He was transfixed by the lake again, and took no notice as we approached him.

'Can't be too careful,' said Smeaton, pulling a face as he holstered his weapon.

The sound of pills sloshing around in a plastic bottle drew us back to Hanley. He was bending down to remove his shoes. Once he got them off, he placed his bare feet in front of a three-bar heater that had only one bar glowing. Smeaton shook his head at this pitiable sight, then he and Bender sat and kept an eye on Hanley while I poked around the room.

A filthy sleeping bag was bunched up on a dark-grey mattress in one corner. An assortment of odd shoes and dirty clothes spewed from a backpack that lay upended next to the bed, and an avalanche of old magazines and newspapers, plus the odd fast-food wrapper, covered most of the rest of the floor.

The only relief from this chaos was the shelf above the sink. There, bags of nuts and muesli bars sat either side of a bowl of fresh fruit. There was even half a bottle of disinfectant. Tom Hanley wouldn't starve, and though his room smelt like his arsehole, it was probably bacteria-free. Someone was taking care of him.

I sat in the chair next to the window and glanced out across the lake. Then I nodded at Smeaton, he hit 'record' and recited the necessaries, and I kicked things off.

'Mr Hanley, where were you between eight o'clock on Tuesday night and eight on Wednesday morning?' I said.

'Here,' said Hanley, sounding more like he was asking a question than answering one. 'Yes. I was here. All the time. I'm usually here.'

'Were you alone during those hours?'

'I live alone. So, yes, I was alone.'

'Did you know Susan Wright?' said Smeaton.

'I didn't know her,' said Hanley, his eyes suddenly more focused. 'But I met her once. My dad used to work for her.'

'And did your sister meet her then as well?' I said.

'Sylvie? Did you know Sylvie?'

'No, I didn't know her. She's dead, isn't she?'

'Sylvie? Yes. Yes, she's dead. She went to Thailand. I've still got the newspapers. You can have a look, if you like.'

He picked up a fat paperback from the floor — *Dune* by Frank Herbert — and took a wad of yellowed newspaper cuttings from inside the book and handed them over. They were from nine years before, and all of them told the same story. Twenty-eight-year-old Sylvie Hanley had been trekking in northern Thailand when the group she was with had stopped at a Karen village for the night. When her fellow trekkers awoke the next morning, Sylvie's backpack was where she'd placed it the night before, but she and her sleeping bag were gone. None of the trekkers had heard anything in the night that might have indicated Sylvie's fate, and a week-long search of the area had failed to find her. The last cutting in the wad was from a Sydney tabloid. It claimed that Sylvie Hanley had been kidnapped by a local warlord, taken to the golden triangle, and forced into sexual slavery.

'Losing your sister like that, Mr Hanley,' I said, 'it must have been very hard on you.'

'That's right,' said Hanley. 'And Mum and Dad are gone now, too. So I'm all alone.'

But right at that moment, he didn't look lonely. Or sad. In fact, his confidence seemed to be building the more he talked.

Perhaps he was relieved, thinking that the interview was going well — maybe better than he'd expected. Whatever the reason, I figured that if he was hiding something, we had a better chance of getting at it if we kept him a bit off-balance. So I dropped some weight on him.

'You know, Mr Hanley, it's difficult for us to talk to you here,' I said. 'And difficult for you, too, no doubt. So maybe we should arrange for you to come into Queanbeyan police station. Just for a chat.'

Hanley's reaction to this suggestion was immediate and extreme. His face morphed into a desperate mask, he pushed himself back into his chair, and he brought his knees up to his chest and hugged them tight.

'I'm not leaving here,' he said, his voice cracking with emotion. 'I haven't done anything wrong, so why would you want to take me away? Why? Why would you do that?'

'It's alright, Mr Hanley,' I said, regretting my impulse. 'We can talk here for now. It's okay. Let's just see how we go.'

I gave him a minute to settle. Maybe it was time to come at him from an altogether different angle. Get a little speculative.

'Mr Hanley, do you ever remember your father talking about a bank called Mondrian?' I said.

Hanley hugged his knees tight to his chest, and his face went red like he was straining to get something out. Or keep it in. It might have been the question that disturbed him. But having already upset him, maybe any question would have had the same effect.

'No, he never said anything about a bank called that,' Hanley said at last. 'Why don't you ask Michael Lansdowne about your bank. See what he remembers.'

'That's a very surprising suggestion, Mr Hanley,' I said. 'What do you think Mr Lansdowne knows about Mondrian?'

'Lansdowne knows everything,' said Hanley, suddenly relaxing his grip on his knees. 'He always did. Because he makes it happen. Like that. And that.'

He jabbed his index finger at the far corners of the cabin, his hold on reality seemingly derailed.

'He knows, but he won't tell,' said Hanley, his eyes red and wide open now. 'When my dad knew, they pulled the rug from under him. And now they're all gone. Except me. And I've *almost* bitten the dust. Because that's how it goes, isn't it? Another one bites the dust. Bites the dust. That's what they say about the lake, too. That it's all dust down there. Well, there's a lot more than dust, I can tell you. There's things you wouldn't believe.'

'Mr Hanley,' I said loudly, to get his attention, and then more softly, trying to calm him. 'Mr Hanley, what does the Prime Minister know about Mondrian?'

Hanley considered my question as though it was the first time I'd asked it.

'Whatever he knows, you'll have to ask him,' said Hanley, gripping his knees again. 'Only he can help you there. Pick up the phone. He'll talk to you, you know. He talks to me.'

'Yeah, right,' said Smeaton in a whisper.

Hanley stared at him blankly, then his gaze slid to the window and he looked out to where a line of dead eucalypts fronted the edge of the dried-out lake bed. In the waning light, the mountains that fringed the far side of the lake looked like they'd been cut from a sheet of purple paper.

Hanley began swaying from side to side in his chair, keeping time like a zoo animal as he bumped against the armrests, wrapped up tight. It was time for us to go. Smeaton leaned over and whispered in my ear.

'If this guy's acting,' he said, 'it's the best job I've seen in a while.'

'It's no act,' I said. 'Though I'm sure he knows more than he's saying. Let's give him a day, then get a psych out for a crack at him. I'm sure McHenry'll want that.'

We left Hanley rocking in rhythm to the waterless lake, and made our way back to the car. The gravel road was even more challenging in the fading light, so I took it very slowly. Bender pointed to a luminous mist that hung over the middle of the lake. It was as though a cloud containing its own light source had descended.

We skirted Bungendore, an old pastoral town that these days accommodated the overflow from the national capital. When our mobiles came back to life on the Queanbeyan side of the ranges, mine rang. It was McHenry, so Smeaton put him on speaker.

'Jean Acheson's running a big story on that "Live" thing she does,' he said, breathless and excited. 'She's claiming that the treasurer's been treated at some sort of addiction clinic in America. The thing is, Penny Lomax from the PM's called a few minutes ago, and she reckons there's only one possible source for Acheson's story, and that's the file that went missing with Susan Wright.'

Blood Oath news flash

Thursday 1 August, 8.30pm

Fair cop? Or is it a raid?
by Simon Rolfe

My colleague and friend, the esteemed Ms Jean Acheson, has done it again. Broken a story that's got the Plod knocking on her door. And her crime? She acquired some documents that the government says are connected to the murder of Susan Wright.

While the Plod needs to sort out this claim, what's definite is that the documents in question reveal that the man in control of Australia's finances is addicted to prescription drugs. And in a person with his responsibilities, addiction is a matter of the greatest public interest.

As one of the local wags here in Isa said to me today, when the prime minister claims that the economy is in a safe pair of hands, should we now assume that those hands have just popped a pill into the treasurer's mouth?

With the election race tightening by the day, Ms Acheson's exposé has done Australia a big favour. The character and competence of both sides of politics is now firmly in focus. Punters, your time to speak is almost at hand. Jean Acheson's story couldn't have come at a better time.

11

JOURNOS GLARED AT us from every doorway as we followed the young production assistant down the main corridor of the press gallery. The radio shock-jocks and some of the political bloggers had engineered this hostile reception by claiming that we were intent on muzzling — or even arresting — Acheson. It had me fearing that she might be full of the same bile when we fronted her. Things would get tricky if she was. But a few minutes after Smeaton and I were shown into the network's green room, Acheson popped her head around the door and beamed a smile at me.

'Ah, Detective Glass, isn't it?' she said. 'And right on time, too. Sorry about this, but I need to lose the makeup. Then I'll be with you.'

And with that she disappeared.

Smeaton cooed in my ear and gave me a gentle nudge.

'Who's a popular boy, then?' he said.

Ignoring him, I took out my notebook and tried to concentrate on the task at hand. But Acheson's greeting had left me feeling strangely embarrassed as well as euphoric, and the clash of these emotions momentarily swamped my ability to think straight. I was still battling to focus when the door opened and she came in, carrying a cup of coffee. She closed the door behind her and sat on the couch opposite me.

'I assumed you'd both want one of these,' she said, lifting her cup. 'They've just put on another brew. It'll only take a few minutes.'

I thanked her, almost stammering as I did. Her apparent calm and simple good manners were unexpected. And Jean Acheson, face-to-face and without makeup, was certainly far more beautiful than any version of her I'd seen on the box. I thumbed through my notebook, still struggling to marshall my thoughts.

'Thanks for seeing us, Miss Acheson,' I said, finally facing her. 'You know why we're here, no doubt. So, can you tell us how you got onto this story? The one about the treasurer?'

Acheson smiled and lowered her cup to the table. Then she lifted her head and drilled me with eyes that suddenly seemed unbelievably green.

'As you'll no doubt appreciate, detective,' she said, 'I'm often asked about sources, and I never co-operate on such things. But this is an extraordinary situation, so I'm making an exception. With one proviso. Please don't let out what I'm about to tell you. At least for a few days?'

'Our lips are sealed,' I said, trying to hide my relief. 'Now, about this story. Did you actually get a document? Or did the information come in some other form?'

'Oh, I've got documents alright. And don't worry — they're safely locked away. I can get them now if you like.'

'Before you do,' said Smeaton, 'could you tell us *how* you got them?'

'Sure. Well, earlier today, reception took a call from a guy who said he had something that'd kill off the government's chances next Saturday. And he insisted on talking to me personally about it. I wasn't too busy at the time, so I spoke to him.'

'Did he give you a name?'

'No, he refused, and I didn't push it.'

'I take it the call came in on the office landline?' I said.

'That's right,' said Acheson. 'Through the Sydney switch.'

Impossible to trace, then.

'What did he sound like?' I said.

'Well, that's the thing,' she said. 'He had a heavy accent that I couldn't pick. I'm pretty sure it was European, but that's all I can say about it. And as for how old he was, I really wouldn't have a clue about that, either. The accent thing, I suppose. But his English was fairly good. And he was very keen for me to get these documents.'

'So, he rang and offered you documents,' I said. 'How did the conversation go from there?'

Before Acheson could answer, her assistant came in carrying two cups of coffee, which she set down on the table in front of me and Smeaton. Acheson thanked her, and waited for her to leave the room before continuing.

'This is how it went,' she said. 'He asked if I'd like to get some documents that'd hurt the government. I said I'd like to see them. He asked if I knew Warrina Inlet. More particularly, he asked if I knew the bridge that goes over the inlet. I said I did. The inlet's that bit of Lake Burley Griffin that separates Government House from the golf course. As it turns out, I walk over that bridge a couple of times a week. Anyway, he said he'd left something for me up under the bridge supports on the Yarralumla side. And then he hung up. I was naturally intrigued, so I drove down there, and, sure enough, there it was — a plastic sleeve, wedged up under the bridge supports.'

'We'll need everything you got from him, including the sleeve,' said Smeaton, barely controlling his excitement.

'Of course,' she said. 'But there's one thing I should tell you. It didn't occur to me that this stuff might be linked to your investigation, so I'm afraid I handled it a bit. I only realised what I had when Penny Lomax called and threatened to have me locked up. That sort of gave the game away. Anyway, it's yours to take, and I hope it helps. I really do. But can I ask you something? Do you really think the person who gave me this stuff is the same one who, you know, killed Susan Wright?'

Her question was laced with story possibilities, but there was also a note of fear in her voice.

'I really don't know,' I said. 'It's possible, but we'll know more once we've examined what you've got. Now, just a few more questions, if I could. You've worked in the gallery for a long time. Do you know of anyone who really had it in for Susan Wright? Someone capable of doing her physical harm?'

'I knew we'd get to this,' she said, settling back in her chair. 'And the first thing I've got to say is "no". I don't know anyone capable of killing her. Then again, she did have lots of enemies. In fact, I can't think of a minister who got more people offside.

'I mean, she was good on urban issues, so she was popular in city electorates. But the interest groups in her portfolio? Like the irrigators, say? They simply *loathed* her. Would you believe that yesterday, a few hours after she was found, the organisation that represents the irrigators issued a statement calling on the PM to overturn her water allocations? And the local property developers? They hated her even more. They're still furious about the building bans she approved for the south coast last year. And she certainly wasn't popular with the Greens, but that was mostly because she was a Lansdowne minister.'

I was about to ask Acheson if anyone other than city people actually liked Susan Wright, but I was stopped by a knock at the door. It was the production assistant.

'Sorry to interrupt, Jean,' she said, obviously very anxious, 'but Jim said to tell you this straightaway. There's a whisper in the corridors about Alan Proctor. Apparently, something's happened to him.'

Channel Four Live Cam

Friday 2 August, 9.00am

Good morning all, Jean Acheson with the Live Cam, and one of Australia's leading criminologists says that the police may have less than thirty-six hours to save Alan Proctor, the prime minister's close confidante who disappeared last night.

Mr Proctor spent most of yesterday in Sydney working on the government's campaign. He flew back into Canberra early last night for a strategy meeting, but failed to show up. And since then he's been uncontactable. Ominously, his abandoned car was found in the inner-Canberra suburb of Yarralumla early this morning.

Bond University's Professor Stephen Billings says Mr Proctor's apparent disappearance is a cause for grave concern, coming as it does just days after the kidnapping and murder of Environment Minister Susan Wright.

The professor says that if Alan Proctor has been taken by the same people who took Mrs Wright, the police only have until tomorrow night to rescue him. This is Jean Acheson. Back with more in a moment.

12

WE SPENT THE night and most of the next morning pulling Alan Proctor's house apart. For all its slick artwork and furnishings, the place turned out to be little more than a crash pad where he kept a few changes of clothes and some basics in the fridge, and not much else. There were certainly no significant documents in his study. And no computer, either. We found no sign that he'd made it home from the airport, and nothing to indicate what had become of him.

As I helped process Proctor's place, my increasing sense of foreboding about his fate caused a knot to take hold of my guts. I was certain that the pair from the lake were also behind his disappearance, and that they weren't just doubling up on their crime. They were issuing a challenge to us, and a warning to all senior ministers and their staff. No one was safe, they were saying; everyone was fair game. Their sheer bloodlessness was perplexing in the extreme. What could have led them to this? What had motivated their outrage? And how profoundly committed would they have to be to plan and execute these high-profile crimes in the way that they had?

Of course, not everyone had such a dire take on things. Initially, there was even talk around that Proctor had done a bunk — disappeared himself, believing that the government was on the way out. But when we canvassed that thought with the party people he'd been working with up in Sydney, they all said he'd been very upbeat about the government's chances.

By mid-morning, I was back in the room scrolling through

PROMIS. I opened a just-posted Forensics file on Proctor's Audi; but the car, like the house, told us nothing about its owner's fate.

Then I went to CCTV footage of Proctor from the airport. It had been captured at six-fifteen the previous evening, as he walked through the terminal concourse. He was carrying a briefcase, and wearing a funny little short-brimmed hat — the sort favoured by Swiss yodellers.

The other vision of Proctor on the system was of him driving out of the long-stay carpark at the airport. And a traffic camera had snapped him as he ran a red light on Kings Avenue. Somewhere between that camera, and the meeting in Parliament House where he'd been heading, Alan Proctor had fallen off the face of the earth. His disappearance had sent the room into overdrive — people now moved in and out of the place at a clip, keyboards clattered with a new urgency, and every phone conversation sounded sharp and to the point. Given Susan Wright's fate, we all assumed that Alan Proctor's time was running out. I turned back to my screen and continued to scroll.

Also up on PROMIS was a Forensics report on the documents that Jean Acheson had received from the European. They turned out to be two receipts from the treasurer's American addiction clinic, and there were three sets of fingerprints on them. One set belonged to the treasurer. The second was from the accounts person at the clinic. The third were Acheson's — and her prints were the only ones on the opaque plastic sleeve that had held the receipts.

As well as Acheson's prints, Forensics had found a small, oblong impression freshly etched into the bottom edge of the plastic sleeve. Their report said that the impression had been made when the sleeve was stored in a tight space next to an object the same size as a small audiocassette case. The plastic sleeve had most recently spent time in the dirt file that Susan Wright had 'pinched' the night she disappeared. If the impression on the sleeve *was* from a cassette case, and if that case and the sleeve *had* been together in Proctor's dirt file, it raised a number of questions.

Assuming the cassette case had contained a cassette, what was recorded on it that needed to be secured with Proctor's dirt? Did the recording relate to the treasurer's clinic visits, or was there altogether different dirt on it? Maybe something related to Susan Wright? Stuff so damaging that when she got the chance, she'd felt compelled to nick it and do a runner?

Only two people knew the answers to these questions. One of them was dead, and the other was missing. But maybe Proctor's staffers, Penny Lomax and Janet Wilson, knew something about the cassette, if indeed there had been one in the file. Lomax was in Adelaide with the prime minister and wasn't due back in Canberra for at least twenty-four hours. I'd been planning to talk to her about Proctor again, anyway, but now I thought I'd get both her and Janet Wilson down to the station for something a bit more wide-ranging and intensive.

I ducked out at lunchtime for a shish tawook from the Lebanese on Northbourne Avenue. As I carried the food back to the station, I put all thoughts of Proctor aside, and instead tried to think through arguments for why we should be talking to the prime minister. They were all pretty obvious, really. His most popular minister had been murdered, right at the business end of an election campaign, and now his closest confidante had disappeared. Surely that was enough for us to seek a face-to-face with the man. Then again, if he agreed to it, he'd probably just spout the same pious rubbish he'd given me over the phone.

For some reason, my thoughts then turned to Jean Acheson.

I pictured her smiling at me from behind the crime-scene tape, and sitting in the green room, nailing me with those eyes of hers. But I didn't get any pleasure from these images. Instead, they added to my sense of foreboding. The nub of it was, the more I thought about the killers' choice of Acheson to publicise the treasurer's drug problem, the more I worried about her safety.

These people were careful and considered in the way they went about things, so they were hardly likely to have dropped the treasurer's drug story on a random journo. So why had they chosen Acheson? Sure, she had a high profile, but so did lots of her colleagues. And some of them had much bigger audiences than hers. It could be that the killers were big fans, or maybe they were fixated on her. Whatever it was, I figured that, having achieved a good run for the story nailing the treasurer, they'd use her again when they next had something to air. And that was a danger for Acheson, as I saw it. If she irritated them in the way she handled one of their stories — or, worse, if she made them angry — they might react in an extreme way, and we'd already seen what they could do. So although I had no evidence to support my fears, I made straight for McHenry's desk when I got back to the room.

'What's on your mind, Glass?' he said, his eyes on me, but his fingers poised over his keyboard.

'There's a few things, actually,' I said. 'So I'll wait till you're finished there before I go through them.'

I took a seat beside his desk, and unwrapped my tawook and took a big bite out of it. McHenry hated people eating in front of him, and he soon pushed his chair away from his desk and told me to get on with it.

'First, why don't we get some European accents on tape?' I said, still chewing. 'Down at the Migrant Resource Centre or somewhere? Then run them past Acheson for a possible ID?'

'Good idea,' he said, writing the suggestion on a pad next to his keyboard. 'Next.'

'I've been thinking about the plastic sleeve that Acheson's documents came in. And the cassette case that might've been stored with it. Janet Wilson's the only one we can talk to now who handled Proctor's file on the night of the party, and she says the thing was closed all the time it was with her. But I think we should assemble the CCTV footage, just to be sure she didn't have a peek inside.'

'Good. I'll get Audio-Visual on to it. Next.'

'You've got the profiler coming in tomorrow. Can I just say that, even without a psych degree, it's clear to me that we're not looking for serial killers here. There's nothing random about what's happening. These people have murdered a cabinet minister. And it's a fair bet they've now got Proctor — the prime minister's top advisor.'

'That's not right,' said McHenry, his voice full of challenge. 'Just think about it for a minute. No one knows where Proctor is, but, given what happened to Wright, we have to *assume* that he's been taken by the same people. That's safety first. But to take it as fact? That's just sloppy.'

I wasn't sure if McHenry was prosecuting an argument, or if he really thought that Proctor could be anywhere other than with Wright's killers. He must have seen the doubt in my eyes because he proceeded to clear that one up for me.

'Look, Glass, let's assume that Proctor didn't do a runner and that he's being held against his will. How do we know it's the same people who killed Wright? Mightn't we be dealing with a copycat here? Or maybe *Proctor* killed Wright, and now someone's doing a vengeance job on *him*. Or if Proctor was in on the Wright murder, maybe his accomplices have decided to do him in for some reason? There's any number of possibilities, so let's leave speculation to the journos. We operate in the real world, and we've got to work this through as though he's been abducted. But don't close yourself off to anything. What else?'

'I think we should interview Lansdowne,' I said — a suggestion that drew a groan from McHenry. 'If you assume for a moment that Proctor *is* being held by Wright's killers, then their real target in all of this is obvious. It's the prime minister. And if he wasn't so well protected, I reckon he would have been their first kill, and probably their only one.'

'And why do you say that?'

'Who's the common link between Wright and Proctor? It's Lansdowne. Who was the source of their power? He was. Were they up to anything that he didn't know about? Probably not. Lansdowne's a control freak. I mean, he *is* the prime minister, so by definition he's into control, but from what I understand ...'

'From your mate Stevo ...'

'No, not from Stevo — from listening to the political commentators and reading what they say. All of them reckon that Lansdowne likes his hand on the tiller. At all times. He's a micro-manager who doesn't let go. So, assuming he knows what's going on in his government, shouldn't we be fronting him as a matter of priority?'

'Anything else?' said McHenry, his eyes flitting between me and his screen.

'I'm also convinced we should be putting surveillance on Jean Acheson. She's spoken to one of the killers, or someone pretty close to them. That makes her the only person with that sort of link. There's also the fact that when they wanted her to have those receipts, they left them in a fairly obscure place, but one that she knows well. That says to me they're keeping an eye on her, and, as you know, predatory killers often end up targeting people they're fixated on. If I was drawing up a list of their possible next targets, I'd put Acheson right up there.'

'Along with Lansdowne,' said McHenry.

'He'd be their number one, as I say.'

'So, surveillance on Acheson, eh?' he said, smiling wearily. 'And if we did tail her, we'd have to tap her phone, too, I guess. And monitor her emails. The question is, where are you going to find a Federal Court justice who'll approve a fishing expedition like that? And even if you found one, you saw how Acheson's colleagues went off when we just wanted to talk to her. Commissioner Brady wouldn't want a repeat of that — not unless we could guarantee him something.'

'Okay, okay. It was just a thought. And what about Lansdowne?'

'Brady's one step ahead of you there. He raised it with the PM's people this morning, and he expects to hear back from them first thing tomorrow. As for who'll be in on it, the commissioner tells me you ruffled the PM's feathers the other day, and he's not keen on a repeat. So, if and when we speak to the prime minister, you should consider yourself a doubtful starter. Now, if there's nothing else …'

There was plenty else, but I restrained myself. My run-in with the PM was always going to come back to bite me, but using it to ban me from the team that would interview him was vindictive and ridiculous. McHenry went back to his screen, but all I could do was sit there, trying to calm myself. There were two other things I'd planned to raise with him. The first was to push him again for access to Proctor's dirt files. But, as I was in no mood for another backhander, I held fire on that one, and moved on to the second thing — getting a psych out to Lake George to have a chat to Tom Hanley.

McHenry said he'd read the Hanley interview, and seen my recommendation, and he agreed a psych assessment was warranted. He said he'd organise it.

Back at my desk, I let the full implications of what McHenry had said sink in. The Lansdowne interview could be crucial to the case, but it looked like I'd be excluded from it, all on the whim of that pumped-up little bastard Brady. The thought of it made me furious. Yes, I'd stuffed up, to a degree, but not so badly that it should limit my role in the investigation.

I took a few deep breaths, trying to put a cap on my anger. But I was too worked up. I went to the kitchen and got a coffee, hoping that the activity and another dose of caffeine would help. But they didn't. In fact, by the time I got back to my desk, my emotions were bubbling close to the surface.

I sat and did more deep breathing, telling myself that my anger would dissipate. It always took time. I had a mantra: these thoughts weren't me; they were external to me; they did not control me; they were mine to control. I knew I could do whatever I chose to do — and, to show it, I gritted my teeth and pushed on with my work. I called Tony McManus, the police liaison at Foreign Affairs, and asked him for a check on Sylvie Hanley. Essentially, I was after confirmation that she was dead. While it was possible that Tom Hanley was one of our killers, he seemed barely organised enough to feed himself. If I could establish with certainty that Sylvie Hanley had died in Thailand, we could probably rule a line under the whole Mondrian business, and Tom Hanley as well, and forget about taking a psych out to see him.

Next, I began writing up the Acheson interview. It was a pretty straightforward account of our contact with her; but the further I got into it, the more it became clear to me that McHenry was making a huge mistake in not backing surveillance on her. If the killers were watching her, our doing the same would get us closer to them. It would also give her some protection.

As the afternoon wore on, my anger at missing the Lansdowne

interview melded with my growing anger at McHenry over his refusal to keep an eye on Acheson. The boss was pandering to Brady's fear of negative publicity. And Brady was being far too sensitive to the needs of his political masters. Especially when it came to who might best interview the PM. These festering thoughts got such a hold on me that I was forced to put the Acheson write-up aside a few times. And by late afternoon, I was furious with Brady, and ropeable with McHenry for having done his bidding.

Then it dawned on me — there was a way of getting around McHenry's ruling. Maybe *I* could keep an eye on Acheson. At night. In my off hours. It would be limited protection, but better than nothing. And the killers moved at night, so if our paths crossed while I was shadowing her, I could nab them, or call in the troops. And even if I just spotted them from a distance, it would at least give us something to go on, which was more than we had now. And whatever way it played out, I was sure I could handle myself.

The main risk was, Acheson might spring me. If she did, I'd no doubt be kicked off the case. Or, worse, it could mean my job. But I was confident I could shadow her undetected. Then it struck me that I'd never risked my career like this before. So why was I considering such a dire move? Did I really think that a limited tail on Acheson could help us solve the case, or was my anger at McHenry and Brady clouding my judgment? And what about Acheson? Was my fascination with her the real reason I was considering this half-baked mission? I mulled it all over a bit more, then I resolved that, despite my misgivings, I had to put some time into watching her. And I felt much better having reached that decision.

I got the make and plates of Acheson's vehicle from motor registry, and took a note of her Kingston address. I was back to reading the latest entries on PROMIS when Tony McManus called with the details on Sylvie Hanley.

'She left Australia thirteen years ago,' he said. 'Almost to the day. She was down as a temporary resident of Thailand. Then she was listed as missing in the north of the country. There was a search for her, and then the file was amended to "Missing, presumed dead". I guess by now we'd say she's definitely dead.'

'Why "definitely"?' I said, taking the photo of the Hanley children out of its plastic sleeve. 'People disappear themselves all the time and change their identities. Why not her?'

'We did look into that, but we found no reason for Sylvie Hanley to slip out of sight. She had no police record. No outstanding fines. She didn't have a family she wanted to escape from. Both her parents were deceased, and the dispersal of their assets didn't cause any dispute between her and her brother Thomas. It seems they were very close. And there was no bank acquittal in the end, which made her debt-free. The thing is, parts of Thailand were very, very dangerous at that time. She was just one of the unlucky ones.'

So, Sylvie Hanley was shaping as another doubtful lead. Then again, a suspected death without a body left a lot of questions hanging, especially when a *live* Sylvie Hanley had a strong motive for murdering Susan Wright. If our other leads didn't start producing soon, McHenry would have to dispatch a team to Thailand to try to establish Sylvie's fate. It would probably prove a futile effort, given the time that had elapsed, and I hoped like hell that if he did send a team over there, he'd leave me at home.

Jean Acheson's face filled the mute TV screen at the front of the room, and then the program credits rolled. She was signing off for the day. I packed my papers away and told McHenry I was taking a few hours off. Then I raced to my car.

It was dark by the time I reached Parliament House. I used a police pass to gain access to the underground carpark on the Senate side of the building, and reversed my old sedan between two media vehicles parked near the boom gates. Fifteen minutes later, Acheson drove by in a black VW hatch, the boom gate lifted, and she turned left onto Parliament Drive. I gave her a ten-second start, and then I followed her.

Acheson drove off the Hill and turned left onto State Circle. She looked to be heading home to Kingston. I slipped in behind a van and changed lanes at the last minute as she turned right onto Canberra Avenue. My only previous experience of tailing a vehicle had been as part of a team, but going solo seemed easy enough. I slowed and followed her into Giles Street, then watched as she disappeared under an apartment block fifty metres further up. I stopped the car a few doors past her place, got out, and saw the lights come on in the penthouse suite.

I needed a hide from which to observe Acheson's building for a few hours. The most obvious place was a native garden fronting a tall brick wall about twenty metres up the road from her block. It had a good view of both the entrance to the building and the penthouse. I slipped in behind the bushes, leaned against the wall, and resigned myself to a couple of hours standing stock-still in the cold.

However, twenty minutes later, the lights in the penthouse went out. A minute or so after that, Acheson came down the stairs at the front of the block. She looked up and down the street before heading off towards the Kingston shops. I gave her a thirty-metre start, and then I followed her through the shadows, avoiding the light of street lamps. I paused regularly to assess the street for any threat, but saw nothing.

From the way she stepped it out, it seemed that Acheson knew where she was going. She slowed when she got to the shopping strip, and paused at a real estate agent's window. After a few minutes, she moved down Kennedy Street, past the gift shops and restaurants. I shadowed her from the opposite side of the street, using an unbroken line of parked cars for cover.

I figured she must be heading around to Green Square, but near the end of Kennedy Street she stopped outside an Italian restaurant. She read a menu tacked next to the door, and went in. Luckily, the Bella Roma had an all-glass frontage, so I was able to watch the skinny waiter show Acheson to a table. She ordered, and then took a paperback from her bag and read it while she waited for her food.

Two groups of celebrity spotters saw her through the glass, and stopped to stare, but she stayed hunched over her book, ignoring them. During the weeks that parliament sat, the better eateries around Kingston and Manuka fed a lot of Australia's most powerful people. These cabinet ministers and senior journos were able to eat and socialise without the locals staring at them. Only tourists did that.

When her pasta dish arrived, Acheson had the waiter bring her a glass of white wine. She made short work of both, paid the bill, and was soon back out on the footpath. She walked to the end of Kennedy, and I lost sight of her as she went around the corner into Eyre Street.

She had to be heading for Green Square this time, probably to a coffee joint. I jogged across the road and raced around the corner into Eyre Street. Then my guts went into freefall — there was no one on the footpath ahead of me. I ran down the street, hit the brakes, and scanned a service lane that ran through the middle of the block of shops. But she wasn't down there, either. Could she really have been abducted right under my nose? Was that even possible? Then came a voice that hit me like a whack on the head.

'Looking for me, detective?' said Acheson, her tone more accusing than questioning.

I swung around and there she was, peering out from behind one of the fat white pillars that framed the entrance to the lane. My goose was cooked.

Blood Oath subscription news

Friday 2 August, 8.00pm

Did Feeney really go the fiddle?
by Simon Rolfe

Having been a victim of false rumours myself, I know how damaging they can be. The subtle rumour eats away at your reputation, reducing it to rusty fragments that blow away on the wind. The massive rumour is like a pipe-bomb that takes your head off.

Well, I can now reveal that someone has lobbed a highly explosive rumour at Opposition Leader Lou Feeney. According to this rumour, when Mr Feeney was at St Phillip's College in Brisbane, he introduced some junior boys to a novel form of show-and-tell that involved fire, dance, and general nakedness.

Given that we're a week out from polling day, with contenders who are almost neck-and-neck, there's no prize for guessing the motivation of the rumour-mongers.

So now I ask you, dear readers, if you've heard details of this Feeney rumour, please contact me. I'd like to know where you heard it, who told you, and where you were when you were told. I make this request, not only to advance the story, but also to uncover the dirty-tricks department that's just reared its ugly head in this campaign.

13

'MISS ACHESON,' I said, catching my breath. 'Fancy seeing you here.'

'Fancy indeed,' she said, looking me up and down. 'Nice night for a jog, detective, but you're being a bit hard on that suit, aren't you? I can hear the seams popping from here.'

I looked down at my suit and then back at her. She was silhouetted against the bright lights of a furniture shop, and though I couldn't see her face, the warmth in her voice told me she was smiling.

'There's nothing wrong with these seams,' I said, smiling back at her. 'And nothing wrong with the suit, either, for that matter. Here. Have a closer look.'

I rubbed one of my lapels between my thumb and forefinger, and took a few steps towards her. I'd been right about the smile. There was a twinkle in her eye, too.

'Pure new wool,' I said.

She was looking at my right shoulder. I followed her gaze to a smear of cobwebs that I'd probably picked up in the garden across from her place. I brushed them off, gave her my best cheesy smile, and continued.

'This venerable suit is from China, via New York,' I said, hooking my thumbs under both lapels. 'Bought off a street rack near Times Square, from some African guy. And, okay, maybe it hasn't aged that well, but it *is* my favorite suit. And it's got a story. Now surely that counts for something.'

She took a step towards me and gave my coat a closer inspection.

'Yes, you're right,' she said, her brow lined with mock concern. 'It hasn't aged that well, has it? But it looks comfortable. And it's a good fit.'

'I guess I should say thanks for that.'

'No, I think you should say, "Would you like to go out for a drink, Jean?" And I'd probably say, "Yes. That sounds like a good idea." Then I could give you the history of *my* outfit. So what do you say? Are you up for it? A Guinness at Mad Dog's?'

'I'm always up for a Guinness,' I said, a bit surprised at how quickly things had moved.

We made small talk as we walked around to the square. I asked her if she'd eaten, though of course I knew she had. She commented on the cold. It was the only bad thing about Canberra, she said. I couldn't help thinking of her down at the lake — especially the look she'd given me. And now this. Was it personal or professional for her? Was it a come-on, or was she just out to pump me for information? Whatever it was, I'd have to let this play out before I could extract myself.

Mad Dog Morgan's was an Irish pub set deep into the corner of Green Square. It had been years since I'd set foot in the place, but it hadn't changed that much. It was still dimly lit, with a down-at-heel look. The same oddments of furniture were crammed into the same wooden cubicles, and the same old maps of the counties were fixed to the walls.

A few drinkers were standing at the bar, and a circle of musicians were thrashing out a jig in one of the cubicles. Other than that, the place was empty. I ordered a couple of pints and took them to where Acheson had settled on a church pew near a wall at the back of the place. We clinked glasses, exchanged smiles, and drank to each other's health.

'Do you play an instrument, detective?' she said, nodding in the direction of the musicians.

'You can call me Darren, if you like, Miss Acheson,' I said. 'And I'll call you Jean.'

'Darren Glass. There's something well-rounded about the name. Do you play an instrument, Darren?'

'I played guitar when I was a kid. Blues and rock — that sort of thing. And a mate gave me a mandolin the last time I was in the States, so I mess around on that a bit now. What about you? My guess is ... piano?'

'No. Violin. I started when I was four. And, yes, my parents were a *bit* keen. Too keen, you'd have to say, because these days I hardly take the thing out of its case. But I still love music, so no harm done really, I suppose. None that you'd *detect*, anyway.'

We laughed, raised our glasses again, and drank. The bar was filling up with young people dressed in black. And public servants, still suited-up, kicking off their weekend. A group of young men stared at Jean and made no attempt to hide the fact that she was the subject of their prattle. Then another wave of people swept into the place, including a fiddler, an older guy with a mandolin, and another guitarist. When this trio joined the circle, the tunes sped up, but the music became much tighter somehow.

'How do you handle the gawkers when you're out like this?' I said, indicating a couple of guys who were still ogling her.

'It comes with the job,' said Jean, 'and I love what I do. If that means being treated like a goldfish sometimes, I'll wear it.'

We listened to the music, sipping stout and keeping time with our feet. Then Jean turned and probed me with those eyes of hers.

'Darren, I've got to ask. Were you out there following me tonight?'

'No,' I said, reeling back slightly, as though the suggestion came as a complete surprise.

'If it *was* you, I wouldn't be angry or anything.'

'I wasn't following you,' I said, putting some steel in my voice. 'I came over to Kingston for some Indian, but I changed my mind and was on my way around here for sushi. That's when I ran into you.'

She examined me closely for a few seconds, and then she turned away and stared without focus into the distance.

'Okay,' she said. 'But there *was* someone out there. Following me. I didn't see them, but it's just like people say. I knew they were there — somewhere in the dark, when I was walking to the shops.'

'Has it happened before? That you thought you were being followed?'

'Yes. I had the same feeling on Wednesday night when I walked down here. Look, tell me honestly. Was it you out there tonight? I won't go off at you if it was. I promise.'

'No,' I said, staring into her eyes. 'I was *not* following you.'

She looked at me doubtfully for a few seconds. Then her eyes softened. My gift for bare-faced bullshit artistry had done it again. I could lock eyes with almost anyone and persuade them that I was telling the truth. It was a useful talent when I needed to convince a suspect that we knew more than we did. It had also proved handy in the odd courtroom situation. Not that I was a chronic liar; I could just be very convincing when I needed to be.

If you're lying to someone who hates or fears you, or who has a strong interest in proving you wrong, you've got to be both convincing and irrefutable. But for a lie to work on a family member, a friend, or a lover, it's got to be both of the above, and they have to *want* to believe you. Now, while I hated bullshitting to Jean, I really liked the fact that she wanted to believe me.

My one cause for worry was that she might be right. Maybe someone else *was* following her. If it was an obsessive fan, as often happened with celebrities, that could be easily rectified. But if it was either of Susan Wright's killers, their motives would be nothing but bad. Then again, if it was them, their obsession with her was making them vulnerable. But as I thought about it, I realised that if someone else was on her tail, she hadn't sprung them like she'd sprung me. This meant they were better at setting a tail than I was. And if that was the case, what else were they better at?

Blood Oath subscription news

Friday 2 August, 11.00pm

Too hot to handle
By Simon Rolfe

A question, dear readers: Have any of you heard of an arcane schoolboy ritual known as 'the rancid' fire dance? Well, rest assured, those of you who haven't will soon be all too familiar with it. Earlier this evening, I referred to a rumour that's been plaguing Opposition Leader Lou Feeney. Now I can reveal that this rumour pushes the view that Mr Feeney is all too well acquainted with 'the rancid'.

As I understand it, to dance 'the rancid', the dancer strips down to his underpants, wedges a rolled-up section of newspaper into his crotch, with equal amounts of the paper protruding from his front and backsides. Both ends of the paper are then set on fire, and the dancer jumps and gyrates until things get too hot for his private parts. He then signals for the dance 'marshalls' to douse the flames.

Mr Feeney has admitted to me that he danced 'the rancid' in front of students of all ages in his final month at school. And while he concedes that it was a juvenile and somewhat dangerous thing to do, he rejects claims that he achieved sexual gratification during the course of the dance. A number of former St Phillips students have confirmed what he says in this regard.

Interestingly, three readers now tell me that the men they heard discussing the dance rumour had New Zealand accents. Fush and chups anyone? How about darty trucks?

14

McHenry wasn't around when I got back to the room, so I immediately checked in with the analyst, Ruth Marginson. A lot of people had recognised Jean at Mad Dog's, and some of them would have recognised me, so I'd been planning to tell McHenry about my 'chance' encounter with Jean as soon as I could. Now that Marginson was my only option, I took a seat next to her desk and gave her the story.

'Did you discuss the case with her?' she said when I'd finished.

'She raised it, as you'd expect. But I didn't get drawn in. One thing I did learn, though. She thinks she's being followed.'

'And is she?'

'Well, she hasn't seen anyone. It's just a feeling she's got. I'll go down in the morning and see if I can spot anything around her place.'

'And you just ran into her, you say? And she invited you for a drink?'

'That's right.'

'Okay, let's leave it for now,' she said, turning back to her screen. 'But make sure you write it up.'

McHenry would have told Marginson that I'd wanted surveillance on Jean, so I couldn't blame her for being sceptical about my story. But at least now I was covered to a degree. And if McHenry wanted to look into the encounter, the only person he could talk to was Jean — and I doubted he'd do that.

I went back to my desk and wrote up the contact. With that done, I tried to clear my head of the whole thing, but a vague feeling of dread was still hanging over me hours later when I crawled into the rec room for some shut-eye.

At first light next morning, I was back on Giles Street, looking for places from which someone could spy on Jean's apartment block. The most obvious spot was the garden I'd used the night before, but the tan bark there was so compressed that I hadn't even left an impression on it.

A lush garden a few doors down provided a view of both Jean's driveway and the footpath in front of her block, but there was nothing to indicate that anyone had loitered there recently, either. I could have draped the area in tape and called in Forensics, but it was best to leave that decision to McHenry.

My stomach was grumbling by the time I finished up, so I stopped at a café in Manuka and checked out the morning papers over breakfast. They all led with previews of the Wright funeral, and each front page had something on Proctor's disappearance. Having the stories side-by-side like that seemed to imply that Proctor would soon share Wright's fate. The media were preparing the public for the worst.

I drove back to the station and called Steve Newings, the deputy registrar for Births, Deaths and Marriages. I wanted him to dig out a couple of death certificates for me — one for the PM's nephew, Mick Stanton, and one for poor old Dennis Hanley. I planned to talk to the doctors who'd certified them, just to make sure they had died in the way people said they had.

Next, I called all the vet clinics on a list Marginson had supplied, and asked them to check their stocks of ketamine for any slippage. They all promised to let me know within twenty-four hours. McHenry walked past while I was on the phone, which made me wonder about the Lansdowne interview, but I wasn't going to ask him. If I turned out to be a non-starter, I'd deal with it. In the meantime, I'd concentrate on what I had in front of me.

I was going through a list of Marie Staples' radical uni mates when the department's profiler walked into the room. Alan Thorne was small and fit, with dyed-blond hair tied back in a ponytail, and a pair of tortoiseshell glasses perched on the end of his nose. He'd studied criminal profiling at Qantico, then done a doctorate in behavioural analysis at the ANU. I'd read his doctoral thesis, and the cop in me had dismissed it as an over-complicated explanation for why bad people did nasty things, mostly to other bad people.

The room was packed for Thorne's appearance. McHenry must have known it would be, because he had even organised sandwiches. He thanked Thorne for joining us. Thorne thanked him for the invite, and said he'd been through PROMIS, and was impressed with our thoroughness to date. Then he lifted his notes to his nose and launched into his spiel.

'First up, let me explain that, in analysing this case, I've assumed that the people who killed Mrs Wright now have their hands on Mr Proctor. So let's get down to business. As many of you will know, when building a criminal profile we employ the same six questions that journalists commonly use — who, what, when, where, how, and why.

'Let's begin with the "who" in this case. Both victims were associated with the government. They knew each other. Were they specifically targeted? Given their association, I think that's probable. Now, if that's correct, then, in purely definitional terms, the perpetrators here are not serial killers. That is, for them this was more than a case of inclination meeting opportunity. Rather, they're spree killers — people who are driven by a single overwhelming impulse to commit a number of murders.'

It gave me a bit of a lift to hear Thorne echo what I'd said to McHenry. I glanced across at the boss, hoping to catch his eye, but he had his head down, taking notes. Regardless, I knew that Thorne's words would register with him.

'The second and most important part of the "who" question comes under the heading "Who dunnit?". And, in addressing that, I think we can broadly say that the people we're looking for here are very organised. Or at least one of them is. Mrs Wright was not an easy target. She was lured, or entrapped, and then captured. Later, she was despatched and dumped. All of the above required considerable planning and effort.

'The perpetrators were probably familiar with her routine, including her usual route home. They knew about her after-work party, and maybe they were even there. And the document they leaked to the media demonstrates a desire to do damage to the government. In other words, at least one of the perpetrators is well informed and probably highly intelligent — just as you'd expect of an organised, violent offender.'

'Just to interrupt for a moment, Alan,' said McHenry, causing Thorne to lower his notes. 'Leaking a document like they did, during an election campaign, not only demonstrates some knowledge of politics. It was a very political act, in and of itself. So is it possible we're looking for some sort of militant political types here?'

Thorne removed his glasses and considered the question for a moment.

'I think it's much more likely to be an avenger,' he said finally. 'Someone whose life has gone bad, who blames the government for it, and who's organised others to help him exact his revenge. It's a simple but common explanation, I'm afraid. These people murdered Mrs Wright, but I believe that any government target would have suited them just as well. And it means that things look bleak for Mr Proctor, too. You see, the government will continue to irritate our avengers, and now that they've embarked on this course, I fear they'll continue with it until they're caught. Or killed.'

'Are you saying the prime minister's at risk here, too?' I said.

'Certainly at risk,' said Thorne. 'Very much at risk. I see his security's tighter than ever, and so it should be.'

McHenry finally looked around at me, and I was surprised to see that he was scowling. Maybe I was getting a preliminary blast for my contact with Jean. Or maybe he was still smarting over my prodding of Lansdowne. Whatever it was, I blanked him out and concentrated on what Thorne had said about people with a grievance.

'Alan, you've no doubt read our interview with Tom Hanley,' I said. 'The guy's barely functional, and, on the face of it, not a fit for the profile you've worked up here. But is there any way he could be involved?'

'Only as a support player,' said Thorne. 'But, of course, if he is a support player, who's he supporting? As I've said, it's likely to be an organised violent offender, with an anti-social personality disorder. His or her profile could include sexual aggression, poly-substance abuse, sexual perversion, and possibly even a history of mutilating animals — all characteristics that the FBI lists as possible markers for this sort of personality.'

'One of them certainly ticks the box on mutilation,' said Smeaton. 'Given what they did to the cat.'

'Possibly, except that the cat wasn't mutilated,' said Thorne, eyeing him over the top of his glasses. 'In fact, it was treated in much the same way as Mrs Wright, which brings us to the question of "what". What was the cause of death? Well, it was highly unusual. That, too, tells us something about our perpetrators, even though what it tells us contradicts the personality markers

I've just outlined. Because one must say that the killers were unusually gentle with Mrs Wright. She was anaesthetised before she was gassed. Her body, when it was dumped, was not presented so as to shock or offend. She was not sexually interfered with. She was fully clothed. Her dignity in death was maintained. That's why I believe this was not so much an act against Mrs Wright, but more an attack on what she represented. So, anomalies abound, but nothing's ever neat, is it?'

The prime minister had given me a verbal whacking when I described Wright's killers as gentle, so he would have hated Thorne's description of her death as dignified.

'Moving on to "when",' said Thorne, jolting me from my thoughts. 'When did the crime occur? Was there anything significant about the time of day, the month, or the year? Well, yes, of course there was. We're nearly at the end of an election campaign, and two significant actors have been removed from the stage. Clearly, not a coincidence. Clearly, connected to the motivation of the perpetrators, as I've said.

'The next question is "where". Where was Mrs Wright murdered? If you can answer that, you've probably found the killers. And where was she abducted? Another big unknown. The third part of the "where" equation is "Where was she dumped?" That we do know. By the lake, of course. So, did the lake mean something to our killers? Or to Mrs Wright? Well, forgive me if I digress into the language of symbolism here, but, in the absence of firm evidence, it's as close a reading of these actions as I could come up with. Lakes feature in the mythology of a number of ancient cultures, where they're generally linked to a transition to death. In Greek mythology, for instance, the god Dionysus descended into the underworld through a lake.'

'If we're talking about symbolism,' said Smeaton, 'any idea what the cat means?'

Thorne stroked his chin with his thumb and forefinger while he considered the question.

'The cat clearly had special significance to at least one of the perpetrators,' he said at last. 'Perhaps they were telling us that the cat's life was of equal value to the minister's. As to your question about symbolism, that's very interesting. The cat was a symbol of cleverness in some ancient cultures. And cats have always been considered remarkable for their powers of transformation. They have fast-dilating pupils. They're able to sheath and unsheath their claws at will. And they can turn from a sleepy bundle of fur into a beast that lashes out without conscience. It's why different cultures have radically different takes on the cat. I mean, it's an animal that was sacred to the ancient Egyptians, but it's never been very popular with Buddhists; in their tradition, the cat was the only creature, other than the snake, that failed to cry when the Buddha died.'

Thorne let that one sink in. Then he scanned his notes briefly before removing his glasses. He was coming to the end of his spiel.

'Finally, there's the "why" of it,' he said. 'What motivated the murderers? Why did they do it? Well, in the end, it could be that they think they're protecting themselves. Or someone they love. That is, their motive is survival. Their other motivation could be the pursuit of happiness. Happiness achieved through an act of revenge against someone who has harmed them, or their loved ones, in the past. There are any number of permutations to these two motives, but I feel the truth lies with one of them. Or somewhere in between, perhaps. Keep them in mind as you continue your investigation, and they'll help steer you towards the perpetrators.

'I'll put these thoughts and some substantiating materials up on PROMIS. I hope they help you in this important task. Now, are there any other questions?'

No hands went up, so Thorne re-scanned his notes to make sure he'd covered everything. Satisfied, he put the notes back in his briefcase, thanked McHenry, and walked from the room.

Channel Four Live Cam

Saturday 3 August, 1.30pm

Good afternoon, Jean Acheson with the Live Cam, and up to half a million people have converged on the centre of Sydney for Susan Wright's state funeral, which is due to get underway here within the hour.

Prominent business people, politicians, and celebrities are still arriving at Saint Mary's, and police have barricaded roads around the city centre to give mourners easy access to the service. Most of Mrs Wright's cabinet colleagues have already taken their seats, and Prime Minister Michael Lansdowne's motorcade is due any minute now.

Meanwhile, giant screens relaying the event have been set up throughout the city in an effort to relieve the crush around the cathedral. And Macquarie Cemetery has placed a strict limit on numbers for the funeral service to be held out there later this afternoon.

For the record, the previous biggest state funeral in Australia was that of Sir John Monash. More than three hundred thousand people lined the streets of Melbourne in 1931 to farewell the World War I leader. This is Jean Acheson. Back with more in a moment.

15

WHILE THE REST of Australia watched the state funeral on TV, everyone in the Major Incident Room was glued to a computer screen, viewing several minutes of CCTV footage that had just gone up on PROMIS. The footage showed that, despite her denials, Janet Wilson had indeed opened Proctor's file as she was bringing it up to Wright's party.

Wilson hadn't rifled through the file as such, but footage from the night showed her getting into a lift on the ground floor. The next shot was from inside the lift as the doors closed: as the lift ascended, she opened the lid of the file and had a lingering look inside; then, as the doors began to open at the first floor, Wilson quickly closed the file. A corridor camera caught her a few seconds later, scooting into the party. The footage finished with her handing the file to Proctor as he stood at the door to Wright's office.

In the segment that followed, Wilson got a drink from the kitchen and returned to reception, where she chatted to various people. Ten minutes later, Proctor's deputy, Penny Lomax, tapped her on the shoulder and the two of them moved into a short corridor and put their heads together for a few minutes.

In the final shots, Wilson returned to reception, and Lomax headed for the toilet. The minister's private office and the staff toilets were the only areas of the office suite not covered by CCTV cameras. This raised the possibility that Lomax had called or texted someone to tell them what Wilson had seen in the file.

When I discussed the footage with McHenry, he was all for going up to the Hill and charging Wilson with obstruction. I advised against it. Yes, she knew things she hadn't told us. In fact, she'd lied. But I didn't see her as one of our killers. And given her nervous disposition, if we made a big show of arresting her, it might tip her over the edge and cruel our chances of getting anything from her.

McHenry heard me out, and then told me to handle it whatever way I wanted to — so long as I got to the bottom of it. That would mean hauling Lomax in again, too, I told him, to see what she and Wilson had talked about after Wilson delivered the file to Proctor. And, more importantly, I wanted to know if Lomax had contacted anyone while she was in the toilets, after she'd chatted with Wilson.

'That's a lot to cover,' said McHenry. 'You'd better get on with it.'

An hour later, when she walked into the interview room, Wilson looked shaky — as though she knew something was up. When Smeaton told her we had new information about Proctor's file, her jaw started to quiver.

'W-w-what information?' she said, her fingers splayed across her mouth.

'It might have escaped your attention,' said Smeaton, leaning across the table towards her, 'but there are cameras all over Parliament House. So what do you suppose those cameras recorded when you were bringing Proctor's file up to the party that night? Think about it — you and the file, in the lift, alone together.'

'Okay, okay,' she said, letting out a giant sigh, as though suddenly relieved. 'I didn't tell you the exact truth the other time. But you already know that. Well, okay. I did look in the file, but I didn't take anything from it. But you know that, too. And the thing with the file is, I didn't really see what was in it. Just some documents, that's all.'

'How many documents?' said Smeaton.

'There were five of them.'

'And what can you tell us about them?'

'Nothing, really. They were in those heavy plastic covers you can't see through.'

'The opaque ones?' said Smeaton.

'Yes, that's right. They were opaque.'

'What about one of these?' Smeaton said, sliding a micro-cassette across the table towards her. 'Did you see one of these in there, too?'

'Oh yes,' she said, looking like she was going to crack up. 'Yes, there *was* one of them in there, too.'

'So, you remember the cassette now, do you? Well, go on then. Tell us about it.'

'There's nothing to tell, really. It was just like that one. Except the one in the file had a word written on it.'

'And what word was that?

'It just said "Mondrian".'

Smeaton and I exchanged a knowing glance. There it was again — Mondrian, the banker's bank. So what, if anything, was recorded on the cassette in the file? Only God knew the answer to that one. And Proctor, if he was still alive.

We told Wilson she'd be charged if she held anything else back. Then I asked her what had made her open the file. She said it had been a rare opportunity, being alone with a dirt file like that, and she hadn't been able to resist the temptation. I asked if she'd told anyone else about what she'd seen in the file.

'Only Penny,' she said, wiping vainly at the tears streaming down her face. 'Penny Lomax.'

'Why her?'

'Because she's my boss, and I tell her everything. What I hear around the place — the goss and stuff.'

'Do your efforts for her often involve sticking your nose in where it doesn't belong?' said Smeaton. 'Like poking around in secured files?'

'No! That's the first and last time ever. And, truly, it's like I said. I never had the opportunity before.'

'So how did Penny Lomax react when you told her what you saw?'

'She was *not* happy. She told me it was the wrong thing to have done and that I'd be turfed out of the office if ever Mr Proctor found out about it.'

Thirty minutes later, when Penny Lomax walked into the interview room, she looked less than poised. As soon as she was seated, she said she had something she wanted to tell us. Then, in what sounded like a well-rehearsed statement, she said that on the night of the party, Wilson had opened up to her about having a peek inside Proctor's file. Wilson had also told her about a cassette inside the file, she said. And that cassette had had the word 'Mondrian' written on its spine. She apologised for having failed to say anything about these things when we'd first interviewed her. These declarations were no surprise, really. Lomax would have known that we were talking to Wilson again, and she would also have known that Wilson was likely to buckle under pressure.

'So why didn't you say anything about this when we first spoke to you?' said Smeaton, a disbelieving smile on his face.

'I didn't think it was important then,' said Lomax, struggling to maintain her composure. 'But thinking about it since, I now recognise it as something you'd want to know.'

'So you didn't think the word "Mondrian" on that cassette case would interest us?'

'I'm sorry, but at the time I was thinking, like, Mondrian? It's a bank — so what? But then I Googled it, and saw how it was linked with Mrs Wright in the past.'

'I don't believe you for a second. So why don't we start again. And this time, I advise you to think carefully before you respond.'

Lomax dropped her head and ran her tongue over her lips. She looked up at Smeaton, and then swung a look my way. The usual hint of defiance was gone from her eyes. She was finally feeling some pressure.

'I'm sorry, I'm sorry,' she said, her voice cracking. 'Yes, I should have said something. I was vaguely aware of the Mondrian thing. But it was so long ago, I didn't see anything in it. And I was more focused on Janet. Alan would have sacked her if he'd found out, and I couldn't let that happen. She's my eyes and ears up there.'

Self-interest seemed a much more plausible explanation than ignorance, but Smeaton wanted to give her another push.

'And when you had your little tête-à-tête with Wilson at the party,' he said, 'did you tell her to keep quiet about what she'd done?'

'Well, sort of. But, not really. I mean, I was angry that she'd been poking around in things that weren't her business. And I told her she'd jeopardised her job and that she should keep her mouth shut about what she'd done.'

'And after you had a go at her, you went to the ladies',' I said. 'Did you call or text anyone while you were in there?'

'In the toilet?' she said, screwing up her face at the suggestion. 'No. Why would I do that?'

That was the question, but in the absence of a ready answer, my only option was to check her phone records to see if they contradicted her. I cautioned Lomax not to hold anything back in future, after which Smeaton saw her out.

Our final interview for the day was with Simon Rolfe, the last of the Early Leavers from Wright's party. Rolfe owned the *Blood Oath* news blog, which, according to my old schoolmate Stevo, had a healthy subscriber base that gave it plenty of clout with big advertisers and the politicians.

When Rolfe entered the interview room, his clothes were the star of the show. Sure, he looked very fit for a man in his late forties, but it was his cream, double-breasted suit, and the white shirt and pink silk tie, that caught the eye. He even had a matching pink hankie sticking out of his breast pocket. He looked crisp, tanned, and freshly pressed. Maybe he was groomed for the interview.

He sat down on the other side of the table and carefully crossed his legs, protecting his creases as best he could. Then he looked us over with a mixture of impatience and world-weariness. Smeaton started off by asking him our stock question. Did he know anyone who might have had a reason to harm Susan Wright? Rolfe took the question as a cue for a speech.

'I *could* say she was a saint and that everyone loved her,' he said, chuckling at the thought. 'But then, why's she dead? Because someone found a compelling reason to kill her, of course. Was it hate? Who knows? Did she hurt someone so badly that they needed to kill her, or was it just a matter of convenience? Something purely practical? I don't know. And, no, I don't know anyone capable of killing Susan Wright.'

'So how'd she get on with her colleagues?' said Smeaton.

'Especially the other members of cabinet?'

'So it's background you want, is it? Ahh well, she was one of three women in cabinet, and all of her male colleagues, including Lansdowne, were blokey blokes. Enough said, really. I mean, that should have been an automatic block on her ambitions. Except for the fact that she was a shining star in a firmament of black holes. And, of course, Lansdowne greased her path, though I've never understood why. So … Susan Wright. She was elegant. She had an intellect. Her judgment was mostly sound. Not everything she did was popular, but she was a good communicator, so the punters thought they understood her. And gender hardly featured when the gallery wrote her up. I guess no one wanted to kill the golden goose.'

'You sound like a big fan, Mr Rolfe,' I said.

'Yes, a big fan. A lot of people had an interest in seeing her fail, but I wished her well. I mean, I'm not crying over her. Not like some of her cabinet colleagues. Boo hoo! *Not*! You see, they never saw her as crucial to their fortunes. To them, she was just another competitor. Another block in the road. Well, she would have got to the top ahead of all of them, had she lived. And it's that sort of loss, detective. Because whoever killed Susan Wright deprived Australia of someone who would have been a great leader.'

'You agree with Mr Lansdowne, then?' I said.

'About what?' said Rolfe.

'That Susan Wright would have been prime minister in a few years. Had she lived.'

'When did he say that?' he said, sliding forward in his chair, suddenly very focused on me.

And then it hit me. I hadn't read anywhere about the prime minister anointing Susan Wright. Nor had I seen him say it on TV, or heard it on the radio. He'd said it to me.

'I, I don't know when,' I said, looking for a way out. 'I mean, it's what everyone thinks, isn't it? So surely he said it.'

It was a pathetic attempt, and Rolfe knew that he had me. An involuntary shiver rumbled from my middle as I imagined the headline in his next blog.

'So you've interviewed Lansdowne since Susan was found,' he said, 'And that's when he told you these things?'

'We … ahh. We … look, Mr Rolfe, we'll ask the questions here, so let's get on with it.'

'You interviewed him,' he said. 'And he told you she'd be in the top job within a few years. Mmm. Not a complete dill then, is he?'

He spent a few moments weighing up what he had. Then he shook his head and gave me a sympathetic smile. I'd engineered lots of 'gotcha' moments in my time, but I'd never been the bunny in one. Until now.

Smeaton cleared his throat and looked at me inquiringly. What he saw told him I was in a hole. He just didn't know how deep.

'Can we move on to Wright's party now,' he said, taking control. 'You were in reception most of the night, Mr Rolfe. Is that right?'

'Yes, we can move on. And, yes, apart from visiting the little boys' room, and top-ups, I was in reception the whole night. It's the best place to be at one of those affairs. No one gets in without going past you. It's the same when they leave. And if there's nothing interesting happening, you can POQ yourself. But there were a few heavyweights in attendance — Susan, for one. So I hung around.'

'And what did you get out of the party?' said Smeaton. 'I mean, did you hear anything, or make any particular observations?'

'Now that *is* disappointing,' said Rolfe. 'And they say *journalists* are slack about research.'

'I've read every edition of your blog since the minister disappeared,' said Smeaton. 'Now answer the question.'

'You say you read my blog?' he said. 'Mmmm! Anyway. The party. Yes. I saw the contretemps between the minister and Proctor. No, I didn't hear a word of what was said. And when Susan left, I didn't see any point in hanging around. Proctor and I don't get on, you see. And, anyway, he was pissed, judging by the way he staggered out of there. So I went home early, too, and indulged in that profound form of rest called sleep.'

'Mrs Wright drove off the Hill using the Melbourne Avenue exit,' said Smeaton. 'Two minutes later, your Citroen came out of the Senate-side carpark and exited the same way.'

'Yes,' said Rolfe. 'But she went back to her pokey little flat in Kingston, and I went home to Yarralumla. You're not suggesting anything are you, detective?'

'Not at all, Mr Rolfe. But do you, uh, "share" your house with anyone? Anyone who can confirm when you arrived home?'

'No. I live alone. But I've got nosey neighbours who observe all the comings and goings on the street. So, if it's really an issue, I can direct you to one of them.'

'We might get you to do that,' said Smeaton. 'Now, finally, do you have any ideas about Alan Proctor's disappearance?'

'None whatsoever,' said Rolfe. 'I've barely exchanged a dozen words with Proctor in all the years we've both worked on the Hill, but I can say this about him: he's a disgusting little man who does the prime minister's dirty work. And we hate each other. He hates me for what I write about the government, and I hate him for the sycophant he is.'

And that was that. Smeaton saw Rolfe out, and I stayed seated in the interview room, ruing what I'd let slip about the prime minister. If Rolfe did get a story out of it, and I was sure he would, it would not only end my chances of being in on the Lansdowne interview, it might also get me kicked off the case. The thought of this filled me with dread. What a careless dickhead I'd been. My life was becoming a series of stumbles and near misses. If I didn't watch it, I might stuff up in a really major way.

Blood Oath subscription news

Lansdowne: Wright was my rightful heir
by Simon Rolfe

As we enter the final week of this election campaign, I can reveal that Prime Minister Lansdowne believed Susan Wright was his natural successor as party leader, and that he also saw Mrs Wright as a future prime minister.

Today, while interviewing yours truly, Detective Sergeant Darren Glass let slip that he spoke to the prime minister soon after the discovery of Mrs Wright's body. According to Detective Glass, it was during that 'chat' that Mr Lansdowne posthumously anointed 'the loved one' for the top job.

This revelation will come as sobering news to Lansdowne's deputy, Malcolm Redding. Mr Redding has always assumed that the leadership would be his once Lansdowne called it quits. The prime minister's frank declaration to Detective Glass indicates that he might look beyond Redding when the time comes for him to nominate a successor.

And while we're talking about the prime minister, isn't it time the police had another chat to him, if only to get his perspective on what's befallen Alan Proctor? Not that I assume the worst for Mr Proctor. Never, dear reader, never. But the signs are not good, and maybe the PM has a perspective that could help. You know his number, Detective Glass. Why don't you give him another call?

16

I TOOK A BREAK and drove over to Kingston. The lights were on in Jean's penthouse, so I parked near the shops and turned off the ignition. But instead of getting out of the car and heading for the hide near her place, I stayed behind the wheel, questioning the wisdom of my part-time, half-baked surveillance effort. Jean had sprung me once, and I'd nearly gone down. Another slip like that and I could fall the full distance. Fatigue was affecting my decision-making, and this extra activity was draining my precious reserves of energy.

On the other hand, I now firmly believed that the killers were keeping their own watch on her. They knew where she walked. If she was right about having been followed on Wednesday night, and if it was them, they knew where she lived, too. The thing was, if one of my surveillance sessions coincided with one of theirs, I could have them taken down in minutes. And given my recent spate of stuff-ups, it would take something of that order to redeem myself with McHenry.

Buoyed by this thought, I got out of the car, scanned the street, and headed for Canberra Avenue. At the service station on the corner, I crossed over and made my way back towards Jean's block. When I was almost there, I took out my phone, plugged it to my ear, and walked down into her carpark, saying 'Yep' a few times as I went — for all the world, a busy man on an important call.

Jean's car was parked against the back wall, which meant, I hoped, she was in for the night. Then again, she might have walked down to Kennedy Street for another meal. I considered going down there and looking for her, but quickly dismissed the idea.

I retraced my steps up her drive and walked back along the footpath to Canberra Avenue. Once there, I crossed the street to the service station, walked back down Giles, and, when I got level with my hide, scanned the street again before quickly slipping in behind the thicket of native bush. I'd brought a heavy jacket with me this time, so my upper body was warm enough as I stood watching the street, but my feet were soon freezing. After an hour, the lights went out in Jean's place. I waited ten minutes to see if she was going to bed or if she was heading out. When all remained quiet, I drove over to Manuka, picked up a pizza, and headed back to work.

When I walked into the room, McHenry motioned me over. As I approached him, he scowled and jabbed his finger at a spare seat next his desk. This could mean only one thing: Rolfe's story was out.

'Tell me it's a beat-up,' he said, swinging his screen around so I could see the offending yarn. 'Please. Tell me it is. I mean, you wouldn't be so thick as to divulge anything like this to a journo, would you? Not about the prime minister?'

'I'm afraid I was,' I said, scanning the words on the screen, aghast at my own stupidity.

'How could you?' he said, a note of despair entering his voice.

'I don't know. Rolfe said Wright was in line to be PM. And I told him Lansdowne thought the same way. That was the extent of it. But it was enough for him.'

'More than enough. And just so you know, I'd fixed it for you be on the Lansdowne interview tomorrow. Well, not any more. Your name's well and truly off that list now. And you can imagine what Brady wants to do to you, but, typically, he's left that decision to me. The thing is, Glass, you've got good instincts, and I value your counsel, so I generally overlook your blind spots. But, right now, you're costing me more than you're bringing in, and I can't have that. Ya get me?'

His words were a kick in the guts, and my emotions quickly became a dangerous mix of extreme anger at Rolfe and severe embarrassment at my stuff-up. I concentrated on being embarrassed. After all, Brady wanted my head. If McHenry detected anything other than absolute contrition on my part, he'd give it to him, there and then.

'I understand, sir, and I'm sorry,' I said. 'Really sorry. It was a monumental mistake, and I wouldn't blame you if you gave me the boot right now. I really wouldn't.'

'And then there's this thing with Jean Acheson,' he said. 'This "chance" encounter. I'd ask about it, but I don't want to hear another lie. So I'm done with you for now. We'll talk in the morning.'

And with that, he flicked his hand at me and turned back to his machine. The whole room had been tuned into our conversation, but every head was down as I walked back to my desk. I switched on my computer and brought up Rolfe's blog. I read it, and read it again, just to make sure it was as bad as it seemed. It was worse. Rolfe had taken my slip and used it to reflect on the future leadership of the country. I'd told him about a micro-shift in Lansdowne's thinking, and he'd turned it into *the* media talking-point for the next twenty-four hours. No wonder the PM's people were furious. They'd hate having to deal with a bolt from the blue like this, especially so close to polling day.

Hours later, when I finally collapsed onto a couch in the rec room, my mind whirled endlessly in a spiral of dread and self-loathing. And though I tried every way I knew to calm myself, I tossed and turned for most of the night.

I struggled off the couch just after dawn, collected my toiletries from my locker, and brushed my teeth. Then, as I was shaving, I remembered something Stevo had said about Rolfe. That he wasn't so much a political journo — more a colour writer with a bitchy turn of phrase. Well, Rolfe had turned out to be a journalistic hard nut, and maybe the disconnect between the Rolfe I'd been expecting to meet and the one who'd turned up had put me off-guard. Whatever the explanation, the guy had picked me like a nose. There was only one thing that could lift me out of a dreadful funk like this, so I went back to my locker, changed into a singlet, shorts, and runners, and headed off for a jog around the lake.

By the time I reached the water, my breathing was in rhythm with my footfalls, and I was feeling much better for the exercise. I leapt up the stairs onto Commonwealth Avenue Bridge, and crossed the lake to the Parliament House side. Then I ran hard — across the grass in front of the National Library, past wrestling dogs on the lawns at Reconciliation Place, and through the sculpture garden, which was deserted as usual. As I crossed Kings Avenue Bridge, the old Tom Jones hit 'Delilah' drifted across the water from the carillon on Aspen Island. The tune sounded strange and discordant, but it lightened my mood for a moment. Why, why, why indeed?

Back on the city side of the lake, I jogged up the rise to the National Police Memorial and scanned the names of the hundreds of cops who'd been killed on duty. As always, my eyes came to rest on the same name, the one that always brought me here — Senior Constable Simon Glass, the father I never met. He had been killed when a domestic dispute turned into a siege, a month before I was born. His name, etched in metal, was a constant reminder of the father I'd been denied, and of the unforgiving nature of the job I'd followed him into.

I did some stretches on a granite seat in front of the memorial, and then jogged down the slope to the water's edge. From there I followed the lake wall past various memorials, in and out of parkland, and back through the now busy streets to City Station. I showered and dressed and headed around to the room, all the time dreading the reception my colleagues would turn on.

Everyone looked up when I walked in. A few of them acknowledged me without speaking, but most of them just registered that I was there and then got back to work. I didn't blame anyone for this group snub, given the general embarrassment I'd caused. Smeaton would have supported me if he'd been there, but he wasn't. I cast a nervous glance up at McHenry. He and Marginson were deep in conversation. I assumed they were talking about me.

The best thing I could do was immerse myself in work, so I got a coffee and a few biscuits, then logged onto PROMIS and surveyed the latest developments. Nothing had come of the door-to-door in Proctor's neighbourhood. And after interviewing everyone who'd been at Wright's party, we had learned nothing new.

The TV in the corner went to a newsbreak. The thing was on mute, but the caption behind the newsreader said it all: 'Wright was my pick: PM'. The report started with footage of me at the crime scene. A guy sitting at the desk in front of me nudged a couple of colleagues, and soon everyone in the room was watching the report. It also featured footage of Lansdowne walking with Wright. Then it cut to Simon Rolfe. He was smirking in front of a forest of outstretched microphones.

It made me feel sick to look at the smarmy little bastard, and I was about to walk out of the room when McHenry called my name. I looked over at him, he cocked his finger at me, and

I followed him outside to a bench under a leafless tree in the courtyard. He checked that we were alone, and then he leaned in close, his voice a whisper.

'I was ready to give you the chop last night,' he said. 'But this morning, you got a reprieve. You can thank talkback radio for that. Seems *everybody* thinks Wright would have made a good PM, and they're patting Lansdowne on the back for saying so. But this doesn't let you off the hook. Lansdowne's people might have calmed down, but Brady's still fuming, and he says to put you on notice. Mess up again in any way, and it's your job. So be very careful.'

'I will,' I said, keeping my voice low and even. 'I promise you, I will.'

'I'm sure that's right. So, to more important things — like the case. You've been through everything. Where do you think we're at?'

The short answer was we were nowhere at all, but I wasn't about to say that.

'Well, excluding Proctor, we've got four Early Leavers who don't have an alibi, but there's not much more than that implicating them. Which raises the question. Why does it *have* to be an Early Leaver?'

'I've never said it did,' said McHenry. 'But someone at that party was involved. Wright left early, and she was either followed by someone who was in on the job, or that person called the perpetrators to let them know she was leaving.'

'Okay, so let's go through who we've got, then, starting with the Early Leavers. And we obviously rule out Proctor now. So there's Sorby. He had a motive, if Wright *was* planning to sack him. But if he did it, I don't think he'd have been able to hide the fact. He's just too nervy. Then there's Staples, the radical greenie who joined the government. But she doesn't feel like a fit, either. And Penny Lomax? She lied to us, or at least she failed to tell the whole truth, but I don't think it's her, either. She's loyal to Proctor. Too loyal, you'd have to say, so it's hard to see her hurting him. And other than them, there's Tom Hanley, mouldering away at Lake George. He's certainly got good reason to hate the government, but he's barely functional.'

'And what about Hanley's sister, Sylvie? Are we sure she's dead and buried?'

'Officially she is, but who knows? She could've faked the whole thing and be floating around somewhere. Up to no good. So it's a long shot, but it warrants a trip to Thailand. Especially with us drawing blanks.'

'And Acheson? Or Rolfe? Have either of our news gatherers become newsmakers?'

'No chance. We've got nothing connecting Acheson, other than the documents that were sent her way. And Rolfe? I was about to start the write-up, but I can tell you now, he was one of Wright's biggest fans. Not that that necessarily counts him out, but I wouldn't be looking at either him or Acheson.'

'So, is it someone we haven't seen yet?'

'Well, there is someone we haven't *talked* to yet, and I'm sure he'll offer some insights when you see him later today.'

'Yes. And what do you think we'll get from him?' said McHenry.

'Wright's dead, and Proctor's disappeared,' I said. 'If you really wanted to hurt Lansdowne right now, taking out his right-hand man and his most popular minister would be a good start. Sure, the sympathy vote's given him a bounce in the polls, but I'm told that won't last. And the thing is, he must know people who'd wish this on him. Well, we need their names, because the names we're working with at the moment are getting us nowhere.'

McHenry was silent, focused on his toes. Then he got up, I fell in behind him, and we headed back to the warmth of the room.

A couple of hours later, as I was finishing my summary of the Rolfe interview, McHenry called the room to attention and got immediate silence. By the look of him, he'd just received the news we'd all been dreading.

'They've found Proctor,' he said. 'Down by the lake. Near where they dumped Wright. I want all seniors down there immediately, while things are fresh.'

Channel Four Live Cam

Sunday 4 August, 2.00pm

Good afternoon, Jean Acheson with the Live Cam coming to you from Canberra's Lake Burley Griffin, and just repeating the news that a body found here a short time ago is believed to be that of the prime minister's missing advisor and confidante, Alan Proctor.

Mr Proctor was last seen leaving Canberra airport on Thursday evening, and police have since held grave fears for his safety. When Susan Wright disappeared under similar circumstances, she was found dead two days later here by the lake.

The police tents you now see in shot are from an area at the edge of the lake. If Alan Proctor's body is inside one of those tents, then it lies about a hundred metres from where Susan Wright was dumped four days ago.

We expect to hear soon about the identity of the deceased down there. When we do, I'll bring it to you on the Live Cam. This is Jean Acheson.

17

THE KILLER'S CALLING card hung from a melaleuca tree that was growing in the hard ground near the water's edge. It was a tabby cat, this time. Forensics had erected a big tent over the cat and the tree.

Alan Proctor's body was inside a smaller tent about ten metres away. His legs were splayed across the shoreline, and his head and torso were partly submerged in the shallows. A couple of photographers from Forensics were still inside the tent, up to their knees in water taking final close-ups. News choppers hovered high over the middle of the lake, their ceaseless whooping adding to my sense of dread.

The similarities between the two crime scenes were obvious. The bodies had been dumped within a few hundred metres of each other, and both had had a dead cat for company. Proctor's coat and trousers were covered in a mixture of fur and blue carpet fluff. The lividity on his cheek and chin had the same cherry-red edge as Susan Wright's. And the body-drag path was littered with bits of blue plastic.

Also, Proctor and Wright had been hauled to the water by one person; the footprints that the hauler had left at both crime scenes were remarkably similar; and no one had any doubt that Forensics would soon be reporting that it was the same person wearing the same shoes in both cases. If it was the same person, they'd struggled a bit with Proctor. Wright had been shortish and slim, and weighed about sixty kilos. Proctor was short but pudgy, and would have weighed about thirty kilos more.

As with the Wright crime scene, we'd found a second set of footprints in and around the drag path, and in the soft ground near the water. From the look of the heel marks and the chunky soles, this second set of prints had been made by someone wearing work boots. Work boots for an accomplice who couldn't, or wouldn't, lend a hand.

There was movement behind me. I turned to see McHenry coming across the clearing.

'What did you call these mongrels?' he said as he neared. '"Brazen", wasn't it?'

'Yeah,' I said, 'but I've amended that to "cocky". I mean, assuming it *is* the same pair, they dump Proctor here? A stone's throw from where they left Wright? It demonstrates a certain sort of arrogance, don't you think?'

'It does that,' said McHenry, watching another chopper join the clatter over the water. 'So, apart from the obvious, what else strikes you about it all?'

The photographers had disappeared into the cat's tent. From the flashes bursting through the canvas, they looked to be shooting the animal from every angle.

'Their footwear interests me,' I said. 'The person who did the heavy work here wore the same sort of joggers as the person who dumped Wright. Now, if the same person dragged both bodies, while wearing the same shoes, maybe he's running the show. He gets to keep his shoes, but the accomplice has to lose his. It means that maybe the lazy one can't be trusted to keep his footwear under wraps, or maybe he's more exposed to us than the workhorse is.'

'Yeah. Good. Anything else?'

'I said I'd amended my description of these guys to "cocky". Well, I think "cold-blooded" would fit just as well.'

'I know what you mean,' said McHenry, eyeing the media

officer who'd emerged from the trees. 'Well, time to face the journos again. But without you this time, okay? Brady's a big fan of these events, and I don't want to spoil it for him. So meet you back at the car in, say, fifteen?'

As instructed, I waited near the car, about forty metres up the road from where the media had massed in front of McHenry. I couldn't hear a word he was saying, so I focused on Jean. She was standing in the front row again, wearing a black biker jacket and black jeans. Rolfe was next to her, dressed in a shiny black suit.

At one point, Jean caught my eye and cocked her head a couple of times at a planting of eucalypts just down the slope from where I was standing. It seemed she was directing me there for a word. McHenry finished his spiel and took a few questions, before his media officer called a halt to proceedings. As the journos and cameramen began to disperse, McHenry clapped a phone to his ear and, with a few members of his entourage still in tow, walked slowly back towards the crime scene.

Jean and Rolfe chatted briefly. Then she joined some of her colleagues and walked towards me, and I made my way down the slope to the stand of trees. A few minutes later, Jean was edging cautiously down the same bit of slope, and within no time she was standing in front of me, close enough to touch. She smiled, but her eyes betrayed a nervousness that I found reassuring.

'I don't envy you,' she said, as we sat on the bench that fronted the trees. 'What I do is a breeze by comparison.'

'I don't envy myself,' I said, checking to see if McHenry was coming.

'No. Well, ahh, look, this is probably not the time,' she said. 'I know it's definitely *not* the time. But, I just wanted to say how I enjoyed the other night. And, you know, if ever we went out for another Guinness, we'd have to make it a rule not to talk shop.'

'Are you asking me out?' I said, turning to face her.

'Well, no. I was just saying that if ever, you know, if ever we did have another Guinness together ...'

'And is that what you want?' I said, smiling at her. 'To have another Guinness. With me?'

'I might like to,' she said, her smile reflecting some embarrassment.

'That's a yes, then?'

'I guess it *is* a yes.'

'I don't believe it,' I said, smiling so broadly that the corners of my mouth felt like they might tear.

Some people might have thought it weird of us to be organising a tentative date at a major crime scene, though it was no weirder than a doctor and a nurse flirting on a cancer ward. I was mulling this over and smiling at Jean when my phone rang. It was Steve Newings from Births, Deaths and Marriages. He had news on two death certificates, he said — the one issued for Susan Wright's former senior person, Dennis Hanley, and the one for the PM's nephew, Mick Stanton. I indicated to Jean that I had to take the call. She smiled, handed me her card, and mouthed the words 'call me'. Then she headed back up the slope.

Newings said the certificates were typically short on detail. Then he told me he knew the doctor who'd certified Mick Stanton. In fact, the doctor was an old mate of his, and he'd called him to see what else he knew about Stanton's death. I told Newings that I hated interfering amateur sleuths as much as I hated murderers. He countered by saying that his mate had told him things he'd never tell anyone else.

'You see, everyone thinks Stanton died of a heart attack,' said Newings, 'but that's not what happened. My doctor mate says that when the patrol car found Stanton up on Mount Ainslie, he had a hose hanging out the window of his car, and the engine was running. The coppers called my doctor mate to certify the death, and of course they also called Stanton's parents. And that Mrs Stanton, she can be just as persuasive as her brother. When she got down to the morgue, she took the doctor and the cops aside, and told them that her son had just broken up with his wife and that he was very depressed. Then, according to my mate, she broke down and begged them not to call it suicide. Being a Catholic himself, my mate understood why. Good Micks don't top themselves. So he got the cops to agree, and then he certified the death as a heart attack. I can tell you it's not the first time it's happened. And it certainly won't be the last.'

Good Catholics might not top themselves, I thought, *but sometimes they are murdered*. And if that's what had happened to Mick Stanton, maybe our killers had form long before they gassed Susan Wright and Alan Proctor.

Blood Oath subscription news

Monday 5 August, 7.00am

Proctor, the dog with bite
by Simon Rolfe

It's now almost a week since Susan Wright's body was found at Lake Burley Griffin, and yesterday, Alan Proctor turned up dead by the water as well. It's probable both were murdered by the same people.

Michael Lansdowne was so shattered when he heard of Proctor's death that he had to re-schedule an interview with the Plod. The PM's people last night described his eventual contact with the police as 'fruitful and co-operative'. I wonder if that's how the boys in blue saw it.

They say that if you want a friend in politics, get yourself a dog. Well, Alan Proctor was Lansdowne's dog. He was loyal and unquestioning, and when it came to protecting his boss, he had a tendency to bite first and ask questions later.

So why doesn't Lansdowne now honour his dead best friend by suspending the campaign for a day, like he did for Susan Wright? An overnight Aztec poll might provide the answer to that question. Aztec now puts support for the government at 51 per cent, with the opposition at 49, two-party-preferred. This turnaround in the government's fortunes owes everything to the recent slayings, and Lansdowne knows that to ride the sympathy vote back into office, he's got to keep his foot flat to the floor all the way to polling day. Sometimes a politician will wrap himself in the flag to get elected. Sometimes he'll smear himself with the blood of others. Michael

Lansdowne enters the last week of this campaign covered in the red stuff.

18

THE WHOLE TEAM had crowded into the room to hear McHenry's impressions of the Lansdowne interview, but first we had a briefing on the Proctor autopsy from Marjorie Rowan. Peter Kemp was there, too, to give us the latest from Forensics.

There were no surprises in what Rowan had to say. She confirmed that carbon monoxide had killed Proctor, that he'd been dehydrated when he died, and that he had canned food and ketamine in his system.

Peter Kemp's forensics summary was even more predictable. His vet was still examining the cat from the Proctor crime scene. She was also looking at the fur from Proctor's clothes. And the fluff that'd been found on the clothes had been sent to the same carpet manufacturer who'd looked at the last lot. It was all required procedure, but no one doubted that Proctor and Wright had been covered in the same stuff. As for the bits of blue plastic at the Proctor crime scene, Kemp said his people were 99 per cent sure it was from the same tarpaulin that had been used to haul Susan Wright's body.

When they'd finished their outlines, Rowan and Kemp took some questions, which only prompted them to repeat themselves. After they packed up their notes and left, we moved onto the main game: McHenry's debrief on the Lansdowne interview.

McHenry began the session by describing the contact with the prime minister as 'not very productive'. It had been hard to get Lansdowne to focus, he said, and they'd been loath to push him, given his obvious distress over Proctor's death. Lansdowne's legal counsel and his senior staff had even helped by prodding their boss a few times, and though the interview had covered all bases, it had unearthed nothing new.

I'd already read the transcript and had found several flaws in McHenry's approach to the contact. But I'd blown my chance to be there, and given the prime minister's state of mind, I probably wouldn't have done much better with him anyway.

Lansdowne had told McHenry and the interview team that he didn't know anyone capable of murder. Nor did he know anything about Proctor's missing file. When asked how he felt about being the only one connected with the Mondrian scandal who was still alive, Lansdowne had started sobbing, so they'd had to break for five minutes.

When the interview resumed, McHenry asked Lansdowne why Dennis Hanley had blamed him for his sacking over the Mondrian affair. Lansdowne said he'd always assumed that Hanley's anger stemmed from the fact that, as the justice minister at the time, he, Lansdowne, had been the one who'd called the inquiry into Mondrian that had brought Hanley undone.

Asked about people he might have riled before he achieved high office, Lansdowne told the interviewers that politics by its very nature involved riling people. But he'd always tried to give the voters what they wanted, he said. Then he'd conceded that some of his past colleagues resented his success, and he'd angered others by not appointing them to jobs they coveted.

And while he was adamant that there'd never been any really hateful outbursts directed at him, he said that, like most of his ministers, he regularly received physical threats, both through the post and via email. As for any connection between Wright and Proctor that might have got them murdered, Lansdowne had come to an obvious conclusion. They were both key personnel in his government, he said, and both of them had been very close to him.

'He answered all our questions,' said McHenry, 'but he supplied no new names, and he was so disconnected that, in the end we were just going through the motions. In short, nothing he said was news to any of us. So, enough of that for now. Glass, I see you've got something new on the PM's nephew?'

Most of the team regularly checked PROMIS for updates, so they would have seen what Newings had told me about Stanton's death. And after another sleep-deprived night, including a couple of uneventful hours outside Jean's place, I didn't feel like a major rehash. So I kept it brief, and then updated them on contacts I'd since had with one of the cops involved and with the doctor who'd certified Stanton.

'The quack admits to falsifying the certificate,' I said, 'but, under the circumstances, I'm not inclined to pursue charges. As for the cops, one's dead, as you know, and the other's retired to the south coast. When I spoke to him early this morning, he said he was still convinced that Stanton killed himself, so who knows? There was no autopsy. And Stanton was cremated. We don't even have forensics for the car. All we know is, the Stantons were trying to hide a family suicide, and in the process they destroyed evidence of what might have been a murder. We could get them in, of course — Lansdowne's sister and her husband — but that wouldn't achieve anything, other than getting the media excited.'

'Another dead end, then,' said McHenry, looking grimmer than ever. 'Well, let me say, if they'd treated Stanton's death as they should have, we might not be investigating a double-murder today. But that doesn't help us. So, moving along, I've got a report here on Jean Acheson's contact with our audio people, and they say that, in the end, she thought the bloke who gave her the treasurer's documents might have had an Eastern European accent. Possibly Polish, but she wasn't sure.'

With nothing else to report, McHenry closed the meeting and everyone either headed off for a coffee or swung around and re-engaged with their machines. Marginson came over and dropped a couple of phone messages on my desk. The psych assigned to assess Tom Hanley had rung in to tell us that she had come down with a lurgy and wanted to reschedule. That was fine with me, as long as I could get someone else to escort her out to Lake George. And the New South Wales copper who was co-ordinating the search of Proctor's north-coast beach house had called. I put in a call to the copper, and spoke to the croaky psych, but all the while my mind was on Jean.

She'd said to call. Her eyes had said to call. I stared at her card so many times during that morning that I memorised her number. But each time I went to dial it, I wavered, feeling confused and a bit apprehensive at the prospect of a date with her — especially with everything that was going on.

The pessimist in me said she'd probably regard any get-together between us as nothing more than a news-gathering opportunity. I worked to convince myself that I should be similarly pragmatic. Time spent with her would give me another insider's view of how things worked on the Hill. And the optimist in me said that if I got lucky, I might find myself knocking on her door at night instead of standing outside it in the cold. But that was getting ahead of myself. Suffice it to say, I had any number of reasons for getting close to Jean, and a lot of them had nothing to do with the case. So, after a lot of dithering, I decided to make contact and see where it led.

I texted her, asking if she'd like to do something later in the week — maybe have breakfast or go for an early-morning walk. The speed of her response was more than encouraging. Yes, a walk would be nice, she said in her return text; but with the election so close, later in the week was out of the question. What about this afternoon? She was taking a break at two, and she'd been planning to go for a walk then. Would I like to join her? And coffee afterwards? I replied that that sounded good and that I'd get back to her with an answer.

When McHenry returned to the room, I raced to his desk before he could settle down.

'Got a minute for a chat?' I said. 'Outside?'

He hesitated for a second or two, eager to return to his machine. He grunted and let me lead him out to the cold bench in the courtyard.

'Okay,' he said, 'what's so important that I have to be dragged out here?'

'There's three things, actually. The first concerns Proctor. The thing is, everyone's got some idea of what he did for the government. The dirt-file stuff. But we've never got into the detail of his work — who he had under pressure, and the exact nature of the dirt he had on particular people. So, yes, I'm still keen to get into his files, because if it *was* his work that got him killed, those files might give us a pointer. And, by God, don't we need one.'

'I've spoken to Brady about the files,' said McHenry, casting a glance around the courtyard, 'and he's confirmed what I thought. They're in constant use during the election campaign, and if we wanted them, we'd have to block all other access while they were examined and copied. As you might predict, Brady's not happy to disrupt the government in that way at this time, so it's no again to the files.'

'Okay, then,' I said, nodding reasonably, as though untouched by this rebuff. 'What about Mondrian? Everything keeps coming back to the bank. Isn't it time we organised some forensic accountants to go through *their* files?'

'I'm not against that,' said McHenry. 'In fact, I've asked Brady about it, and he's got someone doing the necessaries. So it'll happen, assuming we can jump the legal hurdles. Anything else before we freeze our bums off?'

'Just one thing. Stevo's been useful, but he's a government staffer, which means he's always putting a slant on things. And we *were* going to diversify our sources. Well, Jean Acheson called half an hour ago to see if I'd have a coffee with her. She's just after background, but you never know. I might get something from it. What do you think?'

'The last time you backgrounded a journo,' said McHenry, 'it was front-page news. And you know what another stuff-up'll cost you. Then again, you might get something useful from her. Okay, do it. But watch yourself.'

I spotted Jean as soon as I rounded the corner at the Yarralumla shops. She was standing outside the supermarket composing a text message. I squeezed into a parking bay and observed her for a bit longer in my rear-view mirror. She was wearing a red down waistcoat with a long-sleeved black T-shirt underneath it, and tight black pants and runners. Her outfit was topped off by a bright red beanie, and she had a water bottle hanging from the belt around her waist. She'd come dressed for a power walk, whereas I was dressed for a stroll. I got out of the car and gave her a wave, and she came over. I put on a sloppy joe while she told me what she had in mind.

Essentially, she wanted to do her regular walk around the Royal Canberra Golf Course. That meant going down to the lake and walking from there to the governor-general's gates. We'd then come back up Dunrossil Drive and cut through the bush that bordered the brickworks. After that, it was an easy walk back to the shops. It would take us about an hour, she said, and we could go off for our coffee afterwards.

We headed up the sloping footpath, side by side. When an overhanging tree or an untamed bit of bush forced us off the path, I let Jean take the lead. She moved at a clip, which I liked, and I was soon swinging my arms in time with hers, warming up on a cold, grey day. We talked pretty easily, ranging over lots of things. We both liked Canberra's clean air, and its four seasons. That it had wide roads, and was relatively uncluttered.

White cockies feasted on the trees around the Forestry School in Banks Street, their discards piled high under every tree. Jean said the birdlife was one of the great things about the city. We talked about our suburbs. She liked Kingston because of the shops and restaurants. Campbell was perfect for me, I said — close to Civic, which meant close to work, and it was an easy jog to the lake.

We crossed the road and walked downhill on a compacted sheep track that meandered alongside the golf course fence.

The fenceline turned a corner near the bottom of the hill, and the track followed it. From there it entered a dense stand of conifers before it descended into a grey gully that was sodden and slippery under foot.

'Do you ever wonder what you'll be doing in, say, ten years' time?' said Jean, treading carefully on the saturated track. 'Do you ever think that far ahead?'

'Sometimes,' I said. 'I mean, I love my work and I wouldn't do anything else, but most people in my game eventually end up behind a desk somewhere. And, you know, it doesn't appeal to me now, but in ten years' time I might want the regular hours that come with a desk job. Especially if I have a family.'

She paused at the bottom of the gully, pulled the bottle

from her belt, and squirted some water into her mouth. Then she passed the drink to me. Drops of water fell on us from the branches above, spotting our clothes. The sweat on my back began to cool.

'And what if you're still unattached in ten years' time?' she said, moving up the slope. 'How would you feel about that?'

'It wouldn't be good,' I said, smiling at her. 'I mean, you should see some of the single blokes at work — the older ones who've let themselves go a bit. They're a great argument for the sanctity of marriage.'

'What?' she said, giggling now. 'You wouldn't want to end up like them? A smelly old fart, in a rotten old cardigan? With your crusty nasal hair merging into your stinking old moustache. Ugh! And the breath!'

'Oh no! My worst nightmare,' I said, laughing with her, while I recoiled at the image. 'I'm settling down tomorrow! I promise! I am!'

'And another one bites the dust, eh? I can see you now, taking the kids to soccer on a Saturday morning — with the dog in the SUV.'

'You're getting well ahead of me there, but I don't mind. Any other predictions?'

'No, not really,' she said, slowing down so that I fell in beside her. 'Except you seem like the sort of man who *should* have kids. I mean, you're honest and direct, and kids really need that in a father. As well as his love, of course.'

'Yes,' I said. 'They absolutely need love.'

The fenceline jinked around another corner, and then it straightened. A golfer on the other side of the wire cursed a ball that wouldn't be found. A cocky shrieked in the treetops.

'I'm sure I'll do the domestic thing one day, too,' said Jean. 'And it'll be great. I'm just not ready for it now.'

'I can understand that. With your career and all.'

'Yeah. And I'm like you. I love my work, and there's nothing else I want to do. Of course, there're times when I feel like I'm just part of a giant sausage machine — churning it out, hour after hour. But when I get onto a big story, one that makes a difference, it's all worthwhile somehow. Not that I've broken anything world-changing, mind you. Not yet, anyway. And now I'm raving, aren't I?'

'No, not at all,' I said. 'Your work's important to you, and it's important work. But it's interesting to consider how you and I view what we do. You say your biggest kicks come from big stories, whereas us cops never hang out for big cases — certainly not ones like what we're working on now. And you want another statement of the bleeding obvious? The world would be a much better place if there *weren't* any big cases. And now *I'm* raving.'

She put her hand on my shoulder and smiled at me as we walked.

'No, you're not,' she said. 'No. You've got a very solid perspective on things, and I really like that.'

We ambled down a grassy slope towards the lake, and for the first time since we'd started out, we didn't talk, and it was comfortable. A dense hedge of cotoneaster blocked our access to the water, so we took a well-worn path around the shoreline till we came to a little beach.

'So, what made you become a policeman?' she said, staring at the rippling shallows.

'My dad was a cop,' I said. 'Not that he influenced me in any direct way. He died before I was born. Killed on duty. But Mum used to talk about him and the things he'd done. And I always wanted to be a cop. I guess a shrink would say that it was my way of getting close to the father I never knew, and that might be right.'

'And your mum? Is she still alive?'

'No. She died a few years ago.'

'Oh. I'm sorry. Were you close?'

'We were until she re-married, when I was eleven. Then her new husband moved us down to Moruya. He and I didn't get on, and that affected my relationship with Mum. So, as soon as I turned fifteen, I left and came back to Canberra.'

'Was it a jealousy thing with him?'

'He was a bullying bastard who threw his weight around if things didn't go exactly the way he wanted them to go. The good thing is, when Mum got sick, she spent her last few months in a hospice up here, so we got to resolve a few things before she died.'

We stood looking out over the lake before a cold gust of wind rushed off the water and I suggested we move on. We headed for the cycle path that circled the lake, and followed it into a dense planting of Monterey pine that filled the space between the water's edge and the golf-course fence. I was conscious of the slack-slack sound of our shoes on the wet path, and of golf balls being thwacked somewhere off in the distance. I looked at Jean, and we smiled at each other again. It was turning out to be one of the best afternoons I'd had in a long time.

She asked if I travelled overseas for work. I rattled off some of the Quantico courses I'd done. That prompted her to launch into a restaurant-by-restaurant account of her latest trip to New York City. As it turned out, we'd eaten at the same restaurant in Harlem. We were comparing notes when we rounded a corner, and Warrina Inlet and its bridge came into view. Bits of discarded crime-scene tape fluttered in the bushes near the foot of the bridge. The sight of the place took the wind out of our conversation.

We crossed the bridge, and Jean stopped on the other side

and squirted water into her mouth, and passed the bottle to me.

'You know, when I got home after Mad Dog's the other night,' she said, staring across the inlet, 'I was thinking about that guy and the receipts he left for me over there. The European. And it was like, I don't know, I was in a bit of a heightened state, I guess, but I remembered something I should have told you when you interviewed me up at the House.'

'And what was that?' I said, in a hard tone that I immediately softened. 'What didn't you tell me?'

'I remembered thinking he wasn't alone — that there was someone else on the line listening in as we talked, even sort of prompting him. You can hear it when that happens. My mum used to eavesdrop on my calls all the time. Do you think it's possible? That there's two of them out there? Two killers?'

Careful! Careful! We hadn't said anything about numbers when it came to the killers, so I couldn't confirm anything about her eavesdropper. Nor could I dismiss it out of hand, as that might make her suspicious. Then it occurred to me that this could all be a set-up. The route she'd selected for our walk included the bridge where the receipts had been left for her. And then, apparently prompted by the place, she'd raised a question that could give her a big headline. But how would she have arrived at the question if she hadn't truly sensed a second person on the line? She was eyeing me intently, eager for a response.

'Two killers?' I said, as though it was a novel thought. 'Mmm. That's interesting. Then again, without a firmer …'

'Look, I know it's flimsy,' she said. 'I should have remembered, so I'm sorry. I guess getting my hands on those receipts shook everything else out of my head. And it was just a sense I had — like when I thought I was being followed. I mean, it's not something I'd do a story on. Imagine how that'd go down: "Now, viewers, I've got this gut feeling I want to tell you about …"'

'Wouldn't do your credibility much good,' I said, smiling at her as I handed her back the water bottle.

We left the cycle path near the governor-general's gates and took a track through a stand of conifers that grew along the golf-course fence. A hundred metres before the end of Dunrossil Drive, the fence did a 90-degree turn and disappeared into the feral undergrowth of Westbourne Woods. Jean and I followed the fenceline into the woods, on a path overgrown with blackberry and blocked by the occasional fallen tree. We finally emerged into a big clearing with a good view of the back of the brickworks, and were admiring the kilns and having another drink when Jean's mobile rang. She eased it off her belt, and I studied her as she took the call.

'Yes, yes, it is,' she said, and her face suddenly turned pale.

'Yes, yes, I know where that is,' she said after ten seconds or so. 'Who is this? Who's calling?'

But they were gone. She lowered the phone, looked at the screen, and then shook her head as she buttoned off.

'He hung up. The European. He says he's left something else for me. And I think we just walked past it.'

Channel Four Live Cam

Monday 5 August, 3.00pm

Good afternoon, Jean Acheson here with this Live Cam exclusive, and the man suspected of the abduction and murder of both Susan Wright and Alan Proctor has contacted me again.

Last week he sent me to a location where I found receipts indicating that the treasurer had put himself through drug rehabilitation in California. It's believed those receipts were with Susan Wright when she disappeared.

Now the same man has directed me here, to Westbourne Woods, where he says he's left more documents for me.

The police are standing by, and we'll soon be going in to recover this latest offering. When I've got it, I'll bring it to you live. This is Jean Acheson.

19

MᴄHᴇɴʀʏ's ʀᴇsᴘᴏɴsᴇ ᴛᴏ my call was as immediate as it was dramatic. Choppers and car sirens homed in on us from every direction as we ran along the fenceline, and by the time we got back to Dunrossil Drive, the whole area was full of cops. They'd blocked off the road with two lines of vehicles and had begun draping the place in long lengths of tape. A couple of choppers buzzed back and forth overhead, adding to the sense of drama. Dog walkers and joggers gawked at the goings-on from behind the newly established cordon.

Jean's camera crew got there soon after us, and she'd already filed a piece by the time McHenry arrived. Within seconds of pulling up, he was on the radio to a patrol car that had been dispatched to the golf club. Once he'd confirmed that all the stragglers were off the fairways, he called a senior cop over and asked about the status of the nearby lumberyard. The cop said the workers there had knocked off for the day. What about the feeder streets, said McHenry. Yes, said the cop, they'd all been blocked off. And the door-to-door in Denman Street, asked McHenry, pointing to the street that bordered the woods. It was underway, said the cop, and the residents there were being warned to stay indoors until they got the all-clear.

This conversation was interrupted by a beep from McHenry's two-way. He put the two-way to his ear, listened for a few seconds, then lowered it. Like the thirty-or-so other people standing around him, I held my breath, desperate to hear the news.

'The chopper's found it,' he said, prompting a cheer from everyone there.

He turned to Jean and patted her shoulder.

'The wreck's where he told you it would be, so well done,' he said. 'And thank you. Now you can go with Detective Glass and observe the recovery.'

He gave a nod, and with a chopper hovering high above us, Jean and I followed Peter Kemp and his Forensics team down a rutted track and into the woods. About fifty metres in, we came to a collapsed section of fence. We stepped over the strands of wire and headed down a disused vehicle track towards the brickworks. Jean and I walked side-by-side in the ruts, with the team in front of us, and a chopper, flying lower now, its spotlight guiding our way.

The berry bushes petered out as we entered another small stand of trees, and then we emerged into a large clearing where bits of buried brick poked out of the hard ground. The chopper moved away, Kemp signalled for Jean and me to halt, and then led his team up through the clearing towards a pile of rusted panels. It was the old car that the European had described.

Kemp positioned himself at one end of the pile of metal, and his people radiated off him in a straight line. Once everyone was in place, they did a circular sweep around the pile, stepping carefully, their eyes to the ground.

'It's been well and truly tramped over,' said Kemp, to no one in particular.

When they got back to where they'd started their sweep, the team sidestepped together, away from the wreck, and circled it again. After they'd been around it five times, Kemp stepped out of the line and put on a pair of heavy gloves. He took out a torch and knelt down next to the hood section of the wreck, and started poking around underneath it.

After another sweep, the officer at the end of the line pulled photographic gear from her backpack and started shooting the wreck. Kemp meanwhile was on his back, edging his body further under the hood. Then he stopped wriggling.

'Amazing!' he said, more in relief than triumph. 'It's right where he said it would be.'

He worked his way out from underneath the wreck, and when he stood up he was holding an envelope wrapped in plastic. He carefully inserted the envelope into a large evidence bag that he handed to a female officer. She slipped the bag under her armpit and closed down on it tightly before stepping off to the side of the wreck.

Kemp took a brush and a container from his belt and focused his torch on the hood. He dusted it for a few minutes, pausing occasionally to examine his efforts. Finally, he turned to me and shook his head.

'Nothing here that I can see,' he said. 'Okay, let's take her apart now.'

The team began separating the wreck into bits. Three of them were all patience and co-operation as they eased a partly buried mudguard out of the ground. They'd just moved on to a bumper bar when the officer holding the document got a call on her two-way. The whole team eyed her expectantly.

'Yes, sir,' she said into the device. 'Will do, sir.'

She buttoned off, and, without another word, she swung around and walked briskly back towards the road.

'Where's she going?' said Jean, turning to watch her leave. 'And, more to the point, where's she taking that envelope?'

'It's a crucial find, Jean,' I said. 'It'll have to be thoroughly examined.'

She stared at me, assessing the implications of what I'd said. Then she swung around and quickly headed off after the officer.

I followed. Jean wasn't gaining ground at walking pace, so she started to jog. But the officer had too great a lead on us, and she was jogging now, too. She rounded a corner about twenty metres ahead of us and disappeared.

We were about fifteen metres from the officer when she handed the envelope to McHenry. He immediately gave it to a uniformed guy who ran it up through the road block and passed it in through the front window of a patrol car. The car then sped off. When Jean stumbled up to McHenry a few moments later, their eyes locked, but she seemed to be smiling.

'You *are* going to let me see what's in that envelope, aren't you?' she said, catching her breath. 'Surely you are.'

McHenry looked at me, then his gaze returned to Jean. But he said nothing, which effectively communicated his answer.

'Ohhhhh, now this really is shaping up as a *big* mistake,' she said, shaking her head. 'Just think what you're doing here. What's this guy want? This European? Well, in part, it's personal profile, isn't it? Publicity. And if I don't give it to him, he'll write me off and find someone else to leak to. And none of my colleagues will call you if he leaks something to them. Not if you do this to me. And nor will I if he decides to keep using me. So if you want to catch him ...'

'What you're saying makes perfect sense, Miss Acheson,' said McHenry, in a calming tone. 'But we've got no choice. We have to examine what we've recovered. Then, hopefully, there'll be a trial in which it's used as evidence. And maybe then there'll be an appeal process. And after that, we'll return it to its owner, as we're required to do. I appreciate your priorities, but this is not a simple matter.'

'But it's not that complicated, either,' she said, her eyes drilling McHenry. 'You'll give that document the once-over, it'll sit in an evidence drawer for a few months, then you'll hand it back to … who? Lansdowne? The government? That way, you'll save yourself a short-term headache, but you'll lose your only link to this guy — the European. What could be simpler than that?'

McHenry was saved from further argument by his phone. He took the call, and Jean turned to me and shook her head.

'It's okay, Darren,' she said, seeming to console me. 'I know you're bound by what this guy says, but it's a big mistake — maybe even a tragic one — and I think you know that. And as for you and me? Well, life's full of possibilities, isn't it, but timing's everything, and now's just not our time, I guess.'

She gave me a weak smile, and turned and walked back to the roadblock where her crew was waiting. She did a brief piece to camera, using a police vehicle as a backdrop, and then walked up Dunrossil Drive alone. She shook her head a couple of times as she went, as though she was trying to free herself of something.

'Not happy,' said McHenry, pocketing his phone.

'And who can blame her?' I said, feeling like I was about to throw up. 'She helps us, and then we see to it that she misses out, big time. I know what you're going to say — we did what was required of us. But how does that help the investigation? Doing the *right* thing! Because what she said is true, you know. She was our best connection to the killers, and now we've lost her.'

McHenry nodded, but I didn't care if he agreed with me or not. Less than an hour before, Jean and I had been on the verge of something. Now she was walking away, robbed of a huge story, and partly blaming me. But no matter how injured she felt, or how high the stakes were for me personally, there was nothing I could have done differently. The document wasn't mine to give her.

'What about surveillance on her now?' I said, trying to settle my guts. 'Brady'd *have* to agree to it, wouldn't he? I mean, they've left two documents for her — both on a route that she walks every other day, so they're obviously watching her. And there's a fair chance they'll contact her again, regardless of what happened here.'

'Maybe they will, and maybe they won't,' said McHenry. 'But Brady's still against it. He says it'll blow up in our faces. So, no.'

I'd normally have responded with fury to such stupidity, but I was totally consumed by a profound sense of loss. And as I watched Jean disappear over the rise on the Cotter Road, I wondered what it would take to set things right between us.

Blood Oath subscription news

Monday 5 August, 4.30pm

A trust betrayed
by Simon Rolfe

The relationship between the police and the news media may seem symbiotic, but don't be fooled, dear reader.

Each regards the other with a high level of suspicion, and when their interests collide, the cost to any journo who gets in Plod's way can be high indeed. Just ask Jean Acheson.

Earlier this afternoon, Ms Acheson helped the police locate more documents pertinent to the Wright and Proctor investigations, and what did she get for her trouble? A kick in the guts, and her story went missing.

Who could blame Ms Acheson if she now avoided all contact with the police?

20

As soon as I got back to the station, I dialled Jean's number. It rang and rang and went to messages, so I hung up. I hit redial, and it rang and rang again, but just as I thought it was going to go to messages again, she answered.

'Hi, Jean,' I said, keeping all emotion out of my voice.

'Oh, it's you,' she said, very snaky. 'And I suppose you're on your way over here with the documents, are you? And that's why you called. To see if I'd be around.'

I couldn't respond to her anger, so I said nothing. After an eternity, she sighed deeply and broke the silence.

'Sorry, sorry,' she said. 'I'm just very frustrated at the moment, as you'd understand.'

'And I wish I could do something about it,' I said. 'Anyway, I just wanted to check that you made it back to your office okay. And I wanted to say that, you know, I thought we had something there, but I can see how it might not suit at the moment.'

'At the moment?' She laughed ruefully, and we lapsed into silence again.

'Look, as for us,' she said, in a small voice. 'Well, it's like I told you. Timing's everything. We're both very busy, and even when things quieten down, it could be hard. Being on opposite sides of the fence.'

She had her anger under control, but she sounded resolved, all the same. Here was the brush-off. I'd set it up for her, and she'd done the rest.

'Okay,' I said, trying to put some steel in my voice. 'But when the election's over, and this case is out of the way, expect a call from me. From the other side of the fence.'

She laughed and said that would be fine, but without enthusiasm. Then she hung up and, immediately, all the hopes I'd had for us, all the daydreams I'd entertained, began whirling around inside my head in a confused mess. Then my guts got involved, and I knew I had to assert control. I told myself that I hadn't won her heart, so I hadn't lost it. And I had a job to do and I had to be effective, not distracted. I had to get back on task. But as the afternoon wore on, in everything I did, my thoughts returned to Jean. And it occurred to me that keeping a tail on her had suddenly become much more dangerous. If she caught me at it again, she wouldn't swallow another half-baked excuse. And she certainly wouldn't be asking me out for a drink.

Luckily, I owned an old GPS vehicle-tracker that I could monitor her movements with. It was another gift from my American friend James — the one who'd given me the mandolin. His tracker wasn't as small or as sophisticated as the type we had in the storeroom, but it worked just as well, with one complication: once I'd got the thing attached to Jean's car, I'd have to call James in Memphis so he could locate the car through his service provider. It was a bit of an imposition, but when he'd given me the device he'd said to call him any time for a reading, day or night. In fact, he'd said he'd be offended if I didn't try the thing out.

It was almost seven when I walked past Jean's place. Her lights were out, so I scanned the road and the footpaths, and then plugged my mobile to my ear and walked briskly down into her carpark. Her car wasn't there, so I decided to give her fifteen minutes. If she hadn't turned up by then, I'd pick up some dinner and go back to work.

I'd decided on stir-fried noodles, and was about to go and get them when Jean's black VW swung into Giles Street. The car slowed as it turned into her driveway, the glow from the streetlight catching her face as she flashed past.

When the lights went on in the penthouse, I took my usual evasive trip down to Canberra Avenue, crossed Giles Street, and walked back up to her drive. I checked the street again before descending into her carpark, where I found her car reverse-parked against the back wall in a numbered bay. When I got to the rear of the vehicle, I removed my backpack and took out the tracker, a torch, and a wire brush. I laid them on top of the pack, and then got onto my back and eased myself under the car.

There was a flat metal plate next to the rear bumper bar that looked made for the magnetic base on the tracker. I brushed the dirt from the plate, then took the tracker in both hands and eased it into place. The magnets and the metal met with a clang; when I tested it, the thing felt like it had been glued there. I turned it on. A dull, red light flickered rapidly next to the switch, and then went out. The job done, I eased myself out from underneath the car, put the torch and the brush back in my pack, and returned to my hide via the usual route. I'd only just settled in there when Jean's lights went out; a few minutes later, her VW emerged from the carpark and headed for Canberra Avenue.

Earlier in the day I'd had an email exchange with James in which I'd spun him a line about my girlfriend's wanderings. I'd told him I wanted to track her for a few nights. It might be completely innocent — I just needed to know the score. James was sorry to hear about my troubles, and said to call him anytime I needed her co-ordinates.

It was three in the morning, Memphis time, when I dialled his number. James picked up after a couple of rings and said to call him back in a few minutes. When I did, he'd already tracked

Jean to Mueller Street in Yarralumla. Rolfe lived in Mueller, so I figured she was visiting him. I thanked James, and as there was no way of telling how long Jean would stay at Rolfe's, I headed off to a noodle place in Manuka.

Back at work, I spent a couple of hours calling Marie Staples' old radical mates, but none of them had seen her in years. Then I called James to check on Jean; after only a brief delay, he told me her car was stationary in Giles Street. I thanked him, and, secure in the knowledge that she'd got safely home, I retreated to a camp stretcher in the rec room and went straight to sleep.

In one of my dreams that night, I was creeping along a low white passageway, Glock in hand, on-guard against some unspecified threat. I came to a door that I opened, and there was a huge room with a big hourglass sitting in the middle of it. The top bulb of the hourglass was almost full, and the sand trickling from it formed a pointed pile in the bottom bulb.

I went back into the passageway and came to another door. The room behind it contained a big hourglass, too, but there was much less sand in the top bulb of this one, and it seemed to be emptying out at a faster rate. I rushed from the room and saw a third door. I knew exactly what I'd find behind it, and, sure enough, there was another big hourglass, except the top bulb on this one was almost empty. I watched the last of the sand fall through it, and then I realised I'd been going into the same room all the time, and seeing the same hourglass. It was just that there were three different doors leading to it. That thought made me panic for some reason. Then McHenry was yelling at me to get out of the building. I smelt smoke and could hear fire crackling somewhere, and I was suddenly very hot. McHenry was yelling, 'Get out! Get out!'

I woke in a sweat in the dark. It was just after four. I could have done with a lot more sleep, but I knew I'd just lie there, so I got up, had a shower, got dressed, and went down to the room. Not much had come in through the night — just a handful of callers to the hotline, mostly insomniacs offering half-baked advice.

At seven, I walked down to Northbourne Avenue for a croissant and a coffee. Just after I got back to the room, McHenry called a team meeting that turned into a talkfest which ate up a big chunk of the morning and got us nowhere. It seemed everything we did and everything that came our way was leading to the same old dead ends and dross. The bosses upstairs would be telling their political masters we were making progress, but the truth was we had two very disciplined predators in circulation, and our hunt for them had all but stalled.

At about one, I got a sandwich from the lunch cart and checked my news sites while I ate it. Rolfe hadn't updated his blog since the night before, which was unusual. He'd been filing a story or a comment piece every few hours since the election kicked off — in fact, with the race tightening, he'd even been updating his site in the middle of the night. I put his failure to file down to a technical glitch, but, only a few minutes later, McHenry called the room to attention. The grim look on his face gave me an inkling of what he was about to say.

'I've just got off the phone with Simon Rolfe's people in Sydney,' he said. 'They can't contact Rolfe. Now, they were a bit cagey, but it seems he goes missing sometimes, without notice, and then turns up after a couple of days. So it might be a false alarm, but we're taking no chances.'

By the time we arrived at Rolfe's house, Peter Kemp and his team had given the place the once-over, and Kemp was looking very frustrated. It seemed Rolfe was a believer in spray and wipe-type products, and as a result his kitchen benchtops were as clean as a whistle, as was every other surface in the house. Adding to Kemp's irritation, the place had been vacuumed within the last day or so, the parquetry floor in the hallway had been mopped, and all the beds had clean sheets.

The porch light had been on when Forensics had arrived. According to a neighbour, Rolfe left the light burning whenever he went out at night, but always turned it off when he got home. Well, by the look of things, he hadn't made it home. What had happened to him? Was he off on a jaunt, or had he been nabbed? And if he *had* been nabbed, why him?

We spent the next six hours pulling Rolfe's place apart. When that proved fruitless, people started to head back to City Station, and I told McHenry that I'd see him back there after I'd got hold of some food. But, instead, I drove over to Kingston to check on Jean. She and Rolfe were friends, and according to the GPS under her car, she'd been in his street just hours before he'd gone missing. She might have been seeing someone else on the street, of course; but if she *had* been visiting Rolfe, that made her one of the last people to lay eyes on him. If my surveillance on her had been above board, I would have brought her in at that stage, but all I could do under the circumstances was to keep shadowing her.

Her lights were out when I drove past her place, so I called James. He already had the GPS site up on his computer, and he quickly located Jean's car: it was stationary near the corner of Tennant and Gladstone Streets in Fyshwick, he said. I thanked him for his help, and drove over to Fyshwick to see what she was up to.

The street corner was occupied by a self-storage facility, and Jean's car was parked under floodlights next to the security office that guarded the place. I stopped outside a mower shop ten doors up, and thought through my next move. In the end, I decided to give Jean half an hour. If she wasn't out of there by then, I'd go in and look for her. The only obstacle to this plan was the young female guard hunched over her textbook in the security office.

As I waited, two lots of people left the facility, and the guard barely raised her head as they walked past her. After half an hour, I walked into the light of the glassed-in security office, my library card up at eye level, hoping that she was habitually slack. She gave me a fleeting glance, and waved me through.

The storage facility was essentially a large area of fenced-in bitumen with three long, squat buildings of brick and steel. Each building had what looked like about fifty storage units of various sizes running along each side. The door to each unit was numbered, and beside each door was a slot with a removable name tag. I worked my way along the first building, looking for light at the bottom of each door, and listening for movement and other sounds of effort.

I'd reached the middle of the second building when a dull thud came from a unit just up ahead of me. Almost simultaneously, I heard Jean shout, 'Shit.' I slipped into the nearest doorway, fearing she was about to come out and spot me. When she didn't materialise, I sidled up to what I figured was her unit. There was a strip of light at the bottom of the door, and I could hear her muttering to herself inside. She didn't sound distressed — just frustrated. I took out my torch and read the name tag in the door slot. The unit belonged to Simon Rolfe.

What was Jean doing in the storage unit of a man who'd mysteriously gone missing? Should I go in and see? She might not be alone; so, if I went in, I couldn't afford to take any chances. I'd have my Glock out, and I'd be ready for anything. But with no warrant and no probable cause, that could open me up to another world of trouble. So, instead, I decided to stick close to her, without getting in her way. If she took anything from the unit, we could always recover it.

The security girl nodded as I walked past her, but returned to her book in a trice. I got into my car and waited. When the cold became too much, I got out and paced back and forth. Within a quarter of an hour, Jean emerged into the light of the security office and walked to her car. She sat with the interior light on, reading something in her lap. Then she started the vehicle and drove back towards Kingston. I waited fifteen minutes, and rang James. It was four in the morning, Memphis time. 'Sorry to get you up,' I said. He managed a laugh and struggled to his computer.

'She's in a suburb called Red Hill,' he said in a croak. 'In a street called Roebuck. The car's stationary. Close to a park that runs down to a Beagle Street. Funny name, that, for a street, isn't it? Beagle Street?'

'Par for the course around here, mate,' I said. 'Look, thanks again for all your help. It's really been important to me. And next time I'm over, we're having a big one out. On me. Okay?'

I took the Monaro Highway out of Fyshwick. I knew Beagle Street, so I had no trouble finding the park that James had mentioned.

I left the car on Beagle and walked up through the frost-covered park to a hedge of callistemons that separated the top of the park from Roebuck Street. I pushed through the hedge, saw Jean's car parked under a streetlight ten metres away, and darted back into the foliage. When my breathing had settled, l listened for any movement and poked my head out again. I was still scanning the footpath on my side of the street when Jean's voice cut through the air. She was stepping out onto a well-lit porch on the other side of the street, just a few doors along from where I was hiding. She had her back to me, so I couldn't hear what she was saying.

The door to the house eventually closed with a bang, and Jean walked down to the footpath, took out a small torch, and scribbled something into a notebook. Then she approached a neighbouring house built of 1960s pink brick. She pressed the doorbell, and an electronic fragment of 'Waltzing Matilda' played faintly inside the house. Jean waited a minute or so, and then she pressed the doorbell again, reprising the tune.

Finally, an old woman in a dressing gown opened the door and stepped out onto the porch. They talked for a bit, and the old girl pointed across the street in my direction. They talked for a bit more, and she pointed the other way. Jean thanked her and returned to the footpath. Once again, she took out her torch and scribbled in her notebook.

Over the next twenty minutes, she approached five more houses, and was answered at two of them. She engaged in a couple of brief chats, and after each she returned to the footpath and added to her notes. Finally, she got into her car, consulted her smart phone for a minute or so, and drove off.

At the end of the street she turned right and disappeared down the hill, and I ran down through the park towards my car, wondering whether to bother James again. As I scurried down the steep bit of the slope where the park bordered Beagle Street, I heard a vehicle, and then saw it, heading down the street towards me. I slipped behind a tree as the car passed under a streetlight about twenty metres away. It was Jean's VW. I dropped to the ground and crawled behind a clump of bushes, and she slowed and then stopped directly opposite me.

Jean stayed in the car and consulted something on her lap. Then she went back to knocking on doors, starting with a two-storey place lit up like a national monument. The owner spoke to her from behind a security screen, but the contact was brief. Next she approached another pink-brick place, but no one was at home, so she walked a few doors along to a dark-brick house with a well-lit porch and garden. She pressed the doorbell, and scanned her notebook while she waited. The door opened, and she spoke to someone on the other side of the screen. Then the screen opened, and she went inside.

Suddenly, all the lights went out in front of the house that Jean had entered. Were they motion-sensitive? They'd been burning brightly well before she went anywhere near them. I studied the place, and saw that not only had the lights gone off outside, but there seemed to be no lights *inside* either. It didn't feel right. Why would they pitch their place into complete darkness when they'd just invited someone in?

If my tail had been sanctioned, I would have called in a team right away and raided the place. But while that remained an option, I wasn't going to exercise it immediately. Instead, I waited. Fifteen minutes. Twenty minutes. Thirty minutes. She'd been in there longer than she'd been on the street. I told myself that an interview could take half an hour or more. But time continued to tick away.

After forty minutes, I seriously considered calling in a team. Jean would either be thankful that I'd gotten her out of a sticky situation, or she'd be very angry that I'd tailed her and disrupted her interview. But regardless of how *she* saw it, Brady would make sure that I was drummed out of the service just for being there. So I decided to scope the place out before doing anything self-destructive.

I moved down to the footpath, my complete focus on the dark house twenty metres away on the other side of the road. Tree by tree, I went, pausing in the shadows, straining to detect any sound or movement as I closed in.

When I reached a tree almost opposite the place, I stepped from the shadows and casually walked across the street as though

I was a man out for a mid-evening stroll. I passed the house and the tall hedge that hid it from the house next door. Then I turned and made my way back. At the border of the two properties, I pressed myself into the hedge and strained to see if there were any lights on inside the place.

Then something metallic banged hard into the back of my head, and from behind me came an accented voice that sounded more like a wheeze than a whisper.

'Don't turn,' said the European. 'Walk now.'

He prodded me so hard that I stumbled forward.

'Walk up to porch and stop,' he said, his voice now an urgent croak.

I did as he ordered. There was no letterbox to identify the place, and no house number that I could make out in the darkness. He prodded me with such force that I stumbled onto the porch, cursing my stupidity and knowing with utter certainty that my life was on the line.

21

BEFORE I COULD regain my balance, the European pressed his pistol hard into the back of my neck.

'Stop!' he said.

I froze, and the front door swung open as if he'd willed it to.

'Open screen,' he said.

I opened the security screen and crossed the threshold into a small hallway, with the pistol still pressed to my neck. The doors closed quietly behind me. A single downlight covered with dark-blue cellophane glowed dimly in the ceiling, above a corridor of polished floorboards that stretched off into a dark interior. The walls were white, and bare of any decoration.

'Kneel,' he said, prodding me with the weapon.

The floorboards were hard on my knees, but the discomfort didn't last long.

'On your stomach. And face door.'

I got down onto the floor and lay with my cheek against the polished boards. A stream of cold air from under the door played against my face.

'Hands behind back.'

He slipped a plastic tie over my hands and pulled it tight. Wide tape went over my eyes and mouth. Then a second person walked briskly down the corridor. From the sound that the heels made, rapping sharply on the boards, it was a woman. Her hands fussed around my wrists as she checked the tie, and tightened it a notch.

The European pressed his weapon hard into my temple as his partner looped ties around my knees and ankles. She pulled them extra tight as well. Then she put a coarse rope through the ties and pulled it so that my feet rose behind me till they met my hands. I'd seen pictures of people who'd been hogtied. Within no time, I found out why they'd always been grimacing — the tension in the rope made the ties cut into my wrists and ankles. The only relief came from arching my back, but I couldn't sustain that position for long. I alternated between pain and extreme discomfort, cursing myself for the bad decisions that had turned my world to shit.

They searched my pockets, under my arms, and in my groin before they removed my gun and holster and put them into something hollow and plastic. It sounded like a bucket. My phone, cuffs, notebook, wallet, keys, torch, and pocketknife went into the bucket as well. The woman then walked, rat-tat rat-tat, back down the corridor. The European followed her almost noiselessly. I strained at the ties, but they cut into my wrists, so I lay still, saving my energy — a trussed turkey, waiting for their next move.

The European and his mate were talking in low tones somewhere at the back of the house. I held my breath, but couldn't hear a word they were saying. Then I remembered Jean. What had they done with her?

They came back down the corridor, and the European gripped my jacket at the shoulders and grunted as he dragged me forward. I slid easily, if painfully, over the floorboards. He stopped after a few metres, adjusted his grip, and then pulled me further. A door opened next to my head, releasing a peculiar amalgam of smells — musty odours mixed with petroleum products. It had to be the garage. He pulled me through the doorway and across a cold, abrasive surface that was probably bare concrete. His partner rat-tatted past us and opened the door of a vehicle. They were taking me for a ride.

The European put his hands under my shoulders and extended his fingers into my armpits. His accomplice looped her hands under my calves. Then they lifted me up and manoeuvred my torso onto a spongy surface, which I took to be the back seat of the vehicle. The woman cradled my legs while the European went around and opened the other door. Then he pulled me across the seat. When I was fully inside the vehicle, they threw some sort of plastic covering over me, and the doors slammed shut. Then someone started whimpering in the back of the vehicle. It had to be Jean. I made the only noise I could with my mouth taped up — a high-pitched bellow through my nose. Jean replied with a mournful wail, which stopped abruptly when the front doors of the vehicle opened and our captors got in.

'Shut the fuck up back there,' said the European.

They buckled up, a roller door was activated, and they moved slowly out of the garage. They turned left onto Beagle, and left again at the end of the street. They drove without urgency, the vehicle moving smoothly through each turn. Fifty metres on, they turned right, probably onto Mugga Way, heading north. As we veered through a roundabout, it occurred to me that if they stayed on this road, we'd end up on the shores of Lake Burley Griffin.

Not the lake! Images of Wright and Proctor, dead-eyed and slack-jawed, cascaded through my brain. The idea that we'd soon end up like them brought on a panic, and I struggled against the ties, which really cut me this time. I shook my head and bit my lip. *Get it together, you idiot!* But to do what? What?

The vehicle slowed and turned left, so maybe we weren't going to the lake. At least not yet. We continued straight for a stretch, then we slowed and turned left again. After ten minutes, the vehicle slowed and stopped. Another roller door clanked, scraped, and was silent, and the vehicle inched forward and came to a halt.

The roller door descended, and the European got out and opened the back of the vehicle. Jean let out a high-pitched squeal through her nose as the vehicle dipped and rose on its suspension.

'Quiet or I throw you on floor,' said the European.

He grunted as he carried her from the garage. There was an echoing sound as metal slid on metal in the near distance. Then came a clicking noise, like a light being switched off and on a few times. A sliding sound of metal on metal again. And another sliding sound that ended with a loud clang.

'Look here, is bad for you,' said the European, his threat laced with contempt. 'Stay at wall!'

I was wondering about this wall business, and who he was talking to, when metal slid on metal again and clanged into place. Seconds later, the door next to my head opened, and hands gripped my jacket and pulled me forward. Then other hands looped around my knees and I was dragged out of the vehicle and quickly lowered onto cold concrete. They pulled me across the floor, through a doorway that banged my knees, and then down a passageway.

Metal slid on metal again. The light switch clicked a few times. The European yelled, 'Face wall!' And then he let me go. Metal clanged, a door opened, and my senses were momentarily overwhelmed by the smell of a blocked toilet. The European dragged me through another doorway and across a carpeted floor. Then he released me and moved away. There were a few popping sounds, and, with each one, Jean grunted.

'No move,' said the European, presumably to Jean. It was more a threat than an order.

He crouched beside me and pressed his pistol into my cheek while he cut the rope between my wrists and ankles. When my feet thumped into the carpet, he cut the ties on my hands and legs.

'You count to ten, *then* you move,' he said, his pistol gouging my cheek. 'Rolfe knows rules. You disobey, you die.'

When I got to three, the door slammed shut. I continued counting as the bolt slid into place. Then I heard someone running towards me. I ripped the tape from my eyes as I rolled over, my arms up, ready to defend myself.

It was Rolfe. He dropped down next to Jean, put a protective arm around her shoulders, and helped ease the tape away from her eyes and mouth. Then he looked at me and shook his head, a tentative smile on his lips.

'So Joe got you, too,' he said, seeming far too upbeat for a man in his position.

'Joe?' I said, eyeing Jean, who looked completely stunned. 'Is that his name?'

'That's what he calls himself,' said Rolfe. 'Anyway, we don't have to worry about him now, do we? I assume your people are right behind you and that they'll be bursting through that door any minute. Right?'

'I'm afraid not,' I said, taking in the blue-grey carpet that covered both the floor and the walls. 'I'm on my own.'

'You're what?' said Jean, open-mouthed with shock at this revelation.

A roller door rumbled and clanged somewhere outside. It was a muted sound, but unmistakeable. I jumped up and raced over to the carpeted wall, and pushed my ear into it. A vehicle fired up on the other side of the wall, the rumbling stopped, and the vehicle moved off. Then the rumbling door came down again.

Were both Joe and the woman going, or only one of them? If it was both — say, if one was dropping the other back at Beagle Street — it gave me about twenty minutes to scope this place. I ran over to the metal door and banged on it as hard as I could, and screamed at the top of my lungs. Then I put my ear to the door and waited.

'You mean …?' said Rolfe.

'Shhh,' I said, batting him away. 'You've both got to be quiet now.'

Thirty seconds passed, and no one came. The door had a horizontal viewing-slot set into the middle of it, about a metre-and-a-half off the ground. I pressed my thumbs against the slot and pushed it this way and that, desperately trying to move it, but it was shut tight. The door itself was made of sheet metal. It was hinged from the outside. I pushed and prodded at every corner of it, but it was immoveable, too.

Jean and Rolfe stood together at the back of the room, both eyeing me with a mixture of fear and bewilderment. After only a day in this place, Rolfe's black suit was covered in blue carpet fluff. I figured there was probably cat fur all over him as well. The source of the fluff was obvious. The floor was populated with little drifts of it, and it massed in the corners of the room.

'They'll be back soon,' I said, trying to sound calm but commanding. 'So, please, some quiet now. It's most important.'

I knew I had to take charge, and what I had to do, because I knew exactly where we were and what being there meant for us. I also knew we had no time to lose, so I immediately began taking an inventory of all the elements of the room. The place was the size of a single-car garage, and the metal door looked to be the only way out. Four thin mattresses were piled up against one of the side walls. There was an empty soda-water bottle next to the mattresses. And in a corner near the door were two rolls of toilet paper sitting next to a red plastic bucket. The bucket was the source of the stink in the place.

I walked to the closest wall and banged on it a few times with the side of my clenched fist. Every blow met solid brick. I took some of the wall carpet between my thumb and forefinger, but it was secured to the brickwork by lines of self-tappers, and it barely moved. Someone had done a thorough job here — so thorough that Joe and his friend were confident they could leave us alone in this room and that it would hold us, unsupervised, for at least a little while.

There were power points set into the skirting board on either side of the room, and two rows of recessed lights shone down on us from the ceiling. Two air vents sat side-by-side between the rows of lights. Each vent had a cover made up of four little louvre-like shutters, and the covers were each secured to the ceiling by four screws.

Then it occurred to me. Why two vents? Maybe one heated the room and the other cooled it. The vent furthest from the door looked slightly discoloured. I stretched up and tried to touch it, but it was well out of reach. I'd get to it later. First, I had to see if Jean or Rolfe had anything on them that we could turn into a tool or a weapon.

'Okay, questions later,' I said, as I joined them on the mattresses. 'First, let's pool our resources and see what we've got.'

They both looked shell-shocked, and they had good reason to be. Jean would only just be realising what had happened to her. And Rolfe would still be grieving for the cavalry that had turned into a one-man band. I knelt on the edge of the mattresses, facing the two of them with my back to the door.

The only thing I had that might prove useful was my ballpoint pen. It had been in the breast pocket of my shirt, and I'd been lying on it when Joe had given me the once-over. It was basically a tapered metal cylinder, half of which was coated with rubber for ease of grip. I dropped the pen into the space between our knees.

'First things first,' I said, trying to sound confident, like a man with a plan. 'Have either of you got anything metal on you? Anything at all?'

'These buckles are metal,' said Rolfe, pulling his shoes off and handing them to me. 'And the heels have metal discs. Stops them wearing out so quickly.'

I removed the solid-metal buckles from the shoes and dropped them, and the shoes, onto the mattress next to my pen.

'My beautiful Alicantes,' said Rolfe, running his fingers over the shoes. 'An indulgence, to be sure, but you can wreck them if you like, and anything else I own. Just get us out of here.'

'Anything in your pockets?' I said, ignoring him. 'And I'll need your glasses.'

'My glasses?' said Rolfe. 'And how am I supposed to see?'

'If we don't get out of here soon,' I said, 'your ability to see will be the least of your worries.'

Rolfe removed his glasses and placed them on the mattress next to the pen, the shoes, and the buckles.

'And Jean?' I said. 'Anything?'

'My studs?' she said, fingering her ears. 'And my watch? Are they any good?'

'Umm, no. You keep them for now. So, Rolfe, these rules Joe talked about. What are they?'

'He really only has one rule. When he wants to come in here, he switches the lights off and on a couple of times, and I have to move to the back of the room and face the wall. Then he opens the door and does what he wants. When he's finished, he locks up and flicks the lights again. Then I'm allowed to move. And he's warned me that if I peek while he's in here, I'll cop it. And I get the sense that he wouldn't hold back.'

'So how often has he been in?'

'Twice. He brought some cheese and dry biscuits a few hours

after he put me in here. And the water. And this morning he emptied the, um, the toilet. Oh yes, and I should say that, other than when he flicks them off and on, the lights stay on all the time. So get used to it.'

I was studying the downlights when it occurred to me that if Joe was intending to gas us like he'd done with Wright and Proctor, why was he bothering to hide his identity? Maybe it was easier for him not to lock eyes with his victims.

'Have you spoken to this Joe in any meaningful way?' I said.

'Not really,' said Rolfe. 'I mean, an hour after they put me in here, he opened the slit in the door and gave me his rule. And then this morning when he came for the toilet, I asked for some blankets and he didn't answer. So I asked again, and he told me to shut up or I'd regret it.'

'Did you ask him why he took you?'

'Oh, I didn't need to do that,' said Rolfe, suddenly looking shamefaced. 'I know how I got here, and I've got no one but myself to blame. And it's probably my fault that you two are in here, too.'

22

I WAS KEEN to hear Rolfe's explanation for why we'd been taken, but I told him we'd talk about it later. My highest priority was to examine our little prison before Joe or his mate returned. I moved the mattresses to the middle of the room and then started working my way around the walls, tapping them high and low with my middle and index fingers, like a doctor examining a patient's chest. The dull, unyielding response supported my initial assessment: beneath their carpet covering, all four walls were solid brick.

With Jean and Rolfe watching silently from the mattresses, I walked the length of the room, bringing my heels down hard on the floor, hoping to find something other than concrete underfoot. When I reached the front wall, I turned around, took a small step sideways, and walked to the back of the room, banging the floor as I went. I covered the whole room that way, and confirmed that the floor was indeed a concrete slab.

Next, I got down on my hands and knees and used one of Rolfe's shoe buckles to probe the hardwood skirting that was nailed to the bottom of the wall. I poked and prodded as I shuffled along the floor on my knees. Then I got to a join where the end of one of the lengths of skirting was slightly bowed. Excited by this find, I poked all around the join till I found a gap between the skirting and the wall wide enough to take the edge of the shoe buckle. It might have only been a minor defect in Joe's home-made detention centre, but, right at that moment, that gap seemed like a lifeline.

I used the heel of one of Rolfe's shoes to hammer the buckle deeper into the gap. That made the gap wide enough to take the edge of the other buckle, which I hammered in as well, widening the gap even further.

Then I sat on the floor in front of the join, settled my feet low on the wall, grabbed both shoe buckles, and pulled. The skirting didn't budge. I adjusted my grip on the buckles and pulled again, pushing with my legs. The skirting moved, but barely. So I began working on it in bursts, and, millimetre by millimetre, it began to come away from the wall. When the gap was wide enough to take my fingers, I eased them into it, up to the first joint. Then I pulled with all my strength while I pushed with my legs.

The nails gave a little screech as the skirting moved a bit more. Encouraged, I adjusted my grip and went at it. The nails gave a piercing screech this time. Then there was a loud crack, the skirting came away in my hands, and I flew backwards with such momentum that I ended up on all fours in the middle of the room.

When I got up and looked back, a metre-and-a-half of skirting lay on the carpet between me and the wall. I picked up the skirting and examined it closely. The end that had formed the squared-off join was a bit bowed. The other end, where it had broken away, was ragged with splinters. And there were three long nails sticking up out of it. One at either end. And one in the middle.

I couldn't have wished for a better outcome. In my hands I held the makings of an offensive weapon. Maybe a waddy, or a club, or even the prisoner's weapon of choice — a shiv. Whatever I made from it, our chances of surviving this place had just improved a little. I piled the mattresses over the gap in the skirting to cover it, and I slipped my would-be weapon under the pile.

'What good's a bit of wood to us?' said Rolfe, as he settled next to Jean on the mattresses.

'You'll see,' I said. 'Now, sorry, but I need some more quiet. Just for a while.'

Rolfe grimaced at this rebuff but said nothing, and I went back to the middle of the room and examined the plasterboard ceiling. I figured there had to be a cavity above it — at least big enough to accommodate the ducting for the vents and the wiring for the downlights. In all likelihood, it wouldn't have a crawl space, but if things got desperate we could tear down some of the plasterboard and have a look. The trouble was, we'd need to get up there to do that, and the noise from any demolition would surely bring Joe running.

A muffled rumble jolted me from these thoughts. They were back. Or, at least, one of them was. I raced to the wall and pressed my ear to it. The rumbling stopped, a vehicle drove into the garage, and the door descended.

It was time to test the soundproofing in this place. I waited a couple of minutes, then I took a deep breath and called Joe in a moderately loud voice. I waited thirty seconds, but he didn't respond. I called him again, as loudly as I could this time, but still he didn't come. So I turned side-on to the door and charged it with my shoulder. I hit it, and, as I expected, I bounced off and landed on the floor, winded. Half a minute later, the slot in the door slid open with a squeak.

'No banging,' said Joe in a rasping voice, 'or you get trouble.'

He shut the slot and was gone. He hadn't heard me yelling because of the carpet on the walls, but he'd come running when I'd thrown myself at the door, probably because the impact had sent a small shockwave through the house. Maybe we could make that work for us. I was mulling that over when the lights went off and on, and off and on again. And stayed on.

We huddled together facing the back wall. When the slot opened, I felt Joe's eyes on me. It was the first time I'd been sized up by someone who I was sure was planning to kill me. The slide scraped shut, the door opened, and Joe dropped something onto the floor. He stood there for a few seconds, scoping the place. Then the door closed, the lights flickered a few times, and something brushed my leg. When I looked down, a ginger cat was staring at me.

The cat scuttled away as I reached for it. Then it rolled onto its back and eyed me while it rubbed itself into the carpet. I stepped towards it, but it darted away again. Wright and Proctor had both had dead cats for company when they turned up at the lake. Was this moggy going to join us down there? That image sent a surge of dread through me, and I closed my eyes and worked to calm myself. I needed to think clearly now — not panic. And the best way to keep panic at bay was to stay occupied. But what to do? For a start, I had to have a closer look at the ceiling vents, and the only one way I could do that was with Jean and Rolfe lifting me up there.

They were both sitting forward, staring at the cat as though it was radioactive. It had me thinking that maybe they knew more about our crime scenes than they'd let on. It was something to explore with them later, but for the moment there were more pressing matters to deal with. I asked them if they could lift me to the ceiling.

'What do you weigh?' said Rolfe, eyeing me up and down, making his own assessment. 'Eighty-five kilos in your undies? Or ninety?'

'Something like that,' I said.

'Well, I've got a dodgy back, and trying to lift you might not be the best thing for it, but if ...'

'Hold on a second,' said Jean, a hint of impatience in her voice.

'If you need to know what's up there, why don't you two lift me?'

It was a fair suggestion. She weighed much less than me, and we'd have a much better chance of getting out of this if all three of us remained fit and able. So I agreed. But first I gave her riding instructions.

'Two very important things while you're up there,' I said. 'First, do *not* touch the ceiling or the vent covers. We can't let Joe know what we've been doing. Grab onto our hair if you're losing your balance, but keep your hands well clear of everything. Second, if the door starts to open while you're up there, we'll have to bring you down in a hurry. You understand?'

She nodded, and I handed her my pen.

'When you get up under the first vent, use this to open the slats a bit so you can have a look up inside.'

I positioned Rolfe underneath the cleaner of the two vents and stood side-on to him. We put our arms over each other's shoulders and squatted. Jean then edged her backside onto our shoulders, we wrapped our free arms around her legs, and we stood up. When we'd steadied ourselves, I asked Jean to open one of the slats and describe what she saw.

'There's a big silver tube going from the base of the vent up into the ceiling,' she said. 'And it bends away towards the back wall. And there's a fan with a little motor attached to it set into the middle of the tube, and there's wires running away from it.'

'Good,' I said. 'Put the slats back where they were, and then we'll move you across to the other vent. You ready, Rolfe?'

'Say when,' he said.

'Okay. Taking it slowly. And, now.'

Jean took more time to open the slats on the dirtier vent.

'There's no motor or anything like it in this one,' she said, finally. 'Just more silver tubing coming down to it. And these slats are covered in some sort of dirt. Like it's caked on.'

'Does the tubing bend away towards the back wall, too?'

'No — it seems to head towards that wall.'

She nodded in the direction of the mattresses.

'Okay. Good. Now I don't want you to leave any evidence of what you're about to do, so be very careful. First, I'm going to get you to fully open one of the sets of slats that face *away* from the door. That's it. Open it up as far as it'll go. Now put your finger up inside it and rub some of that black stuff onto it. That's it. Good. Now close it up, like it was. Well done.'

Once we'd lowered Jean to the floor, Rolfe put his hands on his knees and drew in some big breaths. The cat, which had been preening itself in the corner, looked up and assessed Rolfe for any threat. Detecting none, it went back to working on itself.

I took Jean's hand and sniffed her blackened finger. It was just as I'd expected — eau de dirty garage. Jean sniffed it and screwed up her face in disgust. Then she put the offending digit under Rolfe's nose. Once he'd had a sniff, they both looked at me enquiringly. Apart from the prime minister, the only people who knew how Wright and Proctor had died were people associated with our investigation. Now these two were about to find out. Would I sugar-coat it for them? No. There was no point.

'The stuff on your fingers confirms where we are,' I said. 'And what this place is.'

'Wright and Proctor,' said Rolfe in a whisper. 'This is where they died, isn't it?'

'Yes. From carbon monoxide pumped in through that dirty vent up there.'

Like most of their colleagues, Jean and Rolfe had badgered us for a cause of death ever since Susan Wright had turned up at the lake. Now they had their answer, and it stunned them.

'That black stuff is a mixture of carbon and unburnt petrol,' I said. 'It's residue from a vehicle exhaust. When these people decide to kill us, they'll rig up a hose between a vehicle-exhaust pipe and that ducting up there. Then they'll turn the engine on, and this room will fill up with carbon monoxide. And that'll be it for us, unless we do something about it.'

'And there *are* things we can do, right?' said Jean, her eyes pleading.

'There's plenty,' I said. 'I figure we've got about a day-and-a-half before they move on us, but maybe a lot less, so we've got to move fast. Our first task is to disable their delivery system. Then we'll get them in here with their guard down and take them on. None of it's going to be easy, but if everything goes in our favour, we'll get out of this.'

23

THE FIRST STEP in disabling our execution chamber was to remove the screws that held the dirty vent cover in place. Once the cover was off, we'd be able to rip into the ducting that had been set up to feed carbon monoxide into the room. Most of the gas would then disperse into the ceiling cavity. To maximise our chances of survival, we'd also have to seal the vent cover somehow before we screwed it back into place. Once that was done, we'd wait for the European to turn on the gas, and then somehow convince him we were dead. And if that all went well, we might get a chance to fight our way out of this place.

Neither Jean nor Rolfe had anything to add when I told them my plan, so I got down to making a screwdriver. Rolfe's shoe buckles were clearly too chunky for the job. I considered honing them down on the concrete I'd exposed in harvesting the skirting, but decided against it. The noise and vibration might have brought Joe running.

The only other possible screwdriver was my pen. I figured that if I could flatten the writing end of it, it should be tough enough to turn the screws without shearing. I removed the ink cartridge and reassembled the empty barrel. Then I put the pointy tip of the barrel between the two shoe buckles and pounded the metal sandwich with the heel of a shoe.

When the flattened tip looked a fit for the screws, I gave it to Jean and repeated my warning not to touch the ceiling. Rolfe and I got her onto our shoulders, and twenty seconds later she let out a triumphant 'Yes!' Not only did the pen fit the screws, she said, but the rubberised coating made the barrel very easy to grip.

I felt like cheering when the first screw hit the floor at our feet. The second one came down a minute after that, but then Rolfe said something about his back, and began moving unsteadily from foot to foot. I tried to steady him, but he was like a drunk trying to mark time. Jean moved her weight onto my shoulders, I helped her down to the floor, and Rolfe dropped to the carpet, jerking in shallow breaths, his eyes closed tight. It was his lower back, he said, and, no, there was nothing we could do. He needed to rest it. We helped him to the mattresses and laid him on his back. He closed his eyes and brought his knees up to his chest. Jean squatted next to him and stroked his forehead. Then she looked up at me.

'We'll have to do this without him,' I said. 'Once you get the rest of the screws out, you can tackle the vent cover. The trick is to get your fingers up inside it so you can ease it out. One side, then the other. But remember, don't mark anything up there.'

Jean stood under the vent. I bent down behind her so she could straddle my shoulders, and I hoisted her up to the ceiling. She was light enough, so, given Rolfe's bad back, I probably should have lifted her alone from the start.

She rocked on my shoulders as she worked away. The third screw soon hit the carpet. Then the fourth. The vent cover took a little longer, but she eventually handed it down to me and I lowered her to the floor. I put the cover face-up on the mattresses. Then I examined the square hole in the plasterboard, and the silver ducting that arced away into the ceiling cavity.

'What now?' said Jean, buoyed by her success.

'Next, you use the pen to shred the ducting,' I said. 'But you have to hold the ducting steady with one hand, and shred with the other, okay? We don't know how Joe's got it rigged up at the other end. If you put pressure on the ducting, or give it a big tug, who knows what it'll do back there. We don't want to alert him in any way to what we're doing. And once you've shredded the ducting, I want you to see how far you can reach up into the ceiling cavity. So, you right to go?'

'Ready when you are,' she said.

Jean felt a bit heavier this time, probably because my energy levels were down. Bits of silver paper fluttered past my eyes as she wriggled and chopped. By the time she stopped to assess her work, my right shoulder had had enough of her.

'I've hacked right around the ducting,' she said. 'I've separated it from this metal plate it was attached to, and I've put big holes in it as far back as I could. Now let's see what's up inside here. I can feel some sort of wiring. And now some long wooden beams, but I can't see them. And that's as far up as I can reach — about thirty centimetres into the ceiling.'

'And you can't feel anything else?' I said.

'Nope. Just fresh air.'

'That's great,' I said, and lowered her down.

Rolfe was still lying on his back, holding his knees to his chest, but he'd stopped groaning. I flexed my shoulders for a while, and then Jean and I picked up the bits of silver paper and shoved them under the mattresses. Next I asked them to give me their socks and undies, and any other small bits of clothing they had. We'd need it all if we were going to block the vent.

Rolfe and I faced the back wall while Jean removed her smalls. Then she and I turned away while Rolfe removed his. After I'd added mine to the pile, I shoved all the smalls into a leg of Jean's pantyhose and compressed the lot into a small, flat bundle. Then I carefully forced the bundle into the back of the vent cover, and used one of the shoe buckles to shape it into a tight, thick seal that I finished off with some wads of toilet paper.

Jean felt heavier than ever when I lifted her to the ceiling for the final time. I handed her the cover, and she wriggled as she manoeuvred it back into the hole and screwed it into place. My shoulders were really aching when I lowered her to the floor. I flexed them for a bit, and then checked the ceiling and the cover. They looked untouched, which meant that Jean had done a great job, and I told her so.

'But what if Joe has other plans for us?' she said, scrunching her face. 'And what if those plans don't include pumping gas at us from up there?'

I gave her a pained smile, but said nothing. I'd already considered that possibility, but all we could do was nullify obvious threats and stay ready for the unexpected. I pulled the top mattress over to the bucket and wrapped the flopping thing around myself while I took a badly needed piss.

'So what now, Mr Fixit?' said Jean when I returned the mattress to the pile.

'Now we convert our skirting into a weapon,' I said.

'And what did you have in mind?'

'I was thinking of something like a morning star — one of those medieval clubs with all the spikes sticking out of them. Only ours will have three spikes, not forty-three. But if it's well put together, it'll be effective enough.'

'So, a homemade club, which you're still to make, against their guns,' said Rolfe. 'Mmm. Sounds like a fair fight to me.'

'Sorry, but that's not quite right,' I said. 'It's their guns against our club, plus our natural advantage.'

'And that is?' said Rolfe. 'The fact that we outnumber them?'

'No. What we've got going for us is the element of surprise. Eventually, they're going to come in here thinking we're dead. And when we suddenly get up and take them on, they won't be expecting it. That's when we'll give them some of their own back.'

24

THE THREE NAILS that had come away with the skirting were about seven centimetres long. My plan was to remove the one at the splintered end and the one in the middle, and bind them somehow to the one I'd leave stuck in the squared-off end. I wrapped the arm of my jacket around the middle nail and began easing it back and forth. As I worked at it, I thought about what Rolfe had said earlier — about him being responsible for our abduction. I looked at him lying quietly on the mattresses. He wasn't a bloke to accept blame easily, and his time had come to tell all.

'Okay, Rolfe,' I said, resting my fingers for a moment. 'Now you can fill us in on how we got here.'

Rolfe knew this had been coming. He took a deep breath, propped himself up on his elbows, and, without looking at either of us, opened up.

'We're here because of a bad decision I made,' he said, shaking his head at the thought. 'And because of a coincidence that I had no control over. The thing is, if I'd gone to tennis on Monday night like I usually do, none of this would have happened. But my back was playing up, so I cancelled. Then I stopped at the supermarket on my way home and ran into an old contact — a senior person at the RSPCA. We chatted about the usual stuff. Man's inhumanity to beast. The latest outrage. But I knew all the while that he was busting to tell me something. And, eventually, of course, he did.'

'And that was?' I said, sensing some loosening in the nail.

'That their cat person had been analysing material that was somehow connected with your murder investigation.'

'What?' I said, so surprised by this claim that I dropped the skirting into my lap. 'He reckoned his mob was working for us? Well, I can tell you now, it's not true. We don't use them.'

'He didn't say you did,' said Rolfe. 'No. You use a forensic vet over at the ANU, and after you found Susan Wright's body, you sent that vet some fur to analyse. The thing is, the brief you sent with it suggested that the fur had come from *one* cat, but when your vet looked at the fur, she was certain it came from several different cats. Given that discrepancy, she was planning to send it off for DNA analysis, but then one of your people called and gave her a hurry along. So she asked a close friend over at the RSPCA to look at the fur for her. On the quiet, of course. And he confirmed her initial analysis — that the fur was indeed from several different cats. So that's what she reported to you. As it happens, that RSPCA vet is a confidant of the contact I ran into at the supermarket. They're a couple, in fact, and they share everything.'

This revelation hit hard. We'd allowed crucial evidence to fall into the hands of someone outside the loop, and they'd gabbed about it to a lover with loose lips. It meant that the fur might be useless if Joe ever fronted a jury. Then it occurred to me that Rolfe would have to escape this place before he could expose our stuff-up.

'Now you'd already know this,' said Rolfe, 'but around the time you asked your vet to analyse the fur, you also sent her a dead cat. Apparently, you wanted to know the animal's age, its gender, and whether it was domestic or feral. That sort of thing. Well, she had her RSPCA mate — he being 'the man' on all things feline — look at the cat as well. Then Proctor turned up dead, and there was more fur to analyse. And another dead cat. And the RSPCA vet got involved there, too. In fact, he was doing so much cat work for you, my contact was convinced that cats were central to your investigation.'

'I've got nothing to say about that,' I said, resuming work on the nail. 'What I want to know is, how does all this connect with us being here?'

Rolfe pulled his jacket tighter around his neck. Maybe he was attempting to keep the cold at bay. Or maybe he didn't like being brought back to the question.

'Ahh, well, when I thought about all this cat stuff,' he said, 'it reminded me of a story I did years ago when I was a junior at *The Digest*. About cats disappearing up in Red Hill. There were twelve of them in all. Beloved moggies, fat and healthy — just like the ones the two vets had examined. Now, call it a long bow if you like, but I thought I could draw a link, storywise, between the two sets of dead cats. A tentative one, mind you, but my update of the old Red Hill story was only to be a sidebar to my lead, which of course was going to focus on cat fur, two dead cats, and the way your people allowed crucial evidence to fall into the wrong hands.'

'When did you do the story on the disappearing cats?'

'About ten years ago,' said Rolfe.

I eased the first nail out of the skirting. It hadn't bent in the process, and it was long enough to do serious damage.

'So how does your storage unit out in Fyshwick fit into this?' I said.

'Ahh, so you know about the unit,' said Rolfe. 'Then no doubt you'll also know that it's where I keep my documents and old papers. And I never discard anything. So when I decided to revisit my *Digest* story, I went out to the unit, dug out the old notebooks, and retrieved the names of the people I'd interviewed back then. And last night I drove up to Red Hill, hoping to catch a few of them at home. I could have looked up a directory and rung them, of course. But I prefer face-to-face contact. Don't you, detective?'

'When you did the original story, how'd you know who to speak to?' I said, going to work on the second nail.

'The RSPCA gave me some names. And there were lost-animal notices plastered up around the shopping centre. And I spoke to people I met in the street up there. Everyone had something to say about the missing cats.'

'And presumably you spoke to someone at the Beagle Street house where they nabbed us. Otherwise you wouldn't have gone back there.'

'That's right. I spoke to a young man. He was working in the front garden.'

'And that was Joe?'

'Yes. As it turns out, he was Joe.'

'And had he lost a cat?'

'No, he hadn't.'

'So why'd you go back there last night?'

'I don't know. I remembered he was nice looking. Very buff. And I thought that while I was up there, why not knock on his door. A fatal impulse, I guess you'd say.'

'I know all about them,' I said. 'But tell me, why'd you go up to Red Hill to talk to people about cats when you knew there was a strong connection between dead cats and our investigation? Shouldn't you have at least told someone where you'd be? I mean, how dumb was that?'

'Ahh, but I did tell someone, detective. That's why Jean's here. And you, too, presumably.'

I looked at Jean. Her face was paler than ever, making her eyes seem even more deeply green. I waited, expecting her to explain, but her eyes didn't leave Rolfe's. She clearly thought it was his story to tell.

'Poor Jean,' said Rolfe, looking as remorseful as any villain I'd ever seen. 'You see, I did think there might be something of a link between my old cat story and the cats in your investigation, so last night, before I went up to Red Hill, I got Jean over for a drink and gave her a key to my storage unit. And I told her that if anything happened to me in the coming days, she should go out to the unit and look for the 'cat'. Yes, I was that obscure, but I'd written the word on the relevant notebooks, and I'd put them near the door out there. That way, I thought, if she did have to go out, she'd find them easily enough. And I fully expected her to call you, if and when that happened.'

'But you didn't call us, did you, Jean,' I said, as I felt the second nail slip slightly in its hole. 'You went it alone.'

'That's right,' she said, her eyes defiant. 'And why *wouldn't* I? After what happened at Westbourne Woods?'

'But this wasn't a story, Jean. It was a police matter.'

'I know,' she said, her defiance waning. 'But I didn't see any real danger in it for me. I mean, okay, no one knew where Rolfey was, but he's taken off before, and he's always shown up after a day or two. And much as I love you, Rolfey, you do tend to over-dramatise things. So when I looked at those addresses, all in up-market Red Hill, I thought that whatever was going on up there wouldn't be dangerous in any way. I mean, Red Hill? Where could you be safer? I know it makes me look like a complete snob. And a careless one at that. But if you …'

'Come off it, Jean,' I said, shaking my head. 'Don't tell me you weren't thinking about the big scoop waiting for you up there.'

'I wanted to see if the addresses in Rolfey's notebooks would lead me to him. And if I got a story out of it, so be it. But what about you, Darren? How did you come to be here alone?'

It was a fair question, but I wasn't sure how to answer it.

I could have said that I'd feared for her safety, and that because the boss wouldn't give her protection I'd followed her into a trap. I could have said that I thought she'd get me closer to the killers, and I'd been dead right about that. I could have said that I had my suspicions about her, so I'd decided to keep an eye on her, but why admit to being a piss-poor protector and a bad investigator?

I had another explanation for how I'd ended up there — one that was much closer to the truth. But I wasn't prepared to voice that one, either. It was that I was deeply attracted to her. I saw her as being at risk, and I'd used that as an excuse to follow her, to try to protect her, to be close to her. And in the process, like her, I'd taken my safety for granted and got myself into the deepest shit.

'Well, seeing as how everyone else has had a turn in the confessional,' I said, stopping work on the nail. 'The fact is, Jean, I've been keeping an eye on you. In my off-hours. Nothing authorised. Just me. I even put a tracking device under your car. It was clear to me that you had the killers' attention, but my seniors wouldn't put surveillance on you. They were worried about the bad publicity if we got found out. Worried that Rolfe here, and your other colleagues, would rip into us. So, in a funny sort of way, everyone who should have protected you, effectively conspired to have you nabbed. Silly, eh?'

'In retrospect, you'd have to say pretty silly, yeah,' she said. 'And silly me, too.'

'I've got a proposition for you, detective,' said Rolfe. 'If you get us out of here alive, I promise not to expose your shambolic investigation for what it is. What do you say to that?'

The second nail came out of the wood in a rush. I looked at Rolfe and tried to muster a smile.

'God, you drive a hard bargain,' I said. 'But, yes, it's a deal.'

25

APART FROM ARMING yourself as best you can, they say that the key to winning a fight is to know your enemy. I didn't have a clue about what made Joe tick, and it was almost time to find out. But first I needed a weapon. It would be no use getting to know him if I didn't have some way of taking him on.

The materials at hand were very basic: a metre-and-a-half of skirting, three long nails, and two shoelaces. I put the two loose nails on either side of the one I'd left in the skirting, and pinched the three of them together, along with the tail end of one of the laces. Then I wound the long end of the lace tightly around the bundle and worked it round and round, all the way down to the wood.

Next, I wound the lace over itself and brought it back up towards the pointy ends of the nails. Halfway there, with the lace running out, I looped it under itself and pulled it tight. I knotted it a couple of times. Then I did the same with the other lace.

When I tested my handiwork, the nails were remarkably firm, and their shiny points looked like little silver teeth. I stood up and swung the club, left and right. It felt well balanced, and was surprisingly heavy. I flailed the air, visualising the fight and the moment of impact.

'Can I have a go?' said Jean.

I handed her my new toy. She swung it back and forth, tentatively at first and then with more vigour.

'You could do some real damage with this,' she said, handing it back to me.

'Let's hope I get the chance,' I said, stowing the club under the top mattress. 'Now let's see if Joe's up for a chat. And just so I can engage him, I'm going to tell him that you've done your back in, Rolfe. I know it's partly true, but I'm going to say that you're in absolute agony and that you need painkillers. Can you turn it on if you have to?'

'Exaggerate, you mean?' said Rolfe, looking from me to Jean. 'Well, according to some people, that's what I do best.'

I went to the door, thumped on it a few times, and waited. There was no response, so I thumped it again. Then the slide opened, but by barely a centimetre.

'Step back,' said Joe, in a muffled voice.

'We need some painkillers,' I said, stepping away and pointing to Rolfe, who was groaning on the mattresses. 'It's his back. Aspalgin would be good. Or Nurofen, if you've got it.'

'I got nothing,' said Joe, slamming the slide shut.

'Wait!' I said, my voice full of emotion. 'Please wait.'

The slide opened again, just a few centimetres. Joe checked my position, and then he opened it a bit more.

'What?' he said.

When I'd thought about what I'd say to Joe, if and when I got the chance, most of what I'd come up with was straight from the textbooks. According to the experts, as a kidnap victim, you should try to build a rapport with your captors. Get to know them and let them get to know you. Show sympathy where possible. Don't complain. Appear reasonable. Remain low-key.

While ours wasn't a normal kidnap situation, I had these sentiments in mind as I considered how to approach Joe. In the end, I decided to try to push his greenie buttons, hoping that a concern for the planet was his motivation for murder.

'I guess you've got your reasons for locking us up,' I said, looking at the eye in the slot. 'But the other two people in here, Jean and Simon? Their stories have nailed dozens of environmental vandals over the years. The illegal loggers. The cockies who bulldoze the bush. If you kill them, the environment will lose two of its best advocates, so you must find a way to let them live.'

I surprised myself with the passion I injected into this little speech. And while Joe didn't respond, he didn't leave, either. After an extended silence, I dangled a second-string argument.

'I'm a policeman,' I said. 'I know the risks, and I choose to put my life on the line. But Jean and Simon here didn't bargain for this …'

'Yeah, yeah,' said Joe. 'Everyone deserve special. And you say you don't want it, but you do. So we see what happen. Okay?'

Joe's voice had a smile in it, like he was enjoying our chat.

'Okay, but just remember,' I said. 'These two didn't sign up for this. And whatever else you believe in, you've gotta believe that their deaths would be nothing but bad.'

The eye seemed to soften. But without its partner, and a face to give it context, I couldn't really assess the impact I was having. There was another prolonged silence. Then Joe spoke.

'When prawn trawler go to sea,' he said, 'it drag in lots they no want. Like small fish and useless sea creature. Even seal and bird. But only prawn is good. The rest, it by-catch, and it stay on deck and die. Then they push it back in water. It victim of stupid system and big waste. You here by accident, like by-catch. I no want you, but you here. For now. Later I push you back.'

'When we're dead,' I said grimly.

'We see,' he said. 'Please understand, human is same like kangaroo. Or tree. Or maybe cockroach. All is okay. Place for everything. But cockroach on food, or in bed, is no good. So must die. People who no good for me, or mine, they's same like cockroach. Only harder to kill. But really same.'

'Is that what Susan Wright did? Threaten you in some way?'

'No,' he said, turning his head away from the slide, distracted for a moment. 'She have something we want. Something hard to get.'

'And Alan Proctor?'

'Proctor? He *was* cockroach. And easy to kill.'

Someone out in the corridor said something to Joe. The voice echoed like an angry hiss. He turned away and said, 'Okay.' Then he shut the slot and locked it. End of conversation. I went back to the mattresses and sat next to Jean.

'I was hoping to give him something to think about,' I said. 'I don't think it worked. Anyway, he's not the one we need to influence.'

'The woman?' said Jean.

'That's right,' I said.

'So what now?' said Rolfe. 'You've got your club. We've blocked the vent that delivers the gas. Shouldn't we be doing something about the other vent up there?'

'No,' I said, looking at the cleaner of the two vents. 'There's an exhaust fan inside that one. It's there to suck the fumes out of this place — when they've done their job.'

Rolfe was unsettled by this explanation, but said nothing. Jean was quiet, too. And so we sat there, silently pondering our fate, hungry and tired. I began to wonder why the team hadn't heard from any of the residents that Rolfe had interviewed in Red Hill on Monday night. Our fears for his safety had received blanket media coverage throughout Tuesday. Maybe his interviewees weren't big media-consumers. Or maybe they hadn't made a connection between the missing journo and the one who'd knocked on their door to ask about missing cats from years ago.

Jean was different. It was still the middle of the night, so it would be hours before it was generally known that she was missing. But once people heard, someone from Red Hill was sure to call the cops to say that she'd knocked on their door just before she disappeared. Then they'd learn that Rolfe had been knocking on the same doors, and McHenry would link their disappearance to my own — especially as I'd been keen to tail Jean. If I were him, I'd assume that the three of us were all in the same place, and in mortal danger. The problem was, this room was miles from Red Hill, and we hadn't found it when we'd been searching for Wright and Proctor. It meant we three were beyond help, and there was no one who could save us but ourselves.

According to the experts, kidnap victims should accept their situation, await resolution, and not attempt any heroics. It was reasonable advice, as only a small number of kidnapped people ever escape their captors. However, the advice didn't apply to us. If we accepted our situation and waited patiently on these mattresses, I was 100 per cent certain that we'd soon be dead. What still wasn't clear was why Joe and his mate had taken so long to dispatch Wright and Proctor. What had they been waiting for? And how much longer did we have?

As if to answer this question, the lights flashed off and on, twice. I knudged Jean and Rolfe, and we trudged to the back of the room and faced the wall. The door opened with a squeak of hinges, and closed in what sounded like the same movement. The bolt slammed back into place and the lights flashed again. Then the ginger cat let out a throaty growl, and the three of us swung around to see a small black-and-white cat in front of the door. It was up on its tippy toes, hissing death at ginger.

'That didn't take long,' I said, stunned by how quickly things were moving.

Rolfe shooed the cats to opposite ends of the room. They soon settled on their haunches, their eyes locked on each other.

'So here we are,' he said, sitting back down. 'Three little

cockroaches waiting to die. Well, surely there's something more we can do! There must be!'

There *was* more, but I'd been keeping it to myself for fear that too much detail might cause these two to drop their bundles. Now the time had come to reveal all.

'Here's the thing,' I said, kneeling on the edge of the mattresses, facing them. 'Joe kept Wright and Proctor dehydrated and food-deprived while they were in here, but both of them had full stomachs when they died. And there was a date-rape drug called ketamine in their systems. In essence, he starved them, then gave them a feast of drugged food, and once they were unconscious, he turned on the gas. You'd expect him to use the same method on all his victims, but maybe he won't with us — he'll know that I know about the ketamine, and he'll expect me to tell you about it so that you don't eat any of the food he gives us. So he might forget about sedating us, and just turn on the engine out there and be done with it.'

'And if he offers us food and we reject it?' said Jean. 'I guess he'll turn on the engine pretty soon after that anyway, right?'

'If he brings food in here,' I said, 'Rolfe should make a big show of eating it.'

'What?' said Rolfe, mystified by this suggestion. 'Why would I do that?'

'Joe will know that I warned you about the food, so when I abuse you for eating it and you keep eating despite the abuse, he'll think we're totally demoralised — that we're in disarray, and that we're even more vulnerable than we appear. And that's how we want him to see us, because that way he'll be much easier to catch off-guard when he comes in here to check on us. After we're supposed to be dead.'

'How dangerous is this ketamine?' said Rolfe.

'Essentially, a moderate dose will put you to sleep in a hurry.

You'll have strange dreams and you'll be wonky when you wake up. But it won't do any damage. I can assure you of that.'

'And you really think it'll help if I do a little performance and eat some of it?'

'Yes, I do.'

'Okay then, I will.'

With that resolved, I suggested we take turns in getting some shut-eye, and I nominated Rolfe to go first. He agreed, and rolled onto his side and closed his eyes. Within minutes, he was fast asleep. Jean edged closer to me so that our shoulders and knees were touching. Despite our situation, I felt strangely at ease sitting there with her.

'What's the first thing you're going to do when we get out of here?' she said.

'I don't really know,' I said. 'Shower, I guess. Change my clothes. And then nail these bastards. What about you?'

'Yeah. The same. Clean myself up. Then tell the world about this place.'

The serious set on her face turned into a smile as something else occurred to her.

'And I'd thank Detective Darren Glass for saving me,' she said. 'And I'd demand that he be rewarded for his bravery. And his nous.'

'And the reward? What would that be?'

'Oh, something appropriate.'

She looked into my eyes, and then she moved her head towards mine, and our lips met. Just brushed together, really. She pulled her head away to where we could focus on each other. We smiled, and then we kissed again. This time, the kiss lingered. And when our lips finally parted, I put my arm around her and she turned towards me.

'You know what they say about kissing and cuddling at times

like these?' I said, as she snuggled into me.

'They have something to say about everything else, so what do they say about this?'

'That people in situations like ours tend to get physically close. But what they're really doing is comforting each other. And themselves. And when their ordeal's over, things usually don't go much further between them. They resume a polite distance. And sometimes they never see each other again.'

'And is that what you want, Darren?'

'No. I want to see you in that hat again. The black one with the feather.'

'You liked that feather, didn't you? In fact, you couldn't take your eyes off it.'

'You were waving that thing at me, weren't you?' I said, totally surprised by this revelation.

'It was shameless, wasn't it?'

The lights flashed off, on, off and on, breaking the spell. We separated, Jean knudged Rolfe, and the three of us lumbered over to the back wall. The slot opened and slammed shut, and then the door squeaked open and quickly closed again. The lights were still flashing as I swung around to see a big black tomcat crouching by the door. He was puffed out, and his ears were pinned back as he eyed the other cats. Then he flicked his bristling tail and retreated to the vacant corner next to the door, gurgling all the while, ready for a fight.

26

WHEN WE SETTLED back on the mattresses, the ginger cat surprised us all by coming over and rubbing itself against Rolfe. Rolfe patted the animal, tentatively at first, and then in long strokes from its head to its tail. The cat was soon curled up on his lap, purring with its eyes closed.

A buzzing noise came on in my head, the type you get on a long-haul flight ten hours from nowhere. I stood up and walked to the other side of the room, and steadied myself against the wall. Then I walked back to the mattresses and lowered myself down next to Jean. She rested her head on my shoulder and dozed for a few hours. She stirred occasionally, and once when she did, she snuggled into me again and I put my arm around her. I feared our sudden closeness might make Rolfe feel a bit excluded, till I caught him smiling as though he found our intimacy somehow reassuring.

At one point, Jean asked if we'd be alright. I tried to sound convincing when I replied that we'd be fine, but I was fighting the growing realisation that our chances of surviving this place hovered somewhere between slim and non-existent.

Later, while Jean slept, Rolfe asked me how I felt about dying. I told him I hadn't thought about it, which was a lie. Then he asked if I was prepared for death. As well as I could be, I said. And it dawned on me that he was readying himself for the end.

He said he would have liked to have left a last note for his sister. I fished around in my jacket for the ink cartridge from my pen and a faded supermarket receipt I'd found flattened in the back pocket of my trousers. I handed them to him, and he thanked me, then leaned the receipt on the bottom of one of his shoes and wrote down his final thoughts. After he handed me back the cartridge, he asked where he should leave the note. I told him I'd put it under the carpet where the skirting had come away.

'Why would you hide it where it'll never be found?' he said.

'Look, even if we don't make it out of here,' I said, 'my people *will* find this place, and when they do, your note will turn up. And, eventually, they'll pass it on to your sister. I promise.'

He accepted this reassurance and handed the note over. I lifted the carpet and pushed the note under as far as it would go. Just as I was settling back onto the mattresses, the lights went out, plunging the room into darkness for what seemed like several seconds. Then they went on again. And off. And on. As we made our way to the back wall, I reminded myself that if I was going to have an impact here, I had to compensate for what hunger and dehydration were doing to my reaction time, my balance, and my strength. It could be the difference between living and dying. The door opened and quickly closed. The slot in it squeaked, and the lights flickered a couple of times.

When we turned around, a plate full of sliced-up pizza was sitting in front of the door. Without prompting, Rolfe let out a cry of joy and rushed to the food. He shoved a couple of slices into his mouth, then hovered over the plate with his cheeks bulging. The slide in the door remained open a pinch so that Joe could assess how his offering was being received. Jean followed me back to the mattresses, and we slumped down together and scowled at Rolfe.

'No one can be *that* bloody hungry, Rolfe,' I said, eyeing him with contempt. 'What a complete idiot!'

Rolfe tweaked his eyes into a smile. Jean shook her head and growled. Then Rolfe stepped over the plate of pizza so that he blocked the line of vision between the mattresses and the door.

'You!' said Joe, opening the slide a bit more. 'Go back your friends!'

'Whatever you say, darling,' said Rolfe. 'But you know, you sound rather tense. Maybe you should have some of this pizza. Better be quick, though! Ohhh, no! Too late!'

Rolfe picked up the last four slices, took a bite out of two of them, and hurled the other two at the cats that were spread out along the back wall. The animals cringed, but held their positions as the missiles hit the floor in front of them. Rolfe shot Joe a crazy smile before skipping over and joining us on the mattresses.

The smell of the pizza was almost unbearable, as was the noise Rolfe made while eating it. I concentrated on the growls the ginger and the little black-and-white cat were making as they hoed into the slices Rolfe had tossed at them. Big tom was the only cat with no interest in the food. He'd given one of the slices a suspicious sniff, and had then returned to the door to keep watch on everyone.

Rolfe turned and saluted Joe with a half-eaten slice. Joe muttered something inaudible. Rolfe saluted the door again, prompting Joe to growl at him. Then the slide slammed shut, and Joe was gone. Rolfe immediately lifted the edge of the mattresses and spat partly masticated pizza onto the floor. He added the uneaten bits of pizza to the pile, and dropped the mattresses on top of the lot.

'So, three-and-a-half slices,' he said. 'If it's drugged, I guess that'll be more than enough to put me under.'

'Let's see how you go,' I said. 'I'm sure you'll be alright.'

'I certainly hope so,' he said. 'And when you get us out of this, remember, I've got first call on the medics when they arrive. Okay?'

'That's only fair, Rolfey,' said Jean, patting his shoulder. 'And we will get out of here, won't we, Darren?'

I nodded, though I now doubted we'd survive this place. I was dehydrated and very tired. I was also very dizzy, and every movement was an effort. Even so, I knew I could muster the strength if ever Joe's head came within range of my club.

Rolfe shuffled to the end of the mattresses, and the ginger cat climbed onto his lap and went to sleep. Then we waited to see if the food was drugged. The answer came about fifteen minutes later when Rolfe's eyes closed and his head slumped forward. I checked his breathing. It was shallow but regular. And his pulse seemed normal.

Then I realised that I hadn't asked him if he snored. If Joe came in, expecting us to be dead, and found Rolfe snoring like a chainsaw, that would be the end of us. I slid the unconscious ginger cat onto the mattress. Then I leaned down and listened to Rolfe's breathing again. It seemed normal, so I rolled him onto his side and spread my jacket over him. The jacket covered his head and his back, but I could still see the slight rise and fall of his chest. I pulled him upright again, removed *his* jacket, and laid him back down. Then I placed the two jackets loosely over him. Layered up like that, his breathing was barely visible.

'It's best now if we all look like we're out of it,' I said, as I settled back next to Jean.

I slipped my hand under the top mattress and took hold of my club, and I was trying to tally how long we'd been locked away when the slot opened and I felt Joe's eyes on me. I stayed as still as I could, and he closed the slot. A minute or so later, an engine started up on the other side of the wall. They revved it a few times and then let it idle. It had the throaty burble of a big unit — bigger than the one that had brought us here. Perhaps it was a van, or a small truck. I squeezed Jean's leg. She moved her head back and forth across my shoulder. So here we were, and the gas was on the way. The most important question now became: how long would Joe leave the engine running?

The ceiling cavity could accommodate lots of gas, but the seal we'd put on the vent was far from perfect, and we'd eventually get seepage from around the downlights. I figured we had about twenty minutes before a significant amount of carbon monoxide entered the room.

Other than the muffled sound of the engine, the only other noise came from big tom. He sat in the corner with his head between his legs, snorting occasionally as he cleaned himself. Then two things occurred to me in quick succession.

First, I remembered the old joke about why *dogs* lick themselves down there. Then I looked at the little black-and-white cat at the back of the room. It was unconscious, a victim of the pizza, like ginger and Rolfe. And I realised that the next time Joe looked in on us, he'd expect everything in the room to be dead and ready for disposal. And there'd be big tom licking his nuts. There was only one thing for it.

I pulled the club from under the mattress, and Jean touched my arm and looked at me inquiringly.

'When Joe comes in here,' I said in an urgent whisper, 'we've all got to look like we're dead, right? So what's he going to think if that cat's still licking its nuts?'

She looked at big tom, and the implications of what I'd said hit home. It had me wishing she'd eaten some pizza. At least then she wouldn't have to witness what I was about to do. I patted her shoulder, pushed myself up, and confirmed that ginger was unconscious. Then I went to the back wall and confirmed that the little black-and-white cat was out to it, too.

I rested the club on my shoulder and walked slowly towards the door, avoiding eye contact with big tom as I closed in on him.

All the while, I was aware of the hum of the engine on the other side of the wall. When I was within a few metres of the cat, he got to his feet and puffed himself up, ready to run. I froze and stared at the door, watching him out of the corner of my eye. He stayed crouched for a while. Then, thinking the threat had passed, he settled back onto his haunches.

There's no right time to strike. The moment selects itself, as it did then. I stepped low towards big tom and swung, but he shot off as soon as I moved, and my club sliced through nothing but thick air.

Then the cat's luck out ran out because, as he raced past the mattresses, Jean suddenly sat up, and, sensing a trap, he hit his brakes and tried to change course. The move put him within range of my club again. I brought the blunt side of the weapon down hard on his back, and he gave a strangled squeal and slumped onto his side. Then his legs flicked the air a few times, and he was dead. I carried him back to the door and curled him up like he was asleep. When I looked over at Jean, her eyes were wide with shock.

I knelt down next to her and slipped the club under the top mattress. When I sat down, she put her head on my shoulder and I gave her a comforting cuddle. Then I eased her off me and moved away from her a little.

'I'll need room,' I said in a whisper.

She rolled towards Rolfe, and I edged away from her a bit more. Then I rolled over so that I was facing her. I slipped my hand under the mattress and gripped the club again, ready for the fight. I realised that I was puffing and sweating far too much for a man who was supposed to be half dead. I wiped my face with my shirt ends, got back into a ready position, and concentrated on deep breaths. Easy in, easy out. In, and out. Within a few minutes I was back to shallow, almost imperceptible, breathing.

The engine on the other side of the wall continued to hum. Then it escalated through a scale of notes till it was pushing red. Just as suddenly, the revs dropped back to the low, steady hum. Then it revved up again. And again it dropped back. By my estimation, the engine had been running for about fifteen minutes. It meant that if we hadn't disabled Joe's delivery system, we would have already been unconscious and close to death. And that, no doubt, was how Joe would expect us to be — nearly gone. The thing was, we'd be okay if he kept the engine going for another five minutes or so. After that, I feared there'd be seepage. And if it went longer than ten minutes, we'd be in very big trouble.

I was stuck on that thought when a headache came on. Was it dehydration, or had I got it from chasing the cat? It could be caffeine withdrawal. Or maybe it was the first stages of carbon monoxide poisoning. There could be more gas in this room than I figured. So what to do? The door was built like a battleship, and the ceiling was full of gas.

I was working to squash these panicky thoughts when I noticed the silence. I held my breath. The engine had stopped. Was it out of petrol? Were they hitching the hose up to another vehicle? No. Why would they do that? Surely they must think it had done the job on us already. As if to confirm that thought, the exhaust fan in the ceiling began to whir.

The fan was still whirring fifteen minutes later ... twenty ... and twenty-five. Then the door slot scraped open. I felt eyes scanning the room, and a palpable presence assessing us for signs of life.

'They finished,' said Joe, turning to someone out in the corridor. 'You go now. I manage here. Yeah. See you.'

He shut the slide, and his muffled voice receded and died as he and his accomplice moved away from the door. A few minutes later, there was the muted clanking of the roller door. A vehicle fired up and departed the garage, and the roller door descended. I remained frozen, my hand wrapped around the club. Would Joe come in now, or would he leave us for hours? If he left it much longer, I'd be too weak to be effective.

The bolt on the door suddenly slid back with a clang and the door opened. A draft of air brushed my face. Someone lingered in the doorway for a few moments and then strode across the carpet towards me.

27

HAVING PLACED MYSELF closest to the door, I'd expected Joe to check on me first, and I was ready for him. But he walked straight past me. I opened my eyes to a slit, and through a veil of eyelashes I got the blurred image of a big, trim bloke moving lightly on his feet.

He stopped at the other end of the mattresses and stood over Rolfe. He didn't look tense, but the old-style revolver he held at his side showed that he was ready for anything. And the longer he stood there, the more it worried me. Sure, Rolfe was covered in jackets, but you wouldn't have to look too closely at him to see that he was breathing. And Joe seemed to be staring at him. Maybe his eyesight was dodgy. Or maybe, because he assumed Rolfe was dead, that was what he saw.

These thoughts hit a wall when Joe suddenly leapt off the floor, karate-style, and kicked Rolfe in the guts. It sent a shockwave through the mattresses, and through me. I closed my eyes and my stomach churned. He was fit *and* he knew how to handle himself. This was going to be much tougher than I'd figured. I tightened my grip on the club.

Then I was taken by a very worrying thought. Was Joe whacking Rolfe for the cheek he'd given him when the pizza was delivered? Was he so into payback that he'd beat up on someone who he thought was dead? I certainly hoped so, because otherwise, if we were all in for the same treatment, Jean was next. She'd managed to remain quiet while Rolfe copped it, but there was no way she'd stay 'dead' if Joe gave her a kicking.

I opened my eyes to a slit again. Joe was side-stepping along the mattresses towards me. I tensed up, ready to take him on, but he stopped in front of Jean and took a step into the space between me and her. He bent over and extended his free hand towards her face. I closed my eyes. Here was my best chance. Then I realised that even if I got the club up for a clean swing at him, he'd react to the movement and drill me before I could land a blow. Game, set, and minced meat. If only I'd converted the skirting into a short-range weapon like a shiv.

I opened my eyes again. Joe's leg was no more than a foot from my face. The bastard was stroking Jean's cheek. In that pose, he was perfectly positioned for a scissor kick. I was visualising the move when he suddenly withdrew his hand and straightened up. Then he edged his front foot even further into the space between Jean and me. He reached for her face again. The revolver rested on his right thigh as he bent forward. *Now!*

I swung my right leg up and drove my heel hard into his chest while my left knee smashed into his ankles. It was a picture-perfect scissor kick. His feet left the ground and he went backwards through the air. But as he flew, his hands shot out ready to break his fall, and he kept hold of his revolver as he went.

Even so, I was on top of him as he hit the floor. I got a good grip on his wrists, but he rotated his hands, and my grip slipped. I grappled for his gun hand, but couldn't get there before he pulled the trigger. The explosion was deafening, and hot residue scoured my face. I gripped his wrists again and leaned heavily on his gun hand as he pushed and lifted with the other side of his body. We rolled, and the momentum took us over until he was on top of me. Idiot that I was, I should have gone for the weapon and not the hand that held it.

Joe threw all of his weight into the fight, while I tried to hold his wrists apart and away from me. But he was very strong. His line of fire was narrowing, and I knew that I couldn't hold him out much longer.

I put my feet flat on the floor and bucked a few times, trying to shake him off. But he wedged his feet underneath me and rode it out. I whacked his lower back with the tops of my thighs, trying to dislodge him that way, but he just laughed. My arms felt like hot jelly, and his gun was almost in line with my head.

'Not so big man now, eh?' he said. 'Say *goodnight*, detective.'

I waited for the flash that would kill me, but it didn't come. Instead, there was a sound like a mallet whacking raw chicken. Joe froze. His eyes looked like they were going to pop. Then he jolted forward an inch and tried to turn his head, but he couldn't seem to move it. Finally, he shuddered and suddenly went limp, and our faces collided as he collapsed on top of me.

I rolled him off me, grabbed his revolver — an old .38 Special — and immediately swung it around to cover the door. When I glanced back at Joe, I saw my club embedded in the back of his head, and Jean standing behind him with her hands to her face.

I kept the gun on the door while I felt Joe for a pulse. He didn't have one. It was a brutal, sudden end to our struggle, and not a great outcome for our investigation, but I was sure even McHenry would agree that it was better to have Joe dead than me, with a bullet in my head.

I put my arm around Jean. She was shaking, trying to hold her tears at bay. I desperately wanted to stay there with her, but Joe might have had mates outside. And I had to get to a phone.

I checked Rolfe's breathing and pulse. He was fine and, incredibly, he seemed to be stirring. I took my jacket off him, and hugged Jean again. I quickly thanked her for saving me, and we kissed before I edged away from her towards the open door, the revolver up two-handed in front of my eyes.

The room where they'd held us was at the end of a long,

well-lit corridor. Halfway along the corridor was a door that I assumed led to the garage. I dreaded being taken from behind, so I stepped up to the door, turned the handle, and gave it a push. I pressed myself into the wall and held my breath and listened, weapon at the ready. All I could hear was the sound of my own breathing and Jean speaking softly to Rolfe in the room behind me. I dropped to a low crouch and pivoted into the open doorway. Then I had an attack of the dizzies, and lost my balance and fell on my arse.

I pushed up to a crouch again, raised the revolver to eye level, and traced a line across the room. It *was* the garage, and it looked empty, except for a dark-green van reversed up against the back wall. A length of silver ducting arced between the van's exhaust pipe and a hole in the ceiling. Here was the weapon that had killed Wright and Proctor, and which had nearly done us in as well. I walked around it, peering in through the front and rear windows, making sure no one was in the cabin or the cargo bay.

On the far side of the van I found a small, home-made cage sitting up on a work bench. The cage had a spring-loaded door that was activated by a metal touch-plate built into its floor. There was still some cat food smeared on the plate. Ginger, tom, and the little black-and-white cat must have found that food irresistible.

I stepped back into the corridor, tiptoed to the end of it, and stuck my head around the corner. In one direction was a short connecting space that opened out onto a lounge room where two couches sat either side of a fireplace. In the other direction was the front door. I went to the front door, deadlocked it, and chained it. Then I walked slowly into the lounge room.

Apart from the couches, the only moveable objects in the room were three oil paintings hanging on the north-facing wall. They all featured far horizons and big skies. None of them were signed. With any luck, someone at the art school might know who painted them.

A set of stairs filled an alcove at the back end of the room, and in front of me was a short corridor which led towards the front of the house. I made my way down the corridor and pushed through the set of swinging doors at the end of it. What I saw in the room beyond stopped me in my tracks. It was Jean, filling a glass from a tap over the kitchen sink.

'How'd you get in here?' I said, truly amazed by her stealth.

'Rolfe was desperate for water,' she said, and she pointed to a full glass beside the sink. 'Here. This one's for you.'

My eyes darted between the glass of water and the phone sitting on the bench near the fridge. I dialled McHenry, sipping at the water while I waited for him to answer. A small pile of letters sat at the back of the bench. All of them were addressed to The Resident, 13 Rodway Street, Yarralumla, ACT, 2600.

'Ah, McHenry,' I said when he finally answered. 'I bet you thought you were rid of me!'

'Glass, it's you!' he said, as though he couldn't believe his ears. 'Are you alright?'

'I'm fine,' I said. 'We're fine. Acheson and Rolfe are with me.'

'They're with you? Where? Tell me exactly where!'

'I think we're at number thirteen Rodway Street in Yarralumla, but I'll leave this phone off the hook in case I'm wrong. Now I've gotta go. There might still be hostiles in this place. And, boss? Bring the full entourage when you come. This is the crime scene we've been looking for.'

28

THE FIRST ROOM at the top of the stairs contained a couple of single beds. The bed linen was clean, and the pillows and doonas were fluffed-up and ready for use. But there were no bedside tables, and the walls were bare. There wasn't even a coat hanger in the built-in wardrobe.

The second bedroom was much bigger, and the king-size bed that filled it looked like it had been slept in recently — the bottom sheet was creased and slightly discoloured, and the doona was bunched up against the wall. There were even some men's clothes in the wardrobe, and an easel and a clean palette were stacked next to the bed, along with a box of brushes and tubes of paint.

A damp towel hung behind the door in the ensuite bathroom, and a toothbrush and a tube of toothpaste sat on a ledge above the sink. In the cupboard under the sink, I found a red plastic bucket containing everything that Joe had taken from me. I fished out my Glock and my phone. The Glock was loaded and ready for action, and I felt much more secure with it in my hands. I tried my phone, but the battery was dead. I pocketed Joe's revolver and my phone, but left everything else in the bucket.

Downstairs, I crossed the lounge room, unlocked one of a pair of glass doors that led outside, and stepped out onto a large paved area. I felt an instant lift just from standing in the late-afternoon sun, breathing in fresh air.

The noise from dozens of police sirens was building in the distance. Then a cocky squawked nearby, and I was aware of everyday sounds coming at me from over the top of the siren noise. The unbroken drone of nearby traffic was probably Adelaide Avenue. Some kids were shouting a few houses away. Then someone fired up a leaf blower.

How would these people react when they heard that they'd shared their street with a bunch of killers? For some, it would be a major jolt to their sense of personal security. It would make others worry about their family's safety. And still others would fret about the value of their real estate. There's nothing like a major crime scene in the street to depress property prices.

The sirens were very close as I stepped back into the lounge room. Then I heard a loud grunt echo from the front of the house, followed by a scuffling noise. I moved quickly through the room, and when I was a metre from the corridor, I pressed my back to the wall, edged forward, and peered around the corner.

It was Jean and Rolfe. He had one arm draped over her shoulders, his legs looked very rubbery, and she was only just managing to stay upright as she dragged him down the corridor towards me. I raced to them and took Rolfe's free arm.

'You did it, Glass!' he said, slurring his words like a drunk. 'Well done, man! Not that I doubted you. But, by God, I *am* surprised to be alive. Happy, but surprised. And, Glass, you should know — my feelings for you at this moment go well beyond mere gratitude. Nothing carnal, mind you. Not like my colleague here. But I love you, Glass. Like a brother.'

'Thank you, Rolfe,' I said. 'For your gratitude *and* your love.'

Jean and I burst out laughing, and Rolfe looked at each of us in turn and then joined in. The ordeal we'd shared had sealed a bond between us, and I knew that they felt it, too. I was about to put this into words when there were a few tentative knocks at the front door.

I'd expected to hear the squeal of rubber when the lead car arrived. I'd also been prepared for Special Operations to break

down the door and wave their weapons around. So what was this
timid knocking?

'That'll be the boys,' said Jean, hauling us faster towards the
door.

'For you?' I said.

'The Live Cam crew. They took a short cut. I wasn't going to
miss the biggest story of my life!'

'You called them?'

'While you were in the garage.'

'Amazing,' I said, and it was.

'I hope their laptop's got an uplink,' said Rolfe, suddenly
much more alert.

'I'm sure it has, Rolfey,' said Jean, patting his back. 'And if
you're really quick, you might even get your story up before me.'

Channel Four Live Cam

Wednesday 7 August, 5.00pm

Good afternoon, Jean Acheson back with you again, here in leafy Yarralumla with this Live Cam exclusive. A world exclusive, really. Because the house behind me is where both Susan Wright and Alan Proctor were murdered.

And how do I know this? Because I've just spent the last 20 hours in the room where they died. With me was my colleague Simon Rolfe, and Detective Sergeant Darren Glass. And what were we doing in that room, you ask? We, too, were waiting to die.

In securing our freedom, it was necessary for us to kill one of our captors. His death will be the subject of a police investigation, so I can't go into any details at this point, other than to say that, in the end, it was his life or ours.

Stay with the Live Cam. I'll be in conversation with Brett Malone throughout the evening, giving a full account of my time in the House of Death. This is Jean Acheson. It's great to be back.

29

THE SIRENS MORPHED into a chorus that became louder and more urgent as the cavalry homed in on Rodway Street. The three of us stood outside the house on a barren nature strip while Jean's crew took exterior shots of the front door. I'd refused to let them inside, and she'd been fine with that.

A patrol car swung around the corner at the far end of the street and fishtailed towards us. Another quickly followed, and then came a slew of vehicles, the last of which was a big blue van.

'No point taking any chances, guys,' I said, lifting my hands above my head. Jean and Rolfe looked at each other, then followed suit — as did Jean's crew — just as the first patrol car squealed to a stop in front of us. The cop in the passenger seat had his weapon pointed at the roof of the car. He and the driver eyed us nervously, both very much on edge.

'I'm Detective Sergeant Darren Glass, Australian Federal Police,' I said, locking eyes with the armed cop. 'The people with me are friendlies — they're Jean Acheson and Simon Rolfe. Please lower your weapons. We are *not* armed. We are friendlies. Please lower your weapons.'

The armed cop waited till his partner was out of the vehicle before he opened his door. Then the two of them stood staring at us while a special-ops team surged from the blue van and swept into the house.

Through the chaos of cops and cars, I saw McHenry coming towards us. His face was alight with the biggest smile I'd ever seen on it. When he got to me, he scooped me off the ground and held me in a bear hug that lasted too many seconds. Then he put me down, and I saw that he'd teared up a bit. I feared for a moment that he was going to kiss me.

'You had us worried there, son,' he said, his hands on my shoulders, shaking his head. 'Very worried indeed. Now, first things first. Are any of you injured in any way?'

'We're fine,' I said. 'But there's another house you've go to get people to, urgently — in Beagle Street, Red Hill. It's where they nabbed us. I don't know the number, but it's an older-style place just up from the reserve.'

'Number fifteen Beagle,' said Jean from behind me.

'We'll get a team there right away,' said McHenry, nodding at a senior officer who immediately headed off. 'Anything else before we get you to your medical?'

'There's a body in the house,' I said. 'It's the European guy who dropped the documents on Jean. And there was at least one other person in the house with him while we were in there. A woman. She left an hour-or-so ago.'

'Do you have a description?'

'No. I never saw her.'

'And you know it's a woman because …'

'She was wearing high heels. And she and the European had a heated discussion in another room when they nabbed me, and it sounded like a woman.'

'And the way she walked in those things?' said Jean. 'No man could do that.'

'I see,' said McHenry, smiling as his gaze turned from Jean to me. 'Well, that narrows the field down. So they're waiting for you at the hospital. And then I'll see *you* back here, Glass. But, before you go, you should know that we found the tracker. Under Miss Acheson's car. And your American friend James has confirmed what you were up to.'

I should have been ready for this. When they found Jean's car they would have gone over every inch of it, and of course they would have found the tracker. I'd survived the impossible, only to go down for my sins in a previous life. In that instant, I resigned myself to losing my job. And I'd face charges over the tracker.

Jean stepped to my side. 'What does he mean, "the tracker"?' she said. 'Is he talking about that little machine we put under my car?'

'Are you saying you *knew* the tracker was there?' said McHenry.

'Of course,' said Jean. 'We were trying it out.'

'And he wasn't tailing you?'

'You mean, following me?' said Jean, a cheeky smile on her face. 'Of course he was following me. He's my boyfriend, isn't he? That's what he's supposed to do!'

'Your boyfriend, is he, Miss?' said McHenry, smiling as he considered this turn of events. 'Well, he's a lucky man then, isn't he? Very lucky indeed. Well, more of this later. Off to hospital with you now. All being well, Glass, we'll see you back here in a couple of hours. And Miss Acheson, Mr Rolfe, my officers will want talk to you after you're finished at the hospital, and they'll be thorough, so please be patient.'

With that, he slapped my back and strode past us into the house, shaking his head as he went. He hadn't believed Jean, but her quick thinking had saved my bacon. And calling me her boyfriend had sent a big shiver through me. She took my hand, but then the medics intervened, saying we had to travel to the emergency department in separate ambulances.

The quacks who saw me at the hospital said I was dehydrated, but otherwise fine. They ushered me into a cubicle, and cleaned and dressed the cuts on my wrists and ankles. Then they put cream on the powder burns on my face, and inserted a drip in my arm. I woke up an hour later with a nurse removing the line.

When I got to the waiting room, Jean was sitting with three cops who had their noses buried in gossip magazines. She got up, went to the counter, and enquired about Rolfe. He was still being pumped with juice, so we asked the cops for some space, and, staying in their line of sight, took a seat in a quiet corner of outpatients. There I put some flesh on the story of how we'd come to be locked up together.

'We'll say we arranged to meet in Red Hill at eight last night,' I said. 'After you'd finished some interviews up there. And, essentially, the story after that is, I knew nothing about anything. Which is, in fact, the case.'

Jean asked if there'd be an inquiry into Joe's death. I said it was likely there would be, but her actions were clearly justifiable and any hearing would be a formality. I said I'd vouch for her and support her, and I put my arms around her and gave her a long kiss. Then, tired but elated, we headed back into casualty and waited for Rolfe.

When he finally emerged from treatment, we ushered him into Outpatients, where I reminded him of his promise not to write anything about cat fur falling into the wrong hands. Nor about Wright and Proctor dying of carbon monoxide poisoning. He told me I was repeating myself, then asked that I not talk publicly about what we'd endured at Rodway Street — at least for a couple of days. That way, he and Jean would have an exclusive on their own story. I was happy to consent to that, and then I signalled the cops over.

They led us through a labyrinth of corridors to the hospital's loading dock, reckoning it was the only exit not swarming with journos. Even so, when we stepped out onto the dock, a dozen reporters and cameramen rushed us, and we had to push through them to get to the patrol cars that were waiting to take us away.

Rolfe clambered into the front seat of the first patrol car, and I guided Jean into the back seat and closed the door. As they moved off through the shouting journos, Jean turned in her seat, smiled sadly, and fluttered her fingers at me.

When I got back to Rodway Street, McHenry sat me down on a couch in the lounge room and gave me a strong cup of coffee. Then he had me go through how I'd been captured, and the details of our incarceration and our escape. He seemed to accept what I said, even the part about my relationship with Jean. And that bit seemed real.

He asked if I was okay to go back into the carpeted room. I said was fine with it, and really thought I was. But my guts tensed up as I followed him down the corridor. When I stepped back into Joe's death chamber, I felt intensely vulnerable, as though I'd been pitched back into mortal danger.

I thought I was going to throw up. McHenry asked if I wanted to get out. I took a minute to steady myself, and then told him that I just wanted to get on with the job. But, as I detailed our time in the room, I started to doubt what I was saying — as though it was a dream, or only half true. It took the lingering smell of the absent toilet bucket to assure me that it had all actually happened.

When we got back to the lounge room, McHenry called the officer who was overseeing the search of the Beagle Street house. Then he signalled me to follow him through the double-glass doors and out onto the paving. I had a feeling I was in for a bollocking. And I was right.

'So, the boyfriend, are ya?' he said, his smiling eyes drilling into me. 'Well, I'd call it a retrospective relationship at best. A love affair backdated to protect the dim-witted.

'Then again, it must be love, because you sure weren't thinking straight. Breaking every rule in the book. And, by God, you were lucky, son, although it looks like your luck's finally run out. But that's out of my hands, thank God. So go home now, get all the sleep you need, and I'll see you tomorrow. And be prepared for a big day when you get in. Do I make myself clear?'

'Yes, sir,' I said.

And standing outside the house where I'd almost died, I mulled over my prospects. More precisely, I pondered the likely death of my career. But that wasn't McHenry's call. Brady and the mob upstairs would make that decision, and they'd have to sniff the wind before they could work out what to do with me.

Blood Oath subscription news

Wednesday 7 August, 9.30pm

Back from the dead
by Simon Rolfe

Hello. Here I am again. Back from my holiday in hell, still wondering how I survived it. Imagine if you will, a garage barely big enough to house a family sedan. Throw in some mouldy mattresses and a plastic bucket for a toilet, and you've got some idea of where I've just spent what could have been the last days of my life.

I thought we were gone. Jean Acheson and me. And I was prepared for it, dear reader. Resigned to it, even. Thankfully, Detective Sergeant Darren Glass was there with us, and his survival instincts proved to be much more acute than ours.

And Darren, in the tumult, I forgot to thank you for saving us. So now, with every fibre of my being, I thank you.

As for Ms Acheson, her network is planning a telemovie based on our ordeal. I won't be tuning in when it goes to air. The past forty-eight hours were the most horrific of my life. I wouldn't want to relive them.

30

One of the uniforms dropped me back at City Station, and though I was tempted to go straight to the room, I did as McHenry had ordered and got into my car and drove home. The first thing I did when I walked in the door was make myself a big bowl of toasted muesli, which I ate while sitting in a hot bath. Then I got dressed and called Jean.

Even though she'd just got home after being on-air all evening, and sounded tired, she insisted that I come straight over. Her invitation, however, came with a warning. Most of her gallery colleagues were still pursuing us, she said, and now the paparazzi had joined the hunt. Their interest had been sparked by a headline on one of the blogs: 'Love lives in House of Death'.

Jean gave me her address, which I already had, and the number of her apartment. She said that when I came over, I should park under her building. That way, I could mostly escape the shutter hounds who were camped on the nature strip across from her place.

Fifteen minutes later, when I drove into Jean's street, twenty photographers rushed my car, their cameras on rapid fire as they pursued me into the carpark under her building. I parked and ran through the carpark; even so, some of them were just metres behind me as Jean buzzed me through to the lifts.

She looked very sleepy when she opened her door, but she gave me a lingering kiss before taking my hand and leading me into a dimly lit lounge room. We sat on a couch facing a big picture window, and she asked what I'd like to drink.

'I've got beer and Guinness,' she said. 'And there's a chardonnay. Or you can have a tea or a coffee, if you like.'

'I'll go the Guinness,' I said, 'if you're having one.'

She smiled and brushed the back of my hand, and I turned and watched her leave the room. Then I looked the place over. There seemed to be framed photos and intriguing bits and pieces on every flat surface. The northern wall was all glass, with sliding doors that led out onto a balcony crowded with potted plants.

Jean came back with two tall glasses of Guinness, and settled down next to me on the couch. We sipped our drinks in silence, staring out at the lights that dotted the slope up to Red Hill. I desperately wanted to take her in my arms, but then doubt assailed me. What if she'd called me over for a 'Dear John' meeting? Was it possible that she was going to thank me and just say, 'See you around'? No. That made no sense at all, and I knew it.

'I've been thinking about what you said in that room,' she said, running a finger around the rim of her glass. 'About life-threatening situations doing strange things to people. And it's true, it made us very close, very quickly. But the thing is, I thought you were a knockout the first time I saw you. And the second. And the way I feel about you now has nothing to do with gratitude. Or, worse still, hero worship. I really like you, Darren, and even if we'd never been locked up together, I still think we would have ended up like this.'

She leaned in and we kissed. Then we put our drinks aside and wrapped our arms around each other, kissing and withdrawing, looking into each other's eyes, saying nothing. It had been a long time for me, and I was glad to go slowly. But then Jean got up, and, still holding my hand, led me down a corridor and into her bedroom.

We slowly undressed each other, letting our clothes drop

where we stood. Then she pulled me towards her, and we fell onto her bed and coiled together, skin on skin.

I woke up alone in her bed. The dull light breaking through the slit in the curtains told me it was morning. Crockery clinked somewhere down the corridor, and then Jean came in with a tray on which she had a teapot, two cups, and some slices of cake on a plate. She set the tray down next to me on the bed, and then she left again. Minutes later, she returned with the morning newspapers.

Most front pages featured big photos of us leaving the hospital. The accompanying stories cast me as the hero who'd rescued Jean, my new love, from the 'House of Death'. I was also credited with saving the 'hapless' Rolfe. None of them had much information on Joe, other than the fact that he was dead. And they all gave front-page treatment to Brady's reaction. He'd told them I'd been well trained for what I'd confronted at Rodway Street, and that I'd done the AFP proud. So it looked like he was holding fire.

Jean turned on the TV, and we watched a segment about ourselves on one of the morning shows. It included a long clip of her from the Live Cam, and a shot of me hustling her into the patrol car at the hospital. We flipped between networks. Each of them had a different shot of my arrival at her place. And every story was a variation on the theme 'From House of Death to Love Nest'.

'And they're still out there,' said Jean, peeking through the curtains. 'Waiting patiently.'

'And what'll satisfy them?' I said, though I knew the answer.

'We've got two options, really,' she said. 'We could tell our story to one of the networks, preferably mine, but there's no guarantee that would kill the story. It could do the opposite. Or we could give the people down there what they want — us kissing on the stairs outside. That would do it for most of them. The thing is, right at this moment, we're the biggest story in Australia. Bigger than the election. Bigger than the murders, even. So they're not going to give up. Not till they get us.'

'So you're saying we should go down there and pose for them?'

'One kiss and we get our privacy back. Mostly. Otherwise, we'll have to skulk around for weeks. And they'll get us in the end, you know. And when they do, it might have an ugly edge to it. And you and me, we don't need that. Not right now.'

'A kiss at the top of the stairs. Mmm. Well, my instincts say, "Stuff 'em." But then again, I'd kiss you anywhere, under any circumstances. And if it means getting rid of that lot? Let's do it.'

Channel Four Live Cam

Thursday 8 August, 9.30am

Good morning, Jean Acheson here, and with the two major parties running neck-and-neck in the polls, Opposition Leader Lou Feeney went on breakfast television this morning in an attempt to break the deadlock.

A panel of interrogators spent an hour grilling Mr Feeney on his policies, then they canvassed his involvement in the so-called fire-dance affair. The studio audience included a group of Mr Feeney's old schoolmates from Saint Phillip's, and to a man, they backed his claim that the 'rancid' fire dance was no more than a harmless schoolboy ritual.

The opposition leader later detailed a number of other rumours that he says the government is spreading about him, and he attempted to debunk them as well.

Meanwhile, despite the government's surge in the polls, Prime Minister Michael Lansdowne appears to have lost some of his trademark poise on the hustings. He's even been snapping at reporters. Maybe the closeness of the contest is getting to him. Or perhaps the loss of Susan Wright and Alan Proctor is taking a personal toll. This is Jean Acheson. Back with more soon.

31

My colleagues stood and applauded when I walked into the room that morning. I automatically backed away towards the door, but that prompted them to rush me, and pat me on the shoulder and slap my back. 'Well done, Glass,' said one. 'You beauty, Dazza,' said another. Dazza? No one had ever called me that. And I certainly wasn't comfortable having my workmates all over me.

I couldn't help thinking of my reception the week before, when Rolfe had revealed Lansdowne's thoughts on Wright, and quoted me as his source. Everyone had avoided eye-contact with me that morning, as though I was the human incarnation of Sodom and Gomorrah. How things had changed.

Given the pressure of the case, the glad-handing was mercifully brief, and everyone was soon back at their desks, either on the phone or focused on their screens. I got myself a coffee, and looked up the latest log on PROMIS. It turned out to be an upload from Brady's forensic accountants. While I was 'away', they'd scoured Mondrian Bank for anything that linked the prime minister's nephew, Mick Stanton, to the bank's purchase of Dolman Holdings and its youth hostels.

The accountants had had access to all Mondrian files, but they'd found little concerning the Dolman purchase, other than the titles, and no one at the bank knew of any other documents relating to the matter.

I scrolled through the tasks the team had completed as they'd tried to find me. As well as searching my desk and my apartment, they'd spoken to everyone who knew me, which didn't take them long. They'd done the same with Rolfe and Jean. I hesitated before looking at the summary of what they'd found at her place, but letters from old boyfriends were as close to bad as it got, and the latest was more than a year old.

The team had also completed title searches for the Rodway and Beagle Street places. Both of them were in Joe's name. His full name had been Jozef Jankowski. According to Immigration, he'd emigrated from Poland eleven years before as a business migrant. To qualify under the program, he'd deposited half a million dollars into an Australian bank account, which had effectively bought him a passport. The money had stayed put for the required four years, and then he'd withdrawn it.

Efforts to track down Joe's other bank details and his work history had so far come up empty. His prints were all over the painting gear and the landscapes I'd seen at Rodway Street. Interpol was chasing up his relatives in Poland.

Next, I went to the search of the two houses. It had turned up a few old toothbrushes and some dirty plates and cutlery, and the DNA from these was already being analysed. I hadn't exactly searched the Rodway Street place — if I had, no doubt I would have looked under the double bed upstairs and spotted the two briefcases that had been found there.

According to the report, the cases belonged to Wright and Proctor. I saw this find as jaw-droppingly significant, so I was surprised that PROMIS only carried a summary of the cases' contents. All it revealed was that Wright's briefcase contained an exercise book in which she'd listed her achievements in the environment portfolio, and what she saw as her 'future challenges'. From the challenges on the list, it was clear that Wright didn't see a place for Ron Sorby in her future. He'd lost her trust. She wrote that he was 'too close to Lansdowne's people for comfort'.

There was also a parcel of documents in Wright's briefcase. The PROMIS summary simply said that they 'pertained to the Mondrian Affair'. McHenry no doubt had his reasons for applying this nondescript summary to these documents, and I was keen to hear it.

According to the summary for Proctor's briefcase, most of its contents related to the electorate he'd visited just before he went missing. There was also a USB drive on which he'd kept a campaign diary, a contact list of party operatives, and a dirt file on opposition candidates in twenty-four marginal electorates.

The final item listed in the briefcase was a document with the mobile-phone numbers and email addresses of twenty New Zealanders, all of them males. The document also detailed a flight schedule for the men, Auckland to Sydney and return, plus an overnight booking for them at an airport hotel in the harbour city. I was mulling these details over when McHenry came in with a couple of takeaway coffees.

'Back in harness?' he said, placing a cup on my desk.

'Like the workhorse I am,' I said, raising the cup in salute. 'Now, tell me. These briefcases from Joe's house — the summary for them's a bit brief, isn't it? Especially the Mondrian stuff. Is it really *that* sensitive?'

McHenry bent over and put his mouth uncomfortably close to my ear.

'You can have a look, Glass,' he said, in a voice barely above a whisper. 'But a word. Ruth and I are the only ones who've seen it all, and I can tell you, some of it's positively radioactive. So you know what I'm saying. Any leaks, and we'll know who to talk to.'

McHenry had the contents of the briefcases locked in a drawer in his desk. It was where he kept confidential material and any items of evidence that we might need to access during the case. I took the bundle tagged 'Susan Wright' to an empty interview room and locked the door. When I opened the bundle, I understood why the summary had been so brief.

As well as Wright's hand-written assessment of her office, the bag contained a big red box file bearing an Australian coat of arms embossed in gold. It was the file that Wright had nicked from Proctor on the night she disappeared. I opened it very slowly, somehow needing to extend the moment.

The file contained three evidence bags, each of which held a thin set of documents. The bags were stacked on top of each other, and there was a note from Forensics on top of the stack. The note said that the documents, when recovered, had been inside plastic sleeves, and the sleeves had been removed when an impression of a cassette case had been found etched into one of them.

That impression had subsequently been matched to the one on the sleeve that had contained Jean's leaked documents. What had the killers done with the cassette itself? Maybe the documents held the answer. I lifted the three bags out of the box and lined them up on the table.

The document inside the first bag was almost fifteen years old. It was headed 'Share Options Offer', and it informed an unnamed beneficiary that they'd receive 25 per cent of Mondrian Bank's shares in Dolman Holdings once they'd completed an unspecified task. The second bag contained a memorandum of agreement on the Dolman shares. It had been signed about six months after the options offer, and it stipulated that the shares would be signed over to 'Beneficiary A' for the same price that Mondrian had paid for them.

In the third bag was a page from Mondrian's accounts, dated eight months after the introduction of Susan Wright's voucher scheme. This document noted that 'Beneficiary A' had paid the bank four million dollars for an unspecified number of Dolman shares. It wasn't clear if all three documents were talking about the same beneficiary, or the same shares. If they were, the voucher scheme would have boosted the value of those shares from four million dollars to something like sixty million.

These were the documents that the accountants had been looking for when they'd raided Mondrian. So how did Proctor get his hands on them? Maybe Lansdowne's nephew had stolen them from the bank and given them to him. But why would he do that? And why had Proctor shown them to Wright on the night she disappeared? Was it to remind her that she was complicit in some deeper way in the Mondrian affair? Or was it to keep her in line on matters we didn't know about yet? And how did the cassette feature? The only thing we knew for sure was that Wright had been desperate to get her hands on this file. And it also seemed clear that the material it contained had got her and Proctor killed.

McHenry was on the phone when I took the bags back to him. He cupped his hand over the mouthpiece, and handed me a photocopy of Proctor's New Zealand file and asked me to look into it.

I phoned Major Crime in Auckland and spoke to Detective Adam Stowe. Stowe had been following our investigation and was keen to talk about it. I batted his questions away, and asked him to get me everything he could on the Kiwis who had featured in the file.

Then I called Jean. She was in Sydney working on a prime-time special with the network's current-affairs unit. She said it was a 'drippy' little tabloid effort they'd titled 'Canberra: Australia's Capital of Fear'. As well as interviews with Wright and Proctor's relatives, the production team had spoken to the dead pair's friends and staff, including Ron Sorby. Jean said Sorby had become quite emotional when he'd been interviewed.

The thought of him crying on camera had me returning to Susan Wright's assessment of him.

Jean rang off and I got my mind back onto the mystery Kiwis. I called the Sydney hotel where they'd overnighted, and spoke to the duty manager. He agreed to dig out the records of every expense they'd racked up, including their incoming and outgoing phone calls. If anyone had asked me where I thought this effort might lead, I would have told them it was just another loose end from a dead man's briefcase that we needed to tidy up.

I was thinking about another coffee when Ruth Marginson suddenly shot out of her seat. Her eyes were wide with alarm, and her mouth quivered as she struggled to speak.

'C-comms just got a call from the PM's office,' she said, a piece of paper trembling in her hand. 'From Adam Davies. Close Protection. It's unbelievable, but Davies says the prime minister's been taken. Or rather, he's been abducted. And it seems that Penny Lomax is involved.'

Blood Oath subscription news

Thursday 8 August, 1.00pm

Where to start ...?
by Simon Rolfe

What can you say when certainty is gone? Who do you call when the wolf breaks down the door? How do you respond to an awful truth? Where is hope when no one is safe?

Prime Minister Michael Lansdowne was abducted from outside his Parliament House office a bit over thirty minutes ago. They've snatched the one person in this country who should have been secure. The police have scrambled to confront this outrage, and while their commitment should not be questioned, their ability to get to the heart of this evil has been found wanting.

Having experienced what the PM is now going through, I could mouth words of comfort for those who know and love him. But I mustn't lie. If Michael Lansdowne is in the hands of those who killed Susan Wright and Alan Proctor, any assessment of his chances must be tempered by their experience and mine.

This is the dawn of a terrible time for this nation. Let's hope the prime minister is found soon. Safe and well. Let's hope.

32

WHEN YOU'RE RACING to a scene where something truly dire
has happened, your body flips into automatic pilot while your
mind cascades with terrible possibilities. I was speeding down
Commonwealth Avenue, part of a convoy of police vehicles
zeroing in on Parliament House. Cars and buses squeezed into
the outside lanes to get out of our way. Some even jumped the
curb as our lights and sirens bore down on them.

McHenry sat in the front with me; Smeaton and Peter Kemp
from Forensics, in the back. McHenry had already radioed ahead
and spoken to Adam Davies from the PM's close-protection
detail. According to Davies, Lansdowne's car had left the Prime
Minister's Courtyard at about twelve-fifteen. Lansdowne and
Lomax had been in the back seat. A close-protection officer and
the driver had been in the front. As with all road travel involving
the PM, they'd had a security vehicle in tow. Davies said that soon
after they'd set out, Lomax had shot the close-protection officer
in the car with her, and had raised a set of bollards between the
PM's car and the security vehicle. She'd then forced the PM's
driver to speed off into the streets of Forrest. Like all vehicles in
the VIP fleet, the PM's car was fitted with a GPS tracker; it had
been located within minutes, outside the girls' school in Forrest.

From the chatter on the police radio, we knew that the prime
minister's driver and the close-protection officer were still in
the car. The driver was alive, but unconscious. The officer was
dead — a head shot. And Lomax and the PM were gone. It was
assumed she'd transferred him to another vehicle, and all the

suburbs south of Parliament House had been shut down. A big team of cops had already descended on Lomax's apartment in Barton, just in case she'd taken the PM there. If we didn't catch her quickly, her next move was a given.

As I drove, I thought through the contact I'd had with Penny Lomax over the past week. She'd made good eye-contact when we'd interviewed her. Her answers had been crisp and to the point, and she'd seemed relatively at ease. And when we'd caught her out, apparently protecting Janet Wilson, she'd confessed without dissolving. At the time, I'd put her equilibrium down to strength of character. I now knew that the stakes for her had been much higher than mere pride.

So had there been any warning signs, other than the Wilson business — some indication of what Lomax was capable of? We'd checked all the calls on her work-supplied mobile. She hadn't used it in the toilet after her huddle with Wilson at the party, so she must have had a dedicated mobile for contacting Joe. And bizarrely, in that first interview, she'd volunteered the fact that she didn't own a cat. Had she been making a reference to her agenda? Even having fun at our expense? Maybe, but we couldn't have taken it any further at the time.

Lomax had played the part of the loyal underling — a woman devoted to the interests of her boss. I was pretty good at detecting bullshit, but she'd totally fooled me. So was she that good, or had my instincts gone to mush? This thought brought on a surge of self-doubt. It was lead in my veins, and then it lodged in my guts. Again, I had to fight to retain focus.

We couldn't automatically assume that the PM's abduction was connected to the Wright and Proctor murders, but a connection was likely. Which meant that, if the same mob had been responsible for all three crimes, their original plan would have been to take Lansdowne back to Rodway Street. I'd spoiled that for them, so where would Lomax take him now? And what was her endgame? Did she have more surprises in store? With Joe out of the picture, was she operating alone, or was there a third party involved? Well, alone or not, in snatching the PM, Lomax had engineered an almost impossible heist.

A clutch of motorcycle cops had strung their machines across the ramp that led up to the House. Our convoy slowed, we killed our lights and sirens, and the cops unblocked the road and waved us through. At the top of the ramp, we wound our way around to the Senate side of the building and headed for the ministerial entrance at the back. Staffers in suits mingled with kitchen hands and gardeners on the footpath, all of them watching the choppers that clattered over the nearby suburbs. Other workers huddled in groups on the sloping lawns. Some cried. Others gave comfort.

When we turned the corner at the back of the building, we saw the close-protection vehicle that Davies had told us about. The front end of the big Fairlane sat up on a line of raised bollards like some sort of retro-rocketship ready for take-off. None of us said a word as we drove by, but the sight of that car, pointed at the sky, underlined the audacity of this crime.

The vehicles ahead of us turned onto Melbourne Avenue to join the search, while I took the road up to the ministerial entrance. A young woman in House livery stood beside the raised bollards at the top of the road. After she checked our ID, she took a small two-way from her belt and gave the okay. The bollards descended into the blacktop.

I parked, and then we followed our escort into the foyer of the ministerial entrance, where she signed us in before leading us down a short corridor that opened out onto a huge courtyard paved with polished granite. Ahead of us were two massive doors made of copper and glass. One of the doors opened from the inside as we approached, and a security guard stepped out and ushered us into a reception hall where Davies was waiting for us.

Our escort took Kemp around to Lomax's office, while Davies led the rest of us to a small lounge room where three blokes sat waiting on plush leather chairs. They all jumped to their feet when we came in, and Davies did the introductions.

Jim Feathers and Tom Edwards had been in the accompanying security vehicle when the PM was taken. They both made reasonable eye-contact when we shook hands, but their faces were ghostly white and Edwards' jaw tremored uncontrollably. Having worked close-protection myself, I had some idea of what these guys were going through. Then again, I'd never lost anyone, so my sense of their distress probably didn't come close.

The third guy in the room was Lansdowne's chief of staff, James Filandia. He looked more impatient than traumatised, as though he had somewhere more important to be. Davies closed the door, and, once we were all seated in a circle, McHenry set up his recorder and gave me the nod. But before I could open my mouth, the door swung open again and a severe-looking chap in a sharp suit walked in. Davies introduced the newcomer as Cliff Bolton from the Security Co-ordination Centre. The Centre was a highly secretive organisation buried deep in Attorney-General's. It handled mega-policing issues such as national security assessments, counter-terrorism, and VIP protection.

Davies didn't give us Bolton's rank, or any other designation he might own. And Bolton looked us over and simply said, 'Afternoon, gentlemen.' Then he sat down next to me and took out a palm-sized pad and began making notes. I glanced at McHenry. He was eyeing Bolton with undisguised contempt, which surprised me a bit. Did these two know each other? If they did, there hadn't been any sign of it when Bolton had first entered the room. What was going on here?

Then the penny dropped. It wasn't Bolton as such who was

rankling McHenry. It was the fact that the Centre had chosen to crash our interview. They had access to PROMIS, and they would have been following our progress very closely. So the fact that Bolton was here in person could mean only one thing: the Centre was about to 'get involved' in the investigation.

This realisation stunned me momentarily, but at another level it came as no surprise. The case had escalated into a national emergency, and the Centre's search-and-seizure powers allowed it to do things that we couldn't. I looked at McHenry again. He was staring forlornly at the empty tabletop in front of him. I cleared my throat, he looked up, and I gave him a quizzical look. He answered with a resigned nod of his head, so I checked that his recorder was still rolling, and then got on with it.

'Officer Feathers, Officer Edwards,' I said. 'I understand you may have lost a close colleague during this abduction. So, first, can I offer our sympathies.'

Feathers looked up and nodded, his bottom lip quivering as he fought for control. Edwards glanced at his colleague, and then dropped his head and worked to control his own emotions.

'Officer Feathers,' I said, 'can you tell us where the prime minister was going when he was abducted, and why Penny Lomax was with him at the time?'

'We were taking him to the mosque in Yarralumla,' said Feathers, his teeth clenched so tightly that I could hear them grind as he spoke. 'The PM was meeting Sheik Khalid el Sheik. It was something Lomax had organised.'

He emphasised the first syllable of her name, as though he was describing her as much as naming her.

'The grand mufti,' I said, turning to Filandia. 'And what was the purpose of this meeting?'

'The sheik is very influential in his community,' said Filandia, choosing his words carefully. 'And his community tends to vote as a bloc. We'd prepared an endorsement from the sheik which we wanted him to run in the media that services his ahh … his people.'

'And in return?'

'We … ahh … we were willing to look favourably on a cultural centre he wants built in Lakemba,' he said.

Filandia grimaced as he spoke, as though this forced disclosure caused him real pain. Bolton lifted his head from his notebook. He looked as if he was about to ask a question, but he went back to his scribbles instead. I turned to Feathers again.

'So, tell us about the lead-up to the abduction,' I said. 'How did it play out?'

'We got the cars up to the courtyard at about noon,' said Feathers. 'Ray was riding up front in C1, and Tom and I were in the security vehicle behind. Once we were set, I went and waited outside the PM's door. A few minutes after that, Lomax came around from the staff offices and went into the PM.'

'Did she have anything with her?'

'Nothing unusual. Briefing notes. And her handbag. It's medium-sized. Black leather.'

'And was the bag in her hand, or over her shoulder?'

'It was on her shoulder. And she had the notes in her hand.'

'Did you hear anything after she went in?'

'No. And I wouldn't expect to. The PM's office is pretty much sound-proofed. But there's six panic buttons in there, and he didn't touch any of them, so I don't think anything was going on at that stage.'

'Did Lomax know about the buttons?' said McHenry.

'I guess so,' said Feathers. 'Everyone in here knows about them, but only a few of us know where they are.'

'So how long were the two of them in there?' I said.

'They came out at about twelve-ten. So, ten minutes at most.'

'Any "tells" from the PM as he walked out?'

'No, nothing. His was to tug his right ear lobe, and he only ever used it once that I know of, and that was a complete disaster. A mozzie bit his ear while he was talking to some senior Yank in the garden over at The Lodge. He gave the bite a bit of a rub, and we all piled onto the Yank. Spear-tackled him, actually. Almost caused an international incident, but the bloke wasn't hurt, so they kept it quiet.'

It was the wrong time for such a tale, but I figured it might help Feathers to tell it. And that's how it seemed, at least until he'd finished talking. Then he looked at me, and, as he waited for the next question, his neck went red, and then it bulged as the pressure built up inside him again.

'So there was no tell,' I said, nodding. 'And when Lomax came out, did she still have the bag on her shoulder? And the notes in her hand?'

'The bag was on her shoulder. The notes had gone. And her hands were in her pockets. The PM was to her left, walking slightly ahead of her. I guess we know why now. They both went through the foyer. I opened the door to the courtyard. They got into the car and it drove off. And we followed.'

'Was there anything strange or unusual about the way all this happened?'

'It was all pretty much a standard exit. Until we got down to the bollards, of course. Then everything turned to shit.'

Channel Four Live Cam

Thursday 8 August, 2.00pm

Good afternoon, Jean Acheson here. Back in Canberra for what must rate as one of the most dramatic and tragic days in the life of our nation.

A little over an hour ago, Governor-General Mark Bradley signed a Minute from the Executive Council appointing Malcolm Redding as Australia's acting prime minister.

Mr Redding's jet is due to touch down in Canberra in twenty minutes. Once he's on the ground, he'll be taken to a security bunker under Parliament House where he'll be sworn in. Then senior police and security personnel will brief him and his advisors on the fate of Prime Minister Michael Lansdowne.

I understand Mr Redding will remain in his bunker until the parliamentary triangle has been assessed for any threat to him and his team. And in news just in, Governor-General Bradley has signed another Minute which effectively puts the army onto the streets of Canberra. The army's orders, and here I quote from the Minute, are to 'safeguard the national interests of the Commonwealth of Australia from criminal activities and related violence.' This is Jean Acheson. Back with more in a moment.

33

LEAFLESS WISTERIA SNAKED in and over the two massive gazebos that ran the length of the Prime Minister's Courtyard. The clouds had descended during our time inside, and the temperature had dropped to single figures. McHenry turned his back on the metal-and-glass doors, and lifted his hands to indicate the space directly in front of him.

'So, the cars stopped here,' he said, puffs of mist coming from his mouth.

'That's right,' said Feathers, buttoning his jacket. 'Close to the doors, as always. And the PM and Lomax came outside, and, oh … there was something.'

Feathers' eyes narrowed, then he grimaced and let out a sigh.

'The PM usually rode up front with Harry,' he said, picturing the scene. 'But occasionally he liked to sit in the back. Well, today, he went to the back door, so I opened it for him, and when he got in, he shuffled across the seat so that Lomax could get in after him.'

'What's the problem with that?' said McHenry.

'A staffer would normally go to the other side of the vehicle to get in,' said Feathers. 'You know, to save the boss having to shuffle across like that.'

'I assume she didn't have both her hands in her pockets at this stage,' I said.

'No. She had her BlackBerry out, but I'm sure her right hand was still in her pocket.'

'A BlackBerry? Was she using it in any way that you could

see? Making a call, or texting or something?'

'No. It was just in her hand.'

'And her other hand was in her pocket? You're sure of that?'

'Yes. And once she got into the car, she sort of swung around in the seat and faced the prime minister. To keep him covered, I guess.'

'So, once everyone was in their cars and you were ready to go, what happened then?' said McHenry, nodding at Feathers.

'Well, the PM's car moved off,' he said. 'And we followed. The guys on the gates opened up. And we drove down the hill towards the bollards.'

'Let's follow your route, then,' said McHenry, tilting his head at the massive wrought-iron gates that dominated the far end of the courtyard.

He led us across the courtyard, through the warm foyer of the ministerial entrance, and out into the cold again. We marched down the hill to where Feathers' Fairlane sat stranded up on the bollards.

'So this is where we ended up,' said Feathers, running his hand over the bonnet of the vehicle. 'High and dry.'

'How'd she do it?' said McHenry, cupping a hand over the top of his tape machine so that the breeze wouldn't blow holes in his recording.

'It was all too easy, really,' said Feathers. 'The security office usually controls the bollards, but the PM's car carries a remote. It's the only one, and it overrides everything else. We were coming down the hill here, behind C1, and we heard a pop. Just one, but it was a firearm, for sure. I tried Ray on the two-way, but he didn't respond. And they were still moving, so I got bumper-to-bumper with them. And then they stopped, suddenly — about a metre past these bollards. That put us on top of the things. And that's when they went up.'

'And while you were being hoisted, what did you do?'

'Tom tried the immobiliser on C1, and I jumped out, but they'd already taken off.'

'So the immobiliser failed?' said McHenry.

'Correct,' said Feathers. 'She must have got at that, too.'

'And, of course, there was no point putting a few rounds into the tyres,' I said, knowing that there wasn't.

'Nup. The whole fleet's got run-flat tyres. I could've filled 'em with lead, and it wouldn't have made any difference.'

'And did you get a good look at the PM?' I said. 'As they were driving off?'

'Yes, I did,' said Feathers, his voice cracking slightly. 'He swung round and looked at me just as the car took the corner down there. And, you know, I've seen plenty of him up-close over the years, and he's always been calm and confident. Projecting his aura. Well, there today, he looked completely flummoxed. No surprise in that, though, I suppose.'

'And you're *sure* it was Lomax orchestrating things?' said McHenry, eyeing Feathers with mild disbelief.

'Who else could it have been?' he said. 'Ray was slumped against the window, covered in blood. And Harry was driving.'

'Why not Harry?' I said. 'What makes you so sure he wasn't in on it?'

'Harry? No way. I mean, I didn't get a good look at him, but as they went around the corner, Lomax was right forward in her seat, screaming at him.'

The late-afternoon sky had greyed out to the horizon, and the moisture in the air had put a sheen on all our faces. I was suddenly hit by the immensity of what had happened here, and I momentarily struggled for a follow-up question.

'So, the car went down the ramp and off the Hill,' said McHenry, taking up the slack. 'And, Officer Feathers, you pursued on foot. Let's go over there now, and you can tell us what you saw.'

The ramp was a nameless two-lane road that arced off the Hill to an intersection and a set of lights. After the lights it became Melbourne Avenue, with two pairs of double lanes separated by a wide median strip full of mature eucalypts. The overhanging trees obscured the upper reaches of the road, as well as the school where Lomax had abandoned the PM's car.

'We had a green-light corridor all the way to the mosque,' said Feathers, pointing to the traffic lights now flashing amber, 'so those ones down there were green. And by the time I got here, the car was through them and barreling up the hill. I lost them when they went over the first rise, and only got a glimpse when they came up over the second one, and then the trees got in the way and they were gone.'

'And how long before someone gave chase?' I said.

'We had three cars and half-a-dozen bicycle cops here in a minute,' said Feathers. 'And they shot up that road like there was no tomorrow, but it was too late by then.'

McHenry nodded, turned off his tape, and we followed him up a steep flight of stairs and back to the prime minister's office. Once we were settled in the little lounge room again, he put his machine back on record and turned to Filandia.

'Lomax would have gone through a security check when she came to work here,' he said, 'so I assume your people discovered nothing adverse about her?'

'That's right,' said Filandia. 'And Senator Chalmers recommended her, so that would have carried a lot of weight with whoever did the check. Admin's digging out her file. We'll shoot it down to you as soon as we get it, but it's ancient history, isn't it?'

'How would you describe Lomax?' said McHenry, ignoring his rhetorical question.

Filandia slid forward in his seat, thinking through his reply. As chief of staff, he was ultimately responsible for everyone in the office, so maybe he feared that some of the blame for what had happened would attach to him. Or maybe he knew less about Lomax than he should have, and dreaded looking like a goose when his ignorance was exposed.

'I came to work for Mr Lansdowne eight years ago,' he said, measuring every word. 'When he had Communications. Lomax came in about a year after that. And, you know, she was extremely intelligent, and she had skills that were in demand …'

'We want to hear about her skills,' said McHenry. 'But, first, tell us about Penny Lomax the person.'

'Well, people who work here are generally judged by what they do. And she was good at her job and generous with her time — no matter who was after it. She wasn't one for small talk. Or superfluous talk of any sort, really. But she was attractive and easy to have around. So she was liked, and she helped people when they needed it. And she always seemed happy somehow.'

'And what about her skills?' said McHenry.

'Well, she knew computers. Better than most of the IT guys. If you had a problem, she was nearly always the one to fix it. And she had a memory for process, which is a valued talent in an office like ours. Then, three years ago, after Mr Lansdowne became PM, Alan Proctor joined us, and he asked if she could help with his files.'

'And I assume her work for Proctor allowed Lomax to get close to the PM,' said Bolton, his pen poised over his notebook.

It was Bolton's first intervention, and everyone looked at him, as if the question were alive with meaning. Filandia opened his mouth to answer, and then closed it again. He'd had something on the tip of his tongue, but he'd swallowed it like an accused person under pressure.

'Alan developed the campaign strategy,' he said, finally. 'And despite what we know about her now, Penny Lomax was his able assistant in that effort. She was a woman on the rise because Alan Proctor valued her. He paved the way for her to attend key meetings. And whenever the PM had a question at those meetings, she always seemed to have the answer at her fingertips. Alan still kept most of his material to himself, of course, but he regarded Lomax as his disciple, and I've no doubt he was grooming her for a seat. So, did her relationship with Alan allow her to get close to the PM? You'd have to say it did. For a start, she picked up most of Alan's early mornings, after he, ahh, after he passed away.'

'Early mornings?' I said. 'What are they?'

'When the PM's in Canberra,' said Filandia, 'early mornings are exactly that. It's a job for the senior people in the office, and when it's your turn, you get in here at about six, and put together cuttings and cables for the PM, as well as any alerts he should read. And then Harry takes you down to the Lodge. Sometimes you have breakfast with the PM. And when he's ready, you drive back here with him in C1.'

Before I could ask a follow-up question, there was an urgent knock at the door and Peter Kemp stepped into the room, his face as pale as his disposable overalls.

'Sorry to interrupt, inspector,' he said, 'But there's something in the staff offices I think you should see.'

McHenry's eyes narrowed as he assessed Kemp for a moment, then he got to his feet and said that only Bolton and I should accompany him so as to minimise traffic through the crime scene. The three of us followed Kemp through reception and down a corridor to a large room full of work stations. The southern wall of the room was dominated by a bank of windows that looked out onto the Prime Minister's Courtyard. The other three walls were lined with small private offices. Kemp led us past a crush of desks, and into an office that had a frosted-glass frontage and Penny Lomax's name on the door.

Two of Kemp's men were kneeling on the floor beside Lomax's desk. One of them gently buffed the carpet with a wide brush, forcing fluff and some grit into a dust pan. The other held a small vacuum cleaner, ready to suck up anything that remained in the carpet pile. A line of heavy steel cabinets stood open along the back wall, exposing files and red boxes of various sizes.

'I profiled some of the material we got from deep in this carpet,' said Kemp, patting a small machine that he had set up on the desk, 'And that material reads as a high explosive — TNT, to be precise. We'll confirm it back at the lab, but I'd say it's industrial grade. And it's spotted all around here. But that's not …'

'TNT?' said McHenry, talking over him. 'Are you sure?'

'The reading's about 98 per cent accurate, sir,' said Kemp, showing a hint of irritation. 'I *could* give a more definitive answer, but I don't have a lighter on me. Anyway, it wasn't the powder I brought you around here to see. It was these.'

He reached into his kit and carefully removed a couple of evidence bags. One bag contained a length of three-centimetre PVC piping. A few nails rattled around inside the other bag.

'This stuff was loose on the floor in the middle cabinet,' he said.

'So why's some piping and a few nails of interest?' said McHenry, transfixed by the bags that Kemp was swinging in front of our eyes.

'Given the quantity of residue we've collected,' said Kemp. 'I'd say someone's been handling a fair amount of explosives in here. This pipe and these nails are presumably part of the same effort. And what do you get if you put explosives, PVC pipe, and a good number of nails together? Pipe bombs are one possibility. But then, how would a pipe bomb or two advance things for Lomax? I don't think they would. No, I think these components are leftovers from something far more complicated and much more lethal than simple pipe bombs. A step up, in fact.'

'And that would be?' I said, dreading the answer.

'A step up from pipe bombs?' said Kemp, eyeballing me over the top of the evidence bags. 'That would be a suicide vest, wouldn't it?'

Channel Four Live Cam

Thursday 8 August, 4.45pm

Good afternoon, Jean Acheson here, and following the shock abduction of Prime Minister Michael Lansdowne, Canberra is getting its first taste of life under a State of Emergency.

All parliamentary staffers and press gallery workers are being cleared from Parliament House, while Acting Prime Minister Redding meets his cabinet in a bunker below the building. The abduction is the only item on the agenda.

From my vantage point up here on Red Hill, I can see some of the hundreds of fully armed troops who will soon be on active patrol in the parliamentary triangle. All access to the Hill has been blocked, and an army command post is being set up on the sports field just below the Senate side door.

Meanwhile, we're yet to hear whether Saturday's election will proceed without the prime minister. We'll let you know as soon as we're told. This is Jean Acheson.

34

Kemp's vest theory accounted for both the residue in Lomax's office and the BlackBerry in her hand when she got into the PM's car. Sure, she might have had the BlackBerry out to call an accomplice; but if Kemp was right, that phone had a much more sinister purpose.

McHenry led us back to the lounge room without comment. Davies was pocketing his mobile as we re-entered the room. The PM's driver was still unconscious, he said, and the doctors who were tending him had no idea when he'd come to. McHenry shook his head and asked me to resume the interview.

'So what about the school where they left the car?' I said, directing this question at Davies. 'Did anyone up there see the transfer to the getaway vehicle?'

'The school's got an athletics carnival off-site today,' said Davies. 'So the place was deserted.'

McHenry raised his hand and called Ruth Marginson. He told her to organise an immediate door-to-door in the streets around the school, and to get some of our people over to Harry's bedside for when he regained consciousness.

'Okay,' he said, closing his phone. 'Continue.'

'Mr Filandia,' I said, 'the office out the back with Lomax's name on the door — was it for her use exclusively?'

'Yes, it was,' he said.

'Did she work with the door closed?'

'Yes. Usually. She even locked it sometimes. But Proctor did as well, and it was a reasonable thing to do, given the nature of the material they worked with.'

So she'd had privacy, a place to store contraband, and somewhere to turn it into who knew what. But how did she get the explosives and the gun past House security?

'Back to these early mornings at The Lodge,' I said. 'What are the security arrangements for the staffers who do them?'

'It's like I told you,' said Filandia. 'Harry takes you down to The Lodge. The Protective Services people there check your ID, and in you go.'

'Do they put your stuff through a scanner, or search your bags?'

'They all know us very well,' he said, 'so things aren't that stringent. But let me tell you, there's no way Penny Lomax got a gun into this building via The Lodge. Just think about it — the sequence involved in early mornings. When it was her turn, Lomax would have come in here first to put a folder together for the PM, and she had to go through House security to do that. Then she would have gone down to The Lodge with Harry, and she would have stayed inside the walls down there till the PM was ready to bring her back. She therefore had no opportunity to smuggle anything illicit in here, believe you me.'

'Mr Filandia, there are only two ways you can get into this place without going through a metal detector. You either get yourself elected prime minister so that you're driven straight past security and into that courtyard out there. Or you join the PM's staff, and you drive in here with him.'

Filandia shook his head and his eyes narrowed. He was getting impatient with me and my line of questioning, and he didn't mind showing it.

'She travelled from Parliament House to The Lodge and back to Parliament House,' he said. 'It's a closed loop, and it can't be compromised in the way you're suggesting.'

Filandia's unyielding defence of House security had me

mystified, but I was finished with him for now. I nodded at McHenry, and he thanked everyone and told them that we'd call if we had more questions.

Bolton remained in his seat while the Parliament House people shuffled from the room. Before the door could close behind them, a big guy poked his head in and gave McHenry, Smeaton, and me the once-over. Bolton nodded at the interloper, and he disappeared. Then Bolton stood up and smiled down at McHenry.

'Thanks for letting me sit in, assistant commissioner,' he said, pocketing his notebook and pen. 'And thanks for your insights. As you've probably guessed, the Centre's about to become much more involved in this investigation, and that'll start with a city-wide lockdown. Then we'll search every room in every house and building in Canberra until we find the PM. And when he's found, if he's wearing a vest, we'll deal with it. There are ways, as you know. So, thanks again.'

After the door had closed behind Bolton, McHenry waited a few seconds and then let out a frustrated growl.

'His mob might have the muscle and the manpower,' he said. 'But if they're sidelining us, they'd best start organising Lansdowne's funeral.'

He got up and stamped out of the room, and Smeaton and I waited a few seconds before we headed off after him. On the way over to Lomax's apartment, I called Marginson to ask who she'd sent to Harry's bedside. Then I got onto the detective doing the job, and told him about the gun and the other contraband that Lomax had smuggled into Parliament House. I also explained how early mornings at The Lodge worked. Finally, I said that Filandia might be right. It might be a closed loop; but if Harry had made any diversions while driving Lomax on 'early mornings', we needed the details from him as soon as he woke up.

If Lomax had found a way to get contraband past House security, she could easily have got the components for a simple vest into the place in one go. A mobile phone wired to a detonator. Some explosives. A few short lengths of PVC pipe. Some nails to maximise the impact of the blast. And the vest itself.

Once she'd smuggled the components inside, assembling the vest would have been easy, especially since she had complete privacy. She would have attached a mobile phone to the detonator, wired it up to the explosives, and then packed it all into the vest. A call to the mobile would send a charge to the detonator. And she could blow the vest from anywhere in the world. As long as the mobile had decent coverage.

'So, boss,' I said, as I swung the car into Brisbane Avenue, 'what do you think of Kemp's vest theory?'

'Not much,' said McHenry. 'Yes, there are traces of explosive in Lomax's office, but she could have got them on her shoes at any mine site in the country. And these pollies and their people visit plenty of those places. And if Kemp went through my garden shed, I'm sure he'd come up with a similar theory about me — I've got fertiliser in there, and fuel for the mower. Combine them the right way, and you could blow anything up. And answer me this. Why would Lomax bother with a vest when she'd already smuggled a gun into the House?'

'Why would she bother?' I said. 'Well, assuming she *has* a vest, I think we can safely say that the PM would now be wearing it. She would have forced him into it just before they left his office, to ensure he was compliant. Why bother? Well, if we back her into a corner, it allows her to kill him with certainty. Or she can use the threat of it for her ticket out.'

McHenry responded with a growl, and we completed the drive in silence.

Lomax's place was in a block of units in Blackall Street, overlooking the lake. We took the lift to the third floor, where a guy from Forensics handed each of us a pair of white plastic overalls and overshoes. When we were togged up, we were ushered down a short entrance hall and into Lomax's lounge room.

The unit looked a bit more lived in than Joe's places in Yarralumla and Red Hill. A couple of spindly chairs bookended an old wooden table. A small television sat on the floor in the corner. And five of Joe's landscapes hung on the walls. They included a vista of the Tinderrys, Lake George full of water, and the Alps under a dusting of snow.

The place had three bedrooms, but only one of them showed any sign of occupation. It was where Lomax had slept when she'd overnighted here. Her bed was a mattress on the floor, neatly made up with a matching pillowslip, undersheet, and doona cover.

The room also had a makeshift wardrobe: a broomstick suspended from the ceiling by a couple of pieces of thick plastic twine. Half-a-dozen conservative suits hung from the broomstick, along with double that number of identical white blouses.

There'd been nothing in the kitchen cupboards, except some plates and a few coffee mugs. There were no cans of food, and no rotting onions or sprouting potatoes. And no spices, either. Usually, an otherwise empty kitchen had salt and pepper dispensers sitting next to the stove. But not this one. Like Joe's places, Lomax's unit was little more than a crash pad. We'd do a title search, but I didn't expect it to reveal anything other than the date she'd bought it and who she'd bought it from.

Then it occurred to me that the killers' other places had all been doss houses like this one. Maybe there was somewhere else that Lomax called home. And in that place, maybe she'd prepared a room fit for a prime minister.

When I emerged from the unit, McHenry and Smeaton were already out of their protective gear, and the boss was itching to leave.

'Let's go,' he said.

I peeled out of the overalls and overshoes, and just managed to squeeze into the lift as the doors closed.

'Is the photo for the door-to-door here yet?' said McHenry, hitting the button for the ground floor.

'Yep,' said Smeaton. 'But none of the residents they've shown it to have ever seen her. Makes you wonder what happened to all those old biddies who used to sit by the window all day watching the world go by.'

'They're on the internet as we speak,' said McHenry. 'Stalking each other in some porno chatroom.'

Smeaton and I managed a smile, but not even a joke from the boss could extract a laugh.

On the way back to the station, McHenry turned on the car radio for the seven o'clock news. It naturally led with the abduction and the State of Emergency. Next story up was Redding's swearing-in as caretaker prime minister. They used a grab of him warning Canberrans about random and repeated searches in coming days. Asked about Saturday's election, Redding said Lansdowne would have wanted it to go ahead, and so it would. There was nothing in the bulletin about any new role for the Centre in the investigation.

When we got back to the station, McHenry postponed a scheduled team meeting, saying it was best we talk in the morning when we had everything in from Forensics. While that sounded like a reprieve, it was anything but, and we all grabbed coffees and dug in for the night.

I had work numbers for the three most senior people in the Titles Office, but no after-hours contacts. I eventually found a home number for one of them, and she agreed to go back to work and look up the title for the Blackall Street unit.

I reviewed the transcript of the Feathers and Filandia interviews, but found nothing new. There was also a transcript of an interview with Sheik Khalid el Sheik up on PROMIS, but there was no more in it than what Filandia had told us. In other words, the contact between the PM and the Sheik would have benefited both men, had it happened.

Jean called just before eleven to see how I was getting on. We were flat out, I said, and we'd be at it all night. She was about to do her last cross, and then she was going home to get some sleep. I told her I'd call her in the morning.

All the news programs throughout the night followed the abduction story. Every time I glanced up at the silent TV in the corner, it featured another scene from the emergency gripping Canberra and the nation. There were wide shots of heavily armed troops manning the roadblocks that ringed the capital, and over-the-shoulder shots of officers from the Centre knocking on doors and talking to residents. There was also extensive coverage of the thousands of all-night vigils that had sprung up spontaneously in towns and cities across the country, with everyone praying for the prime minister's deliverance. And there was footage of bewildered-looking people being bundled into unmarked vans. Most of the detainees were either crims with a history of violence, fruitloops, or serial complainers. If the Centre didn't get a breakthrough from that lot, I expected them to round up the greenies next, and any other fringe politicos with an axe to grind.

Just before four, McHenry called me over to say that he'd spoken to the pysch — the one we'd lined up to assess Tom Hanley. She'd confirmed that she'd be out at Lake George at three o'clock that afternoon. McHenry said he'd decided to send Smeaton out to meet her. He then swiveled in his chair and re-focused on his screen. I waited a moment, expecting him to say something about the arrests we'd been witnessing on TV all night, but he waved me away. I headed off for a few hours' sleep, knowing that the investigation would probably be out of our hands by the time I woke up.

Blood Oath subscription news

Friday 9 August, 7.45am

The price of saving Prime Minister Lansdowne
by Simon Rolfe

Coming home from work last night, did you spend an hour or more sitting in your car at an army checkpoint? I did. If you got home okay, were you stopped by people in khaki when you went out for the evening? Or maybe they knocked on your door after midnight and had a quick look around. They only spent twenty minutes at my place, but the experience cost me four hours sleep.

We all want to find Michael Lansdowne. And we want to get our hands on Penny Lomax, too. But I'm wondering if this State of Emergency and the consequent roll out of troops across Canberra is helping or hurting that effort.

Yes, I know what Mr Redding says. The AFP used all of its powers and yet it failed to get to the heart of this widening conspiracy. And time is tight, and cracking this thing may require a heavy hand.

What I'd say to Mr Redding is this. The people of Canberra are feeling very insecure in the wake of these murders and abductions. They're also very angry with the perpetrators. Combine anger and insecurity, and what do you get? Hysteria, of course, and the symptoms of it are everywhere in this town. The cops saw more rage on our roads last night than they'd usually encounter in a month. Hospitals are reporting a dramatic spike in drug ODs. And Lifelink's phone system went into meltdown this morning. So, Mr Redding, as you consider your next move, please be mindful of the impact it'll have out here in Australia-land.

35

EVERYONE WAS GLUED to the TV when I entered the room early next morning. Justice Minister Simon Black was on some news program. The caption at the bottom of the screen said it all: 'Lansdowne Abduction: Centre takes charge.'

Black was being asked if the decision represented a vote of no confidence in the Australian Federal Police. No, he said, the AFP enjoyed his full confidence, and they'd still be working on the case. So why hand the investigation over to the Centre, asked his interrogator. Because the abduction of the prime minister threatened the security of the nation, said the minister, and national security was the province of the Centre, especially given its experience in large-scale logistics. The last part of his response could mean only one thing. Black had approved Bolton's plan for a blanket search of the city — to enter every house and building, and to interrogate every citizen.

When the interview ended, Smeaton came over and gave me the latest. Bolton had established a Major Incident Room over at the Centre's Northbourne Avenue offices, he said. And Brady had agreed to the AFP handling any overflow, and for us to assist Bolton's people as required. So that was it — we'd been officially sidelined. It was a bastard of a decision, but fully expected. I clapped Smeaton on the shoulder and headed out to the kitchen for a coffee.

When I returned, I ignored all the huddles that had formed around the room and headed straight to my desk. We'd have plenty of time for post-mortems and hand-wringing once we'd been reassigned. Until then, I intended to stay focused on the case. I grabbed a bunch of newspapers and flipped through them while I drank my coffee. They'd all thrown the kitchen sink at the story, with wrap-around editions and special supplements detailing the abduction. 'The crime of the century' they were calling it, and most front pages featured the same smiling photo of Penny Lomax.

Other pictures featured uniformed cops from Victoria manning a checkpoint in the city centre. Another had a flight of army choppers taking off from Ainslie Oval. And there was an aerial shot of the Hume Highway with a massive convoy of police vehicles heading south towards Canberra.

Lomax's boltholes had all been close to Parliament House, so leads mentioning the inner south were being pursued with maximum vigour. I was reading about a raid in Forrest when a call came through on my desk phone. It was Adam Stowe from Major Crime in Auckland. He sounded like he was bursting with big news — which, as it turned out, he was.

'When I looked at the names you sent,' he said, 'the link between them jumped straight out at me. They're all Special Brethren, and by the looks of it they were up to something very curious over your way.'

'Just a minute will you, Adam,' I said, and I cupped my hand over the receiver.

The thing was, I knew I should be transferring Stowe straight to the Centre, yet that didn't seem right somehow. I'd asked him for this information, so why shouldn't I take his call? I could transfer him to the Centre if it seemed warranted.

'Okay, mate,' I said. 'What have you got?'

'Well, after I got your list,' said Stowe, 'I contacted the local Brethren, and as expected they claimed ignorance of any jaunts to Sydney involving their people. But, as luck would have it, I've got this nephew who's been seeing a Brethren girl. On the sly, of course. So I got him to raise it with her, discreetly like. And he came back with a very interesting tale.

'It seems the girl's brother and twenty other young Brethren men flew to Sydney on the date you mentioned. They spent a day at a hotel near the airport, and, while they were there, they learned a spiel from some spiv, and got fitted out in new suits. Early next morning, they were split into pairs, and each pair flew to one of your state capitals.'

'And what were they up to?' I said, completely gripped by the yarn, but expecting a letdown somewhere before the end.

'Each of the pairs had been given a list of major office buildings they had to visit. Their job was to go into those buildings first thing in the morning, get into a lift full of people, and go through the spiel they'd been taught in Sydney.'

'And that was?'

'Ohh, very nasty stuff. Essentially, they had to pretend they were having a chat, and one of them would tell the other that your leader of the opposition over there, Mr Feeney, was a paedophile, that he was involved in sexual stuff with little boys during his school days — something about a dance he'd done in front of them — and that he wasn't fit to run Australia.'

I thanked Stowe for his good work, and, after he gave me contact details for his nephew, I transferred him to a liaison officer over at the Centre. Then I thought through the implications of his story. Essentially, it was confirmation that Proctor had hatched the paedophile rumour against Feeney. He'd had the authority, the ruthlessness, and the necessary dirt to get it off the ground. And he'd had the list of Brethren members in his briefcase, of course.

However, there was one other possible rumour-monger in the mix — Penny Lomax. What if the 'Fire Dance' had been her little project? If Proctor *had* given it to her to manage, she would have kept a file on it. He would have insisted that she did. The thing was, if she had managed that file, she would have been working on it at around the same time that she and Joe were planning their crime spree. In which case, that file might contain more than just the government's attempts to brand Feeney a kiddy fiddler. Not that Lomax would have written anything specific in it about her crimes, but if she had worked on it, her words might tell us something about her state of mind at the time. She might even have made an oblique reference to her intentions, or pencilled in an aside. There was even a chance she'd slipped up in some way when she'd had the file open.

I'd once nailed a blackmailer because she'd leaned on the cover of a cookbook to pen her demands. What if Lomax had stuffed up in a similar way with the rumour file? And what about the other files she'd worked on in Proctor's dirt collection? Might she not have inadvertently left a clue in one of them? It was a cardinal rule that an investigation should turn over every stone, yet those files remained undisturbed. And Bolton wouldn't be going there. The government would whack him down if he tried, and Redding certainly wouldn't have appointed him if he was anything less than compliant.

It meant that the Centre's handling of the investigation would be dogged by the same handicaps and roadblocks that had held us back. As I saw it, that left us with only one option. Given the extreme turn in events, the Australian Federal Police, as the original investigating agency, had to lead the charge to open up all of Proctor's files — even if that meant raiding the prime minister's office.

Channel Four Live Cam

Friday 9 August, 11.30am

Good morning, Jean Acheson here, twenty-four hours on, and the search for Prime Minister Michael Lansdowne continues.

As part of that effort, the Security Co-ordination Centre last night shut down the mobile-phone network covering the ACT and southern New South Wales. But most of you will already know that.

Now while no one doubts the need for the roadblocks and the house searches that the Centre has instituted, the shutdown of the mobile network has everyone confused, and a little bit angry. Local talkback was flooded with callers this morning. Some said the shutdown had put their businesses at risk. Others with health problems said that a functioning mobile phone could be the difference for them between living and dying.

Campbell resident Margaret James had another argument against the shutdown. She said that anyone who now spotted Lomax in and around Canberra wouldn't be able to alert the police in a timely way. This is Jean Acheson. Back with more soon.

36

DESPITE BEING SIDELINED, McHenry was as busy as ever, tapping away at his machine and dealing with a constant stream of phone calls. I decided to wait till things calmed down for him before I made a final push for Proctor's files. In the meantime, I trawled through PROMIS to see what sort of start Bolton had made.

In a memo discussing his manpower needs, Bolton said he'd already 'imported' an extra eight thousand state coppers into Canberra, and he had more on the way. He'd also commandeered a couple of sanitation trucks to collect the rubbish of high-interest individuals. And he'd accessed bank activity statements for a range of people, most of whom we'd spoken to during our investigation. There was little out of the ordinary in the document attached to this memo. Except, perhaps, for Tom Hanley's bank statement. His account seemed surprisingly active for a man who spouted gibberish.

Bolton had also circulated the letter he'd written to Malcolm Redding requesting the shutdown of the local mobile network. The letter didn't mention suicide vests, nor any other reason for the request.

Just before midday, I ordered in two coffees, a couple of tawook rolls, and an assortment of baklava. When the food and drink arrived, I took it over to McHenry's desk and put it down in front of him. He peeked into the bag of sweets and flashed me a helpless smile. I said we should eat somewhere out of the room. He nodded, got up, and took off with the food, leaving me to carry the coffee.

It was a cold day but warm in the sun, so we ended up on the bench in the courtyard, chomping through gristly bits of chicken wrapped in pita bread, and talking about everything from the weather to the weekend footy.

I asked McHenry how he felt about losing the investigation. He said he felt a bit like the winless coach who gets replaced mid-season. I faked an offended look, and he immediately stressed that there'd been nothing wrong with the team's performance. It was just that the investigation had been blocked in fundamental ways. I used that as a cue to introduce Adam Stowe's story about the origins of the fire-dance rumour.

While I recounted the tale, McHenry worked his way through the tawook, nodding and grunting occasionally. But his jaw stopped moving when I suggested that Lomax might have managed the rumour campaign against Feeney. And he put the remains of his tawook down when I said that if she *had* run the thing, she would have created the file that documented it. But the spell was broken when I told him that we had to convince Brady to go after the file, and everything else in Proctor's dirt collection, as it might give us a clue that could lead to Lomax. Bolton would never do it, I said, so, as the original investigating agency, we should do it for him. McHenry nodded and exhaled loudly, the reason for his free lunch having finally been revealed.

'You might be right,' he said, popping a piece of baklava into his mouth. 'Lomax might have managed the dance rumour. So let's assume she also kept the file on it. What are the chances she'd leave a clue in that file about the abduction? Slim to non-existent, I'd say. And if we *did* get our hands on it, or any of the other files she kept, and we found something that seemed relevant, how would we know it was a genuine lead, and not something she'd dreamt up to put us off the trail?'

It was a reasonable question, I said, but I'd only be able to answer it once I'd been through Proctor's files. McHenry sighed deeply and cast his eyes to his feet. Then he downed the rest of his coffee and studied the bottom of the cardboard cup as if reading the grounds.

'Okay, Glass,' he said. 'Let's suppose that, by some sort of magic, we were able to convince Brady that this rumour business changed the status of these files. And as he never flies solo on anything, let's say Brady then took it up with Bolton and convinced him as well. If that ever happened, Brady would see to it that I wore every negative that came out of it. And there'd surely be plenty. Particularly if we upset the applecart for no result. So, given the slim margin of probability you're working with here, and given the few good years I've got left in me, would you still have me sticking my neck out like you're suggesting?'

'Absolutely,' I said. 'I mean, it could be the breakthrough we're looking for.'

'I doubt it. In fact, it's one of the thinnest possible leads ever. But a lead it is, and all leads must be exhausted. However, if I agree to set up a meeting with Brady on this, I don't want you talking about raids on the PM's office or any such thing. You simply put your argument, then suggest that he raise the matter with Bolton. Right?'

'Yes, sir.'

Taking that as an assurance, McHenry led me inside to his desk, called Brady's office, and asked the PA for an immediate appointment. As he put the phone down, he looked at me and shook his head.

'My God,' he said. 'What are you gettin' me into here?'

Brady didn't interrupt as I put my argument, but he looked distracted the whole time, as though he was willing me to finish.

'Quite a set of connections, detective,' he said when I did. 'But I don't think we'll bother Mr Bolton with this right now. You write it up, and we'll see how the Centre responds.'

And with that he swung around to his computer screen, jabbed at a few keys with his index finger, and then turned to us again.

'If that's all, gentlemen,' he said, with a why-are-you-still-taking-up-my-valuable-time look on his dial.

Brady was not a superior to push, nor did he look ripe for turning on this. So I'd *have* to push him, up to a point. But not so far that I'd rile him.

'With respect, sir,' I said. 'We know this investigation better than anyone else, and this lead is definitely worth pursuing. But if we leave it up to some nameless person over at the Centre to assess its value, without giving Mr Bolton a briefing first, it's sure to end up in the too-hard basket. So I urge you, sir. Please talk to Mr Bolton.'

Brady dropped his eyes to the desk in front of him, took a deep breath, and shook his head. And I realised then that he'd never push for access to Proctor's dirt. The reason? When it came to Pandora's Box, those files were the real deal. If we trawled through them, we might or might not turn up a rumour file, or anything else Lomax had worked on, but we'd definitely find information on plenty of other government activities, and some of them were sure to be highly illegal. When that happened, we'd be duty-bound to investigate the lot. A government groupie like Brady could never allow that to happen.

Under normal circumstances, this realisation might have prompted me to concede defeat and slip away quietly. But Brady had been at me since the start of this investigation, and now I saw his refusal to talk to Bolton as him washing his hands of Lansdowne. Just who did he think he was protecting?

A government in its death throes? What was the point? Surely, saving the prime minister's life trumped any other consideration? And before I knew it, I was firing more questions — ones that I knew would push Brady too far.

'Mr Brady, what if Lou Feeney's in power by this time next week?' I said, giving voice to a prospect he dreaded. 'And what if his people get their hands on Proctor's files? Before Mr Redding can destroy them? They might find something in those files that could have saved Mr Lansdowne. I guess the ultimate question is this: When people ask you if you did everything possible to save the prime minister, what will you say? Because, with respect sir, this is a reasonable lead, and even if ...'

'I think you've had a good hearing, detective,' said Brady, his whole being bristling now.

He picked up a wad of papers and banged them down so hard on his desk that he bent the edges he was trying to straighten. The meeting was over. He wanted us out. But I wasn't going anywhere.

'Sir, they call the stuff that Proctor collected on people his dirt files,' I said, taking a step towards Brady's desk. 'I guess they call them that because of what it would mean to a person if ever their file saw the light of day. And they say Proctor had dirt on most people in public life. Both friends and enemies. Is it possible he had a file on you, sir? And could that be the reason you won't act on this?'

Brady turned red with anger and spat out the word 'You!' He rose in his seat, but slumped back into it just as quickly. Then he looked at McHenry as if he expected him to jump on me, but the boss was studying a spot on the carpet just in front of his feet.

'How dare you, detective,' said Brady, when he was finally able to speak. 'No wonder we're three steps behind this bitch, with you on the job. Inspector, I want Detective Glass out of my office and out of this building as soon as possible. And maybe you could start organising his future. A couple of years on court duty might be a good start.'

'Yes, sir,' said McHenry, looking up from his spot. 'I'm sorry, sir.'

And with that, the boss slipped a hand into my armpit and marched me from the room.

'That really achieved a lot,' he said. 'What you need, son, is some country air to clear the shit from your brain. So, instead of Smeaton, why don't *you* go out to Lake George and meet the psych? Then, with any luck, when she's done with Hanley, she might have a bit of time left over for you.'

So that was it. I'd failed to gain access to Proctor's dirt files, and I'd stirred up the commissioner again into the bargain. And for all my stuff-ups and mis-statements, I'd been sentenced to an afternoon in the country. It was 'punishment lite' for the hero from the House of Death, and I accepted it without further argument. To kick up another stink would have been self-destructive in the extreme. It was best for me to keep my head down and do the job I'd been given. That way, I might limit my stint in the courts. I *did* regret the way I'd carried on with Brady, but more for the emotion of it than the arguments I'd put.

I followed McHenry back to the room. He had a brief conversation with Marginson, after which she got on the phone and cleared my 'assignment' with the Centre. Then I called transport to organise a vehicle, but the out-of-towners had snaffled every car and cycle at City Station, and all they could offer me was an old trail bike they'd just serviced for Search and Rescue. I went out to the transport hutch and looked the bike over before starting it up and letting it blow a bit of smoke. It went okay, so I sorted out a leather jacket and jodhpurs, and found myself a helmet. I got onto the machine, adjusted the mirrors, tested the radio, and rode it out of the yard.

I didn't get far. Road blocks at either end of Northbourne Avenue had reduced traffic flow in the city to a crawl. If I joined the slow-moving stream of vehicles heading north, I wouldn't make it to the lake before dark. So I activated the blue light on the back of the bike, jumped the curb, and ambled up the generous median strip that separated the north and south lanes. When I reached the main intersection at Dickson, I took to the shoulder of the road and skirted the traffic till I got to the last roadblock outside the Exhibition Centre. From there the traffic thinned out, and by the time I was on the Federal Highway, I had the bike up to speed and it was rolling along nicely.

I was back on Mack's Reef Road and heading east towards Lake George when I remembered what McHenry had said about country air — how it could promote clear thinking. You could heighten that effect, I thought, by taking a two-wheeled machine down a winding country road you'd never ridden before. Few things got you thinking clearer than that.

Perhaps if my thinking had been a bit clearer back at the station, if I hadn't given way to impulse and emotion, I might not have been on that country road. Maybe. But I'd had no choice. As for McHenry, he knew there was bad blood between me and Brady, so he must have anticipated a clash between us. Well, in the end, he'd probably pay more for my little outburst than I would. After all, he'd set up the meeting. And what about this Hanley job? Well, it was just another 'i' in the investigation we hadn't dotted. Another 't' to cross. And from what I'd seen of Hanley, that psych was going to more than earn her money.

The turn-off to Bungendore seemed to come up much faster than I remembered. And when I leaned into the corner for Lake Road, it was like I'd taken it a thousand times before. I even anticipated the road for Hanley's place, and slowed down well before I got to his gate. Lucky I did. The gate that had been wide open when I'd come out with Smeaton and Bender was now closed, and secured with a padlock and a chain. Maybe Hanley had gone away for a few days. Maybe, but I'd come too far to ride back without checking.

Under the provisions of the State of Emergency, I no longer needed a New South Wales copper with me to enter Hanley's property. Nor did I need one to escort the psych on to the place. As long as I was on legitimate police business, I could go anywhere, at any time, unchallenged.

I killed the engine and removed my gloves and helmet. I was forty-five minutes early for the psych, so I took out my phone to tell her I was going onto the property, but the phone had no signal. Damn it, I'd forgotten about Bolton's shutdown. I switched the police radio to a Queanbeyan frequency and listened to a bit of voice traffic. Reassured that I still had some form of communication, I killed the radio, and tried to work out how best to get over the rusty old gate without wrecking my borrowed leathers.

I made it over the gate unscathed, and then walked along the rutted vehicle track towards the cabins. Hanley's old BMW was still parked under the tree in the clearing. It didn't mean he was around, but it was a good sign that he might be. I considered going back to the road to wait for the psych, but, as she wasn't due for forty minutes, I pushed on.

I took the path to Hanley's place, and when I emerged at the clearing I paused and surveyed the cabins and the ridgeline above them. Then I climbed to Hanley's cabin. There was no answer when I knocked, so I turned the handle, gave the door a push, and went inside. The place looked much as it had when I first saw it — except that most of the food above the sink was gone, and the backpack in the corner had been secured for travelling.

Was he coming or going? I didn't really care which. The fact that his pack was here meant that he was probably still around somewhere. I sat on the mattress, undid the straps on the pack, and lifted back the flap. The foul smell that whooshed out of it forced me to turn away.

A dull thudding came from somewhere down the hill — just a few raps, like wood hitting wood. I got off the bed and walked quickly to the window. All I could see was the dense canopy of trees below me and the expanse of the dry lake-bed beyond it. The waning light lit the purple hills on the far side of the lake.

I hesitated for a moment, deciding whether to search the pack first or investigate the noise. If it was Hanley down there, I'd be better off searching his stinking belongings before he came back. And if it wasn't Hanley, there'd be an innocent explanation for what I'd heard. Like a cabin door slamming in the breeze. Or a tree dropping a branch.

I stood for a moment, eyeing the massive eucalypts that struggled for life at the lake's edge. Then I suddenly recognised the view in front of me, and I was transfixed. I'd seen it frozen on canvas, at Lomax's Blackall Street unit — a painting of the lake from this same perspective. I recognised the bush in the near distance: the same struggling trees, the line of hills like purple cutouts on the horizon. Joe the jailer had stood at this window and painted the scene below. Only his lake had been full of water, while the one below was bone dry.

Blood Oath subscription news

Friday 9 August, 3.00pm

Lansdowne brings the biggest bounce
by Simon Rolfe

Acting Prime Minister Malcolm Redding says tomorrow's election must go ahead. He says criminals can't be allowed to disrupt the democratic process. But is it possible his resolve is informed by a new poll which shows the government slightly ahead of the opposition for the first time in more than a year?

For all but the last day of this campaign, we've had two contenders slugging it out, giving as good as they got. Then, just before the last round, one of them was abducted and taken to a place unknown. Now all debate is dead, and a nation is left holding its breath.

But life goes on, one step at a time. And the people will vote tomorrow. They'll stand in a polling booth, sizing up the government and assessing the opposition. And when they do, their thoughts will turn to the party leaders. They'll think of Lou Feeney and they'll remember his courage in the face of the rumour campaign that nearly ended his race. Then they'll picture Michael Lansdowne, locked up in a place inconceivable, somewhere dark and distant where he's fretting for his life.

And when that image of Lansdowne enters their consciousness, I believe the Australian people will vote for him, in absentia, and for his government. It'll be partly out of sympathy for the leader, but they'll also be expressing their contempt for Penny Lomax and all her works. So when that happens, as I believe it will, spare a thought for Lou Feeney, whose only crime was to stay free and viable until the end.

37

I TRAINED MY Glock on the door while I upended the pack with my other hand. The contents spilt out onto the floor, and I used my foot to separate the congealed clothes from the mouldy towels and dog-eared novels. Then an opaque plastic sleeve slid into view from between two filthy T-shirts. The sleeve was a match for those that had housed Proctor's dirt. I held my breath, and removed five sheets of paper from it and lined them up in front of me on the mattress.

Each sheet had the same header: 'Mondrian'. It was the transcript of a meeting. The participants' names were written in full when they first contributed to the discussion or asked a question; after that, they were simply noted by their initials. Those named as attending the meeting were Michael Lansdowne, Alan Proctor, Dennis Hanley, Susan Wright, and Lansdowne's nephew, Mick Stanton. All of them were dead now of course, except for the prime minister. And even his fate was uncertain.

My first instinct was to pocket the document, race for the bike, and call in the cavalry — quick smart. But if I ran into Tom Hanley on the way, or even Penny Lomax, it might be handy to know what had been discussed at that meeting all those years ago. So I quickly scanned the pages.

According to the date on the transcript, it had been almost fifteen years since the meeting, so Lansdowne and Wright were shadow ministers at the time. The first couple of pages were taken up with Mick Stanton explaining the bed voucher scheme that was later to embroil the government in such controversy.

The rest of the transcript was mostly questions from Lansdowne, Proctor, and Wright. Stanton and Hanley supplied the answers. They all recognised that they were doing something highly illegal, but they were mostly focused on the rewards they'd reap if the scheme was implemented.

Those rewards included cut-price shares, which Stanton said would net each of them ten million dollars. They could also take up a directorship with a Mondrian-owned company within four years if they wanted. Stanton said directors were paid two hundred and thirty thousand dollars a year for attending quarterly meetings and for providing advice on request.

Towards the end of the meeting, Dennis Hanley had said he doubted Mondrian could keep its ownership of Dolman a secret. Stanton had dismissed his concerns, saying the bank would purchase Dolman using a shelf company, and that it was perfectly legal for it not to disclose the purchase.

Like Stanton, Wright had been very upbeat about the 'opportunity' that they'd all been given. And she said that the voucher scheme represented humane policy, and any party that embraced it should be congratulated.

So this was what had got them all killed. No wonder Susan Wright had been desperate to get her hands on the Mondrian tape on the night she disappeared. If this was a transcript of that tape, and I had no doubt it was, then it damned her, and Lansdowne, and everyone else who was in on the Mondrian conspiracy.

And it meant that even if we were to rescue the prime minister, it was not going to end well for him. He'd effectively go from one prison to another. I was dealing with that image when a car fired up down below. It could only have been Tom Hanley on the move.

I gathered up the document, shoved it into my jacket pocket, and dashed for the open door. A long, thin cloud of dust rose through the treetops below, marking the progress of Hanley's BMW as it roared along the track towards Lake Road. I glanced up at the three cabins coming off the stairs above me, and then I jumped down the stairs, two and three at time, and sprinted through the trees towards the road.

My best chance of stopping Hanley was to get to him before he opened the gate. But by the time I emerged into the clearing that bordered the fenceline, the gate was already open, and Hanley was getting back into his car. He gunned the engine, his vehicle fish-tailed in the loose stones in the driveway, and then it rocketed down Lake Road like a car half its age.

When I got a direct line of sight on it, I raised my Glock and took a bead on the head behind the steering wheel. Hanley looked to be alone in the car, but if the PM was trussed up on the backseat, I might hit him. As I stood there, immobilised by this dilemma, the car rounded the corner a hundred metres away and disappeared behind a stand of conifers.

I lowered my gun and raced back to the bike, hoping that Hanley had been too concerned with his getaway to tamper with it. No such luck. Every exposed hose and cable on the machine had been severed. The microphone for the radio was gone. He'd even bent the aerial for good measure.

I tried kick-starting the bike, but couldn't raise a spark, so I slumped onto the petrol tank and considered my next move. Just then, an old Monaro, blowing heaps of smoke, came around the same stand of trees that had swallowed Hanley.

I stood in the middle of the road and waved the car down, obliging the young woman driver to bring the thing to a shuddering halt a few metres in front of me. A fag hung from her mouth, and the dark rings under her eyes magnified the stress she was obviously feeling at being stopped by a cop in full leathers.

She wound down her window and I showed her my badge. That seemed to stress her out even more, so I assured her that she wasn't in any trouble. I considered commandeering her car to pursue Hanley, but the old bomb looked too far gone for that. Instead, I told her I was dealing with an emergency, and that I needed her to drive me to her place so I could use her phone.

'Sorry, I can't help you there,' she said, taking the fag from her mouth. 'The lines along here went down yesterday, and they reckon they'll be out for another day at least. You after that bastard in the Beamer? The one who nearly side-swiped me back there?'

She drew on her fag and eyed me expectantly. I ignored the question and tried to think through the situation. I knew now that Tom Hanley had been consorting with Joe, a fact that put him in the frame for the murders and the abductions. The transcript in his pack was another indicator of his involvement at a high level.

If Hanley was also in league with Lomax, as I strongly suspected he was, there might be something back at the huts pointing to Lansdowne's whereabouts. In fact, that might be where they were holding him. I had no choice, really — I had to get back there in a hurry. But first I had to trust this raggedy woman with one of the biggest jobs I'd ever given anyone. She shrank back as I leaned in her window.

'What's your name?' I said.

'Jenny Smith,' she said, more edgy now than ever.

'Jenny, the life of the prime minister could depend on your doing exactly what I ask you to do right now. I need you to get into Bungendore as fast as you can, and get to a phone and call this number.'

I wrote McHenry's name and number in my notepad, and jotted down a series of dot points that I wanted Jenny to read to the boss when he answered. Essentially, I told McHenry to send a SWAT team out to Tom Hanley's place with extreme urgency. I knew this might not be warranted, but I wasn't taking any chances.

I told him Hanley was armed and dangerous, and I supplied the details of his car. I said he might have vital information concerning Lansdowne's whereabouts, and that he was on the road somewhere in the Bungendore–Lake George area.

I wrote my name at the bottom of the page, and ripped the page from my notebook and gave it to Jenny Smith. Then I gave her some coins, thanked her for her help, and waved her on her way. She did a perfect three-point turn on the narrow road and took off towards Bungendore, trailing a cloud of smoke and dust. When she was out of sight, I ran back up the track towards the cabins.

I was almost out of breath by the time I got to the foot of the stairs, so I gave myself a minute to recover before making my way up, step by step, holding my Glock two-handed in front of my eyes. I was ready for anything — or so I thought.

The first cabin off the stairs was as bare as it had been when I'd first visited with Smeaton and Bender. So was the next one up. And the one after that. I had another quick look in Hanley's cabin, but it was unchanged from a few minutes before. I was closing the door to the cabin, and questioning the wisdom of trusting Jenny Smith, when I heard a loud grunt from somewhere above me.

I ran to the stairs just as the prime minister staggered from the shadows of the next cabin up. He was hunched over, his suit was filthy, and he looked sickly and weak. A hand holding a revolver came around the corner of the cabin. Another Cobra .38 Special, it was pointed at Lansdowne's head. Lomax didn't show herself. She simply shouted.

'Throw your gun into the bush! As far as you can! Now, or he dies! Do it!'

I hurled my Glock at a tall tree about twenty metres away, and forlornly watched it bounce off the trunk and drop into the scrub below. Lomax stepped from the shadows, lowered her weapon to Lansdowne's back, and prodded him forward a few steps.

'What kept you, inspector?' she said, looking down at me with a half-smile on her face. 'I told Michael here you'd be back in five minutes. And that was what? Eight minutes ago?'

'Are you okay, Prime Minister?' I said, though the answer was obvious.

'I …' said Lansdowne, and he spluttered and clamped both hands to his mouth, attempting to suppress a cough. 'I can't …'

But before he could get anything else out, he was taken by a coughing fit that bent him over and wracked him so completely I thought he'd collapse. When he finally got his breathing under control, he spat out a gob of phlegm, then looked at me, his eyes begging for deliverance.

'He's fine,' said Lomax, pushing her glasses up the bridge of her nose. 'It was cold out here last night, wasn't it, Michael?

'What's the prime minister done to deserve this?'

'What's he *done*?' she said, as if it were the stupidest question in the world. 'Don't play with me, detective. You've seen the transcript. You know about the meeting — the one our friend here taped on the sly. What's he *done*? Well, for a start, he killed my dad with his scheme. And that ended it for my mum. Then he set Proctor onto my brother, Tom, and look at poor Tommy now. Then there's me — your worst nightmare. This guy can take credit for me, too. What's he done? Well, he's done quite a lot, hasn't he?'

'You're Sylvie. Sylvie Hanley.'

'Give the man a prize,' she said.

Her gaze seemed to harden, and there was a tremor in her chin. I had to keep her talking, but I'd have to be careful. If she thought I was stringing things out, she'd bring our little chat to a quick end, and by the look of her that could happen at any moment.

'So this was your objective, was it? To kill Lansdowne? Like you did the other two?'

'We only wanted the tape,' she said, patting the breast pocket of her jacket. 'And we definitely never planned to kill Susan. But once we got her back to Rodway Street, she went all Catholic on us. You know — reckoned she had to confess everything and accept her punishment. I didn't want to hurt her, but there was no talking her out of it. Proctor was a different matter. And this guy. But we didn't want to hurt Susan.'

'So why did Proctor have to die?'

'Like I said, our friend here set him onto Tom, and once he got his claws in, he wouldn't let go.'

'But what did Proctor actually do to him?'

The very question seemed to provoke Lomax. She raised her revolver back to Lansdowne's head, took a deep breath, and then squinted in anticipation. This was it. Lansdowne sensed it, too. His face creased up, then he bent over and spluttered as his body was wracked by another coughing fit. Lomax looked at him with contempt, and lowered her weapon. Then the anger went from her eyes, replaced by an almost sorrowful look.

'Mum's last mistake was to tell Tommy about Mondrian,' she said, her voice cracking. 'And what it had done to Dad. She'd already told me. That's why I went overseas — to escape the whole business. Then, when she died, Tom and I went through her things, and found Dad's transcript. They all had one, but only Proctor had the tape. After we buried Mum, I went back to Thailand, and Tom shifted out here.

'When I'd been gone a couple of weeks, Tommy phoned Proctor and abused him for what the scam had done to our parents, and he threatened to give the transcript to a journo. Well, Proctor knew how to handle that. He told Tom that these cabins and everything else we owned were proceeds of crime, and that if ever the Mondrian story got out, we'd lose the lot. And he told Tom that if that happened, he'd end up tied to a bed in a psych ward somewhere, covered in his own shit.'

'That was cruel.'

'Yes, but then Proctor started coming out here every couple of months, just to remind Tom of what he stood to lose. And he badgered him for the transcript, which Tom refused to hand over. By any measure, detective, Proctor was torturing my brother at that point. Of course, he denied it when we got him back to Rodway. He said he was protecting himself. And Michael here ...'

She jammed the revolver into Lansdowne's spine, and he grunted as he stumbled towards the edge of the landing. His hands were pressed to his mouth, ready to smother a cough. I had to keep her talking.

'No doubt this all had a big impact on Tom,' I said.

'A very big impact,' said Lomax. 'I know this place doesn't look like much, but it anchors him to the world. Especially the lake down there. And Tom knows it, too. That's why he'd call me whenever Proctor visited. He was desperate for me to sort it out. And I couldn't let it go on. Especially after what they did to Mum and Dad.'

'So you decided to kill Sylvie and come back to Australia as Penny Lomax?'

'Yes. I came home as Penny. And Penny had one aim — to do whatever it took to protect Tom. And I knew that, in the end, that would probably mean killing Proctor. And this guy.'

So, finally, here we had it — an explanation for the audacious crime spree that had already taken two lives and could soon take more, including my own. It was a vendetta that had overtaken an election campaign, shocking the nation and making Australia the centre of world attention. Was this what it was all about? A sister's love for her vulnerable brother, and her determination to protect him, no matter what the cost?

'But you worked with Proctor for a couple of years,' I said. 'You could've taken him out loads of times. Why'd you wait till now?'

'Lots of reasons. He'd pretty much stopped coming out here by the time I was working for him. And having me around made Tom feel much better about things. And while I hated these people, I enjoyed the job. But then Proctor's tape appeared at the party.'

'And you thought that if you could get your hands on the prime evidence of the Mondrian conspiracy, Proctor wouldn't have anything to hold over Tom. So why'd you have to kill him?'

'Because after we dumped Susan's body, he came out here and accused Tom of killing her. It had moved beyond the tape for him by then, so I had no choice. Anyway, I hated Proctor, so it wasn't hard to do him.'

'But a gas chamber?' I said. 'Why didn't you just shoot him? Or hit him over the head with something?'

'The room was Joe's idea,' said Lomax. 'He'd already soundproofed it for his music, so converting it took no time. And he always said that if gassing cats was the humane thing to do, why would we do any less for humans.'

'Ah, yes. The cats. What was their significance?'

'Joe's idea as well. He said the cats would confuse you. And he was right, wasn't he?'

'And was there a real Penny Lomax?'

'Of course. She was an Aussie junkie I met in Chiang Mai. An only child, with dead parents like me. It was too hard to resist, so I helped speed things up for her. And once she was gone, I had her passport, so I got her face, too.'

'In Bangkok?'

'That's right.'

'And who was Joe?'

The question touched a raw nerve. Lomax's eyes narrowed as she lifted her revolver over Lansdowne's shoulder and aimed it squarely at my head. Then she squinted slightly as her finger tightened on the trigger.

'Ahh! There you are,' said a woman's voice from below. 'Sorry I'm late.'

I looked down, and there was the psych standing at the edge of the clearing. She had a big smile on her face, and she started walking towards the stairs. Then a loud crack rang out from behind me.

The bullet hit the psych in the chest, jolting her backwards a couple of steps. She looked up at us again, this time clutching the hole that Lomax had made in her. She lifted her hands away and studied the blood dripping from them. Then she dropped to her knees, saying nothing, her eyes wide with surprise.

I dived for the side of Hanley's cabin as a couple of bullets whizzed past my back. I had to escape while I still had the cabin for cover, and the trees bordering the path below looked like my best chance. I leapt off the paving, landed in a stumble-run, and ran down the slope with my arms whirling, fighting to keep my feet, heading for the trees, and expecting a bullet in my back.

Lomax's first shot cut down a sapling a few metres ahead of me. She cursed loudly. The next shot would have pleased her more. I heard it, and simultaneously felt the bullet tear through my side. I threw myself forward and seemed to fall forever. Then my shoulder hit the ground, and I went head over heels all the way down the rest of the slope. A third shot rang out, and I tumbled into a dark thicket at the bottom of my fall.

Channel Four Live Cam

Friday 9 August, 4.30pm

Good afternoon, Jean Acheson here with hot news of a possible breakthrough in the Lansdowne abduction.

Just moments ago, ten police helicopters took off from Fairbairn Airbase bound for a property near Lake George about thirty-five kilometres north-east of Canberra.

I understand an arrest warrant has been issued for a resident of the Lake George property, a Mr Tom Hanley, and more than a hundred law officers have been mobilised to hunt for this Mr Hanley in the area around the lake.

Meanwhile, for those still interested, a poll conducted overnight and this morning shows the government jumping to a two-point lead this election eve. Let's hope and pray that Prime Minister Lansdowne survives to celebrate what appears to be his impending victory. Here with the Live Cam, this is Jean Acheson.

38

THERE ARE FEW things more shocking than getting shot. But I can tell you that if you're still conscious and you're able to move, you don't rip back your clothes and immediately check out your wound. You're desperate to know how bad it is, of course, but you're unlikely to rush the self-examination. Most shooting victims take time to accommodate what's happened to them, as I did then.

The injured area was hot, and it throbbed like hell. I put my hand under my jacket, and it came out wet with blood. I pressed the palm of my hand hard against the wound and took some deep breaths while the pain subsided. Then I eased myself up to my knees and crawled forward through the thicket till I had a view of the cabins and the stairs.

I spent a minute studying the slope, looking for movement, but I saw none. I would have taken a sounding, but there was a whirring in my ears that was getting louder the longer I crouched there.

After considering various courses of action, I decided my best option was to climb to the ridgeline above the cabins and drop down on Lomax from above. But first I'd have to deal with the damage that her bullet had caused. I slumped back against a tree trunk, unzipped my jacket and pulled my shirt out of my jodhpurs.

The bullet had ripped through my jacket and shirt, and punched a channel through the skin, fat, and flesh at my side. Technically, it was a graze, but it was bleeding freely and it could slow me down, even incapacitate me, if I didn't deal with it properly.

I put pressure on the wound and crawled deeper into the trees till I found a fallen log to sit on. I took off my jacket and shirt, and held the shirt by its sleeves and spun it around on itself to create a wad of cloth. I pressed the wad into the wound, wrapped the arms of the shirt around me, and tied them into a knot at my good side. Then I put my jacket back on and sat for a minute, catching my breath and settling my nerves.

When I was ready, I moved deeper into the trees, making my way in the semi-darkness, putting distance between myself and Lomax. Once I was far enough away to be safe, I headed out of the trees into another clearing and started climbing the slope I'd so recently fallen down.

The going was easy at first, but then the ground got much steeper, even precipitous in places. And each time I stretched for a branch or a bush to pull myself upwards, a jagged pain exploded from the wound at my side.

By the time I scrabbled up over the rim of the ridgeline, I was puffing like a smoker, and my shirt was soaked with sweat and blood. I took half a minute to catch my breath, and was soon staggering through a stand of banksias on a well-worn track that ran parallel to the drop. From there I stumbled towards the cabins, certain that Lomax was lying in wait for me somewhere up ahead.

I was dealing with this fear when the bush began to thin out, the track started to veer back towards the edge of the ridge, and the top cabin came into view. I dropped to the ground and remained prone for a few seconds as I assessed the track ahead. Then I crawled to the edge of the stairs and examined each of the seven cabins below me. I tried to take a sounding, but the whirring in my ears made that impossible.

What next? Did I go down without a weapon? I'd be very exposed if Lomax *was* waiting for me down there. Then I noticed that the whirring in my ears had become more intense, somehow, and the nature of it had changed — to a chopping noise. And I recognised what I was hearing. Jenny Smith and her old bomb had made it. I had choppers on the way.

I swung around and faced the far-off whoomping noise, and, as I did, the faint sound of someone coughing came to me from further up the ridge. It had to be Lansdowne. Without thinking, I jumped up and ran as quickly as I could in the direction of the cough. Then I saw something move in the middle of the rock formation that dominated the highest part of the ridge. It was there for an instant and then gone. I stared at the spot for a few seconds, but saw nothing more. If it *was* Lomax and Lansdowne up there, they had quite a lead on me. On the other hand, Lansdowne's condition meant that they wouldn't be travelling very fast. Spurred on by that thought, I took off after them.

The track became steeper and changed from dirt to rock, and I was soon scrambling up a huge granite outcrop that arced gently to the top of the next ridge. Halfway up the incline, I stopped to catch my breath and to check my wound. The bandage was secure enough, though it was wet with blood, as were my trousers. I knew that if I thought too hard about the injury it would rob me of vital energy, so I closed my eyes for a few seconds and drew strength from the sound of the choppers in the distance.

I was down on all fours as I pulled myself up onto the ridge. From there I followed the track through a series of granite boulders and out onto a giant ledge that afforded a full view of the length of the lake. I walked to the edge of the ledge and took in the dramatic vista for a second. And as I moved off, a metal click stopped me in my tracks.

'Stay right where you are,' said Lomax, 'and raise your hands, very slowly.'

I did as I was told, and she stepped from behind a rock wall about ten metres away, her revolver aimed at my chest. I glanced over the ledge but saw no escape there — just a short, steep incline to the rim and a forty-metre drop onto boulders below. I bent my knees and got ready for her to fire. I felt like a soccer goalie defending a penalty kick, except that my aim was to miss the ball rather than stop it.

The noise from the choppers was building. She glanced in their direction, then turned and gave me a hard stare. She squinted slightly, and I pushed off to my right as she squeezed the trigger. The bullet missed me by millimetres, but she swiveled fast, and the pistol followed me.

I readied myself again. I doubted I'd be so lucky a second time. She squinted. I pushed off to my left as she squeezed the trigger, and all she got was the dull click of metal on metal. She hadn't reloaded! I steadied myself, and then I rushed her.

She side-stepped and tried to hit me with the pistol as I charged through, but I grabbed her gun hand and used my momentum to pull her off balance. I hauled her towards me and jabbed her on the nose a couple of times, sending her glasses flying, and then kicked her left knee, hyper-extending it. She screamed, but somehow slipped out of my grasp. She staggered backwards, then stopped to gather herself, close to the edge of the incline.

It was never going to be a fair fight. She had the revolver up again, ready to club me. I moved in and feinted a punch to her left side, and she pushed off on her right leg to avoid the blow. Then I feinted a punch to her right side, and when she pushed off to her left, the knee I'd kicked collapsed beneath her. She fell onto her stomach and then slid down the steepest part of the incline. The revolver fell from her hand and rattled down the rock past her. She watched it fall over the edge and clatter onto the boulders below.

Lomax struggled to stop herself joining it, her attempts to claw her way back up the incline only increasing the impact of gravity. She grasped at a small bush growing in a crevice, but it gave way, and her hands were still scrabbling as she went over the edge.

I held my breath and waited for the thump from below, but it didn't come. So I dropped to my knees and eased myself down the gentlest part of the incline. I tested the staying power of the biggest bush near the edge, and I held onto it tightly while I peered over.

Lomax's fingers were wedged into a crack in the rock face, and she was hanging on grimly, trying to catch her breath. She sensed me above her, but she didn't look up.

'I suppose you reckon this is it,' she said, struggling to get her words out. 'Copper gets his woman, and all that.'

The choppers were only minutes away now. If she could hang on, they'd save her. Then again, did she want to spend the rest of her life in a cell? There was a shuffling noise on the ledge above me. I turned so fast that I almost lost my balance. It was Lansdowne. He looked exhausted and a bit bewildered. He nodded, but I barely acknowledged him. I faced Lomax again. She was eyeing the drop.

'It's up to you,' I said. 'And your fingers. You can relax them now, or you can hang on and we'll save you.'

She adjusted her hold, one hand at a time, swallowed hard, and looked down at the drop again. I don't know what made me do it, but when she took her eyes off me, I quickly bent down and grabbed one of her wrists, and her hand came away from its niche in the rock.

I had a good grip on her, and I was certain I could save her. But then she let her other hand fall out of the crack, and it flopped to her side, forcing me to cope with her full weight. I couldn't hold her for long, so I let go of the bush that had been my insurance, and I got hold of her forearm in both hands and began pulling her up.

Lomax hung limply in my grasp until her chin was level with the rim I was crouching on. Then she walked her feet up the rock face, and when her knees were almost touching her chest, she flexed her legs and pushed off, forcing me to let go of her. Our eyes met briefly as she flew backwards. She looked calm in that moment, resigned to her fate. And, seconds later, she hit the boulders below with a grunt.

It was no easy job getting myself back up onto level ground. I took it slowly, and Lansdowne helped me the last little bit of the way. Then we stood near the edge, looking down at Lomax. The thudding chorus of choppers was almost upon us now.

'The cavalry arrives when it's all over,' I said with a mirthless laugh. 'At least they can go and find Hanley now.'

'Hanley?' said Lansdowne, his face contorting as he wrestled with a memory. 'I think Lomax told him to drive around to Geary's Gap. Then he was supposed to meet us.'

'Where?' I said.

'Oh! Somewhere around here, I think ...'

As if on cue, Tom Hanley stepped from the rock wall into view. He had both hands wrapped around a semi-automatic pistol that was pointed at Lansdowne. Hanley took a few steps towards us. Then he bent down and picked up his sister's glasses.

'What've you done to her?' he said, suddenly wild-eyed and ready to explode.

As if in answer, Lansdowne looked down at Lomax, broken on the rocks. Hanley followed his gaze and gasped.

'You bastards!' he said, again lining the prime minister up in his sights.

Hanley swallowed, and his weapon moved in his hands as he readied himself to fire. The choppers were close, but death was closer. I looked at Lansdowne. If he'd only opened up to us, even a few days ago, we wouldn't have been facing this. But while I knew that Lansdowne had brought this on himself, and on me, I was also convinced that I had a duty here.

When I'd trained in close protection, our instructor had always said that we shouldn't think of ourselves as protecting a person — it was the person's high office we were there to protect. And right then, I knew I had to do something, anything, to save the prime minister.

I lifted my arm and made as if to throw something at Hanley. He swung his aim my way, saw that I was bluffing, and immediately moved his pistol back onto Lansdowne. So I decided to become a goalie again. Except, this time, I had to stop the ball.

I forced my gaze away from Hanley's pistol and focused on his eyes. He squinted slightly, like his sister had, and I flew in front of the prime minister as Hanley's pistol flashed. The bullet hit me in the chest, my world exploded into colours, and everything slowed. The rock ledge moved up to meet me, and I seemed to fall through it. I fell further — much further than I thought I could fall. Then everything went black.

Epilogue

IT WAS LATE NOVEMBER before I was able to walk from my apartment down to the police memorial by the lake. As I stood there in the morning sun, reading the names on the lines of plaques, I visualised my name up there in bronze, and the image didn't trouble me anymore. It had been that close. Hanley's bullet had smashed my collarbone, taken out an artery, broken a rib and collapsed my left lung. It had missed my spine by millimetres, and for that I thanked my luck every day. I had already thanked the sniper in the chopper who had pinged Hanley before he could get off a second shot.

Lansdowne had escaped with barely a nick on his body, but his life was in tatters. The bloodied transcript in my jacket, and the tape they'd found on Lomax, combined to seal his fate. He resigned soon after the polls closed on Saturday night, and he was formally charged on the following Monday. His case is yet to be heard. It's said he'll plead guilty to all charges flowing from the Mondrian conspiracy, so he'll lose everything. And he'll do time. But at least he's alive — not like the rest of his cabal.

Kemp turned out to be wrong about the death vest. Lansdowne never got to wear a bomb, but he very nearly rode in one. They found Hanley's BMW at the top of Geary's Gap, about three kilometres from where he'd shot me. The car was packed with nails and explosives. Lomax had made a very big bomb for the prime minister, and she'd planned to have him strapped into it when it blew.

When Harry the driver regained consciousness, he confirmed my theory about how Lomax had got her contraband past House security. He said that when he drove her down for early mornings at The Lodge, Lomax would occasionally divert the car to her Blackall Street unit, saying she'd left documents there.

The team investigating the Mondrian conspiracy finally got access to Proctor's dirt files. Media pressure on the new Redding government saw to that. As it turned out, Lomax hadn't handled the rumour file. Not that Brady made any mention of that when he visited me in hospital a few weeks after the shooting. He just smiled for the cameras, pinned a medal on my chest, and left. We're yet to see if any prosecutions flow from the files, but the word is that some bigwigs like Brady have reason to be worried. As does Mondrian itself. The Securities Commission has been through the place like a dose of salts, and it's said to be preparing some huge briefs.

Lomax's cat-killing friend Joe turned out to be a Polish national called Stefan Falat, a one-time foot soldier for an Athens-based heroin cartel. Falat had dropped off Interpol's radar in Bangkok shortly after Sylvie Hanley 'disappeared' in Thailand's north. At the time, Falat was known to be in possession of a big wad of his bosses' cash. Interpol had always assumed he had been caught and killed by his own. We now knew that he'd hooked up with Hanley while they were both 're-badging' themselves in the Thai capital.

As a mere copper, all I could think of was what a mess it had all turned out. Greed had led to grief, and that had led to mayhem. The whole country had suffered a trauma that seemed so unnecessary.

Jean was sitting next to my bed when I first regained consciousness. She spent most of the next week there, before I told her to go back to work — at least for a few hours a day.

When I was discharged, she drove me to her apartment and set me up on the couch with the view of Red Hill. Later, when we were having a cup of tea, she asked what I'd do while I was recuperating. Rest, I said, and then get bored. She had a different idea — she suggested that I find a way to tell my story. You could even write a book, she said. I thought about it for a while, and then found myself agreeing with her. A book, eh? I might just do that.

Acknowledgements

MY THANKS TO all those who advised and guided me in the writing of this novel. They include close-protection specialist, AFP Federal Agent Vince Parnell; the former head of ACT policing, Detective Superintendent Ray Sweeney; the senior Crown prosecutor for NSW, Mark Tedeschi QC; the director of the National Institute of Forensic Science, Dr Tony Raymond; the senior instructor in Military Self-Defence and Close Quarter Fighting at ADFA, Warrant Officer Anthony Berne; the dean of the ANU College of Business and Economics, and professor of business administration at the ANU, Professor Keith Houghton; the political editor of *The Canberra Times*, Ross Peake; and ABC political reporter Alex Kirk.

Special thank to my agent, John Timlin, for believing in this book. And to my publisher and editor, Henry Rosenbloom, who seamlessly smoothed the text and taught me to value omissions. And to my good friend and writing mentor Kel Robertson, whose insights and input helped me keep my chins up in the hard times. And, finally, my love and thanks to my wife, Claire Tedeschi, without whose encouragement and support this novel would never have been.